With all the attention focuse̶d̶ ̶
breakups these days, we th̶ ̶
series of novels about love and the pressures of Hollywood fame,
which we call ROMANCE IN THE SPOTLIGHT.

In this year's summer series, we asked some of romance's
bestselling authors to pen stories of love, intrigue and
sizzling romance set against the backdrop of the tabloid media
and Hollywood.

The month's novel in the ROMANCE IN THE SPOTLIGHT series
is *Love, Lies & Videotape* by Kayla Perrin, a torrid tale of
a young actress on the verge of big-time success who is
plagued by an unseemly videotape from her past. Sandra Kitt's
Celluloid Memories, which came out in July, tells the story of an
aspiring screenwriter who finds herself on the brink of success as
she tries to unravel a family secret. And in June, we kicked off the
summer series with *Just the Man She Needs* by Gwynne Forster,
which tells the story of two high-profile yet private people who
reluctantly find themselves the subjects of intense publicity. In
September, look for *Moments Like This* by Donna Hill, a steamy
romance about an established actress looking to make the ultimate
comeback.

We hope you enjoy *Love, Lies & Videotape,* and be sure to buy the
other titles in the ROMANCE IN THE SPOTLIGHT series. We welcome
your comments and feedback, and invite you to send us an e-mail
at www.kimanipress.com.

Enjoy,

Evette Porter
Editor, Arabesque

KAYLA
Perrin

Love, Lies & Videotape

ARABESQUE®

LOVE, LIES & VIDEOTAPE

An Arabesque novel

ISBN-13: 978-0-373-83016-9
ISBN-10:   0-373-83016-5

www.kimanipress.com

Printed in U.S.A.

For Mike Ward.

Not only do you take a great photo,
you're an all-round terrific guy.

You served your country with honor and dignity.
You raised two beautiful daughters.
And you've got one heck of a smile.

Kudos to you for being perfect hero material.

Acknowledgment

This is not so much an acknowledgment as a "shout-out."
If you attended the *Romantic Times BOOKreviews* Convention
in 2006, you'll likely recognize the man on the cover of this book.
I first met Mike by chance at the *RT* convention in Kansas City
years earlier, in his full military uniform, and we became fast
friends. No, he wasn't there for the convention, but a friend and
I encouraged him to crash one of the parties! He was a hit
in his "costume" and a natural in the world of romance.
So when the convention was being held in Florida, near his
home, I persuaded him to enter the 2006 *Romantic Times
BOOKreviews* cover-model contest. No surprise to me, he won
the "Reader's Choice" award—the popular vote.

This is Mike's first romance cover, and I wanted to publicly
give him a shout-out. Congrats, Mike. I'm honored to see
you representing the hero in my book!

Chapter 1

In life there are moments of pure bliss and moments of utter despair. The day Jasmine St. Clair realized her biggest dream, she experienced both.

That day, from sunrise till sunset it rained, making the August day in Los Angeles abnormally cool. The wet weather hadn't bothered her at first, not like it usually did. Jasmine had been in a giddy state of elation, the rush of delicious emotions so strong as she anticipated the coming evening that she'd hardly noticed the summer shower. Hours before the hairstylist and makeup artist arrived—two of the best in the business—her mind had danced with thoughts of how extraordinarily beautiful she would look at the gala event, how incredible she would feel. But when by late afternoon the sky grew darker and more bleak with heavier rain, Jasmine took notice, her excitement quickly fading. Instantly her skin prickled as she felt the familiar chill take hold of the base of her neck, slowly creeping across her shoulder blades and down her spine. But before it could totally overpower her and take her to that dark, cold place, she fought the chill with three shots of brandy and thoughts of her mother. Her mother believed that rain was a blessing. Despite the fact that it rained the day her younger brother had been killed in a senseless hit-and-run incident and didn't stop raining until after his funeral, her mother still believed that. Today, the most important day of her life thus far, Jasmine needed to believe it, too.

But if Jasmine had been looking for a sign that her success would be short-lived, the rain should have been it. With the rain normally came an inexplicable feeling of cold so deep inside nothing could warm her. The cold could last for hours or even days, until something ultimately went wrong in her life. Something major, like when her brother died. Or something minor, like when her fingernail caught in her car door and completely tore off.

Jasmine had moved from Florida to California to escape frequent showers, and today she refused to see the weather as a bad omen. Today, she *knew,* was different. Not even the unexpected downpour could dampen her sweet mood.

This was why, as she followed her boyfriend into the lavishly decorated penthouse suite later that evening, a glass of champagne already in hand, Jasmine felt a rush of excitement. Like a woman thrown into a time warp she was in awe, examining everything around her with the interest of someone seeing it for the first time. Her eyes surveyed the mahogany-hardwood floor partially covered by a giant Persian rug, the gold and crystal chandelier in the center of the room, the textured cream-and-rose-colored wallpaper, the French Provincial furniture and Victorian era paintings. It was all so incredible. And it was all, for one night, hers.

Jasmine's cell phone vibrated in her palm. She glanced at the screen and saw her agent's number, and decided to ignore it. She wanted nothing to interrupt her emotional high, not even another congratulatory call from the woman who'd booked her the audition that had landed her this major film role.

As Jasmine continued walking into the suite, she was aware of sounds around her, but they were drowned out by the intense pounding of her heart. Mesmerized, she took tentative steps toward the floor-to-ceiling window, placing her fingertips on the cool glass as she scanned the wide expanse of the city. Rain trickled down the glass like teardrops. She traced the path of one raindrop, suddenly wondering if it was a tear of joy or sadness. *It's just rain,* she thought, quickly halting the direction of her thoughts. It wasn't a blessing or a curse; it was just an evening shower.

That decided, Jasmine saw past the rain, enjoying the view of the city below. Had she ever been this high before? Thirty-five stories up, the world below seemed abstract, like a different planet. An infinitely friendlier, more attractive place. Certainly not the Los Angeles she knew, where people smiled to your face while they stabbed you in the chest. This world seemed like one she could control, like her own personal playground.

And in the night, the glittering streetlights below looked like a carpet of stars. Stars laid out just for her.

The corners of her lips twitched, wanting to smile, and as Jasmine splayed her free hand on the window, she finally released the scream she'd held inside for hours. The carpet of stars *was* for her—to walk on, sit on, roll around on. Because tonight, this high in the sky, she was literally on top of the world. She had made it! Conquered the dream she'd once believed impossible. Tonight, the world was hers and nobody else's. She was the queen of the universe.

Downing a liberal gulp of champagne, Jasmine smiled, laughter bubbling from her throat like the tiny bubbles floating to the surface of the champagne. God, this feeling of success was so incredible she could savor it for days and days. She'd done it— she had reached a point in her career where she could go nowhere but up. The options were boundless now, as limitless as the stars in the sky. She had dreamed of this day since she was a child, had practiced the appreciative wave for her fans, had strutted the seductive, actress walk. She even had her Oscar award-winning speech memorized. Though tonight she hadn't needed it, she knew one day she would.

Her life was as wonderful as she'd always known it could be. It had taken thirty-one years, but finally she had achieved her ultimate goal.

She was now a verified movie star.

Jasmine, what a fabulous performance! You are destined for super stardom!

Ms. St. Clair, please, your autograph?

Jasmine, over here. Just one quick picture...

The lights had flashed around her all night; the buzz had surrounded her wherever she walked; she had been the center of attention, sometimes so crowded by fans and industry people that she hadn't been able to move. But she hadn't minded. It was her life's ambition to be surrounded with love, to know that people thought she was special, a somebody.

Some people craved money, and yes, money came with a successful acting career, but that wasn't what it was about for Jasmine. She just wanted to know that she would never go back to that lonely place. And now, she wouldn't. That lonely place of her childhood was finally locked away, forever hidden in a dark corner of her past.

Glancing heavenward, she wondered what her brother would think of her now, of how far she had come. Her gaze fixing on a star brighter than the rest, Jasmine imagined that it was her brother, Rickey's, star, that he was smiling down at her, happy that she'd finally gotten out of life what she wanted. When he was alive, she had been happy. Her whole family had been. But after his death, her parents had become so lost in their despair that life in the St. Clair household had changed drastically and permanently. Jasmine's parents hadn't been there for her the way she'd needed them to be. They hadn't been able to smile at her achievements without remembering Rickey and what should have been. They hadn't been able to smile, period. The grief had been overwhelming, and unlike most families that found a way to go on after tragedy, Jasmine's parents hadn't been able to do that. Jasmine had lost Rickey physically that day, but she'd emotionally lost her parents.

Her parents… Jasmine felt only a moment's regret that she hadn't invited her mother and father to the screening, easing her conscience by telling herself that they were so far removed from Hollywood life that a shindig like this one would bore them. Besides, they wouldn't know what to say to people. The troubled world of Miami's north side was a far cry from the glamour and glitz of Hollywood. Her father would no doubt embarrass her with talk of what she'd been like as a child, how she'd been so poor she'd had to wear hand-me-down shoes a size too small. Her mother, sweet but clueless, would have gawked at the likes of Denzel Washington and Brad Pitt, surely humiliating her.

But the truth was, Jasmine feared that if her parents had been at the screening of her first blockbuster film, the memory of their missing son would have ultimately depressed them, and as a result, depressed her. And that wasn't something she'd wanted on such an important night.

No, she'd done the right thing by not inviting them.

"Come here."

Startled, Jasmine giggled as Allan's firm hands circled her waist from behind, pulling her buttocks against his arousal. Champagne spilled from the crystal flute as she gained her balance, settling against him. All thoughts of guilt fled her mind. "Allan…"

His tongue found her ear, gently licking the lobe the way one would lick honey from a rose petal. Jasmine closed her eyes, gripped his thigh…and wondered why she wasn't getting turned on. Her ear was a definite erogenous zone, but as she opened her eyes, she realized that his tongue wouldn't do the job because her mind wouldn't let it.

She wasn't ready.

"Damn, Jasmine, you taste so good. You feel so good. Come to the bedroom."

"Not yet," she replied, then sipped more champagne, hoping it would relieve the sudden annoyance she felt at Allan's impatience, his one-track mind. Recently he'd been cutting short the foreplay and going straight for the main event. He always wanted her in his bed, and yes, he was a great lover, but didn't he realize that she wanted to enjoy this feeling for as long as she could? That not even an orgasm could be better than the natural high she felt right now?

Jasmine heard the faint sound of her cell phone vibrating, and while she hadn't wanted to answer it before, she reached into her purse and pulled it out. Once again, she saw her agent's number.

"I should—"

"Ignore it," Allan told her, pulling the phone from her fingers. He tossed it onto the nearby chaise, then continued trying to seduce her.

His breath hot on her ear, he ran his hands over her ribs and firmly cupped her breasts. Finding her nipples, he tweaked them through the fabric of her one-of-a-kind sleeveless silver gown. "Tell me what you want, Jasmine. I know you love my tongue. Where do you want it?" He lapped at her neck. "I've waited all evening for this. God, I'm going to explode with lust if I don't have you soon."

Jasmine let Allan grope her, hoping his hands would ignite her body, but they didn't. Still, she faked a moan, all the while wishing he would find something else to entertain him until she was ready. Finally she said, "Allan, I—"

"Tell me, Jasmine…"

The sound of Allan's heavy breathing was interrupted by a knock at the door. He froze. Jasmine released a sigh of relief, thankful for the opportunity to escape.

"Did you order room service?" he asked, moving his hands to her shoulders.

Turning in his arms, she faced him. "No…but Ron knows we're up here," she said, referring to the director of *The Game,* the blockbuster movie in which she'd starred. "It would be just like him to send something special up for us."

"You're right."

Jasmine framed one side of Allan's golden brown

face. Having shaved earlier, his skin was smooth and soft. He wasn't the most attractive man—his face was too narrow and his nose too broad—but he was extremely good to her. She planted a soft kiss on his lips, then gave him her glass. "You open another bottle of champagne. I'll get the door."

As she hurried across the large suite to the marble-layered foyer, her eyes misted at the thought that she had truly escaped her past. Risen from the ashes of pain and achieved all she'd ever wanted. She had a man who loved her. She had a fabulous career. She had respect, fame. She had a raison d'être. She was finally, truly happy.

Giggling, Jasmine allowed herself a girlish twirl of delight before answering the door. It was silly, she knew, but damn it felt good.

She swung open the mahogany double doors. Seeing the hotel manager—who had welcomed her upon her arrival—her eyes narrowed with confusion.

"Mr. Healey?" she said, concern in her voice.

"I'm sorry to disturb you in your room, Ms. St. Clair, but your agent, Victoria Graydon, has been trying to reach you. She said you haven't been answering your cell, and your room phone is set up to go straight to voice mail."

"I was hoping to have some privacy," Jasmine explained, and as if to emphasize that point, Allan appeared, slipping his arms possessively around her waist.

"Of course." Mr. Healey looked from Jasmine to Allan, and back to Jasmine again. "I wouldn't disturb you, but your agent said it's absolutely urgent that you call her."

"All right," Jasmine said. If Victoria had important news, it wouldn't hurt to call her before she and Allan ended up in bed. "I'll give her a call. Thank you, Mr. Healey."

"Your agent's trying to reach you?" Allan asked as Jasmine closed the door.

"Apparently. Guess I'll give her a call."

"You do that." Allan kissed her forehead. "I'll get more champagne, and set the mood a little—so we can continue where we left off when you're through with your call."

Jasmine sauntered back into the living room and picked up her cell phone. Seconds later, she had it at her ear.

Victoria answered on the first ring, exclaiming, "Jasmine!"

"Hey, Victoria." Jasmine grinned when she heard the first notes of Sam Cooke's "Cupid," followed by Allan doing a sexy strut toward her with two champagne flutes in his hands. "What's up?"

"I'm sorry to have to track you down like I'm the FBI, sweetie, but I have been fielding calls for the past forty minutes."

"The press hasn't had enough of me yet?" Jasmine asked, feigning annoyance, but in reality, she was elated to be getting this much attention. It was further proof of how far she'd come.

Victoria blew out a loud, frustrated breath. "Hardly. And it's about to get a lot worse."

Worse? Jasmine accepted the glass of champagne Allan handed her, then said, "Victoria, what are you talking about?"

"Something's happened. Something serious."

"Are you planning to fill me in?"

"Sorry I've been beating around the bush. But I was trying to feel you out."

"Feel me out?" Beating around the bush wasn't Victoria's style.

"The truth is, if you didn't plan this, then there's no easy way to tell you what is now making news."

"Just be as direct as you normally are," Jasmine told her. "I'm a big girl. Am I getting some bad reviews already? I can handle that."

"This is far worse than a bad review." Victoria paused. "A tape just surfaced, Jasmine. Of you."

Jasmine scrunched her forehead as her agent's words settled over her. "I still don't get your meaning."

"Think Paris Hilton, Pamela Anderson…*Girls Gone Wild.*"

Jasmine stood stupidly for a moment, thinking. Then horror slammed into her rib cage with the force of a baseball bat. "You mean, some kind of *perverted* tape?"

"You're absolutely sure you didn't plan this?" Victoria asked. "As a way to maximize your publicity surrounding this film?"

"Plan this? Are you kidding?" Jasmine's heart started to pound out of control. "You think I'd release some sort of scandalous tape of myself?"

"The timing is very suspicious. I had to ask."

"What exactly is it?" Had some pervert stuck a camera in her dressing room, or, God forbid, in her hotel bathroom while she'd been shooting *The Game?* "A tape of me getting dressed? Of me in the shower?"

Jasmine saw the shock in Allan's eyes at her questions, and she turned so she wouldn't have to face him. Until she had answers herself, she couldn't be giving them.

"Worse."

"Worse? What could be—" But Jasmine didn't even finish her statement before the awful reality hit her. Victoria had referenced Paris Hilton and Pamela Anderson. Good God in heaven. In a hushed tone she said, "Don't tell me it's a tape of me being… intimate."

"Sweetie, I just got a call from CNN."

"Oh my God." Jasmine crumbled onto the sofa, dragging her hand over her face as she did.

"Damn, do you hear that? The call waiting beep? It's been nonstop for the last forty minutes."

"CNN?" Jasmine asked, her voice barely a whisper.

"That's why I was desperate to reach you," Victoria explained.

"How could this have happened? How could this be *possible?*" Jasmine's mind frantically searched for an answer. She hadn't had sex with Allan in her dressing room, but he had visited her while she'd been on location. Had some overzealous tabloid reporter worked his way into her private space, hidden a camera in her hotel room, and taped her while making love?

Now she looked at Allan again, who was staring at her with concern. She said softly, "Allan. Damn."

"I haven't seen the tape yet," Victoria said. "And I hope to God that the networks have the decency not to air even one small portion of it. It's late, but I'll put a call in to my lawyer and see what we can do to stop this."

Allan mouthed the word "what," raising his hands in question.

"Allan's here with me," Jasmine explained. "I've got to go."

"I would advise checking out of the hotel. If the media knows you're there—"

"I hear you. And I'm gone."

"Stay strong, sweetie."

"Thanks."

No sooner than Jasmine ended the call, Allan landed on the sofa beside her. "What is it, babe?"

Jasmine groaned. It was hard for her to accept the reality of what Victoria had told her, much less to share the story with Allan.

But she had to. He deserved to know as much as she did.

"Something's happened," Jasmine began slowly. "Apparently some sort of sex tape has surfaced. Oh my God, I think I could die!"

Allan pulled her into his arms. "You're sure?"

"Victoria said reporters have been calling her. Even CNN."

"Damn."

Now Jasmine looked into her boyfriend's eyes.

"Why, Allan? Why would someone do this? Who hates me so much?"

Allan shook his head. "I don't think this is about hate. It's probably someone who's obsessed with you."

"Or someone's misguided attempt at achieving fame." Jasmine gripped the collar of Allan's shirt as her heart started to race. "A sex tape, Allan. This is going to end up on the Internet! Oh God. We have to do something to stop this. I was just at the screening for my first major film role! The media loved me. I've been on four magazine covers because of this film, all touting my girl-next-door image." The reality of what this could do to her career made Jasmine's body freeze. "I have finally achieved success in my career. Real success. This could destroy me."

When Allan didn't say anything, Jasmine assumed he was lamenting the situation. Then he stared deeply into her eyes and said, "You sure it's me on the tape with you?"

The question was so absurd, Jasmine couldn't answer for a minute. "Excuse me?"

"You heard me."

"Don't tell me you still think I had an affair with Terrence Green," she said, referring to her co-star. *The Game* was an action-adventure romance starring Hollywood's current It boy, Terrence Green. Terrence had made a huge name for himself in the past couple years, and had reached a status that every black actor hopes to. He'd broken the color barrier. Directors didn't see Terrence Green as a black lead actor, but as a lead actor, period. Which was why Jasmine was suddenly getting so much attention as Hollywood's most talented new black actress. She had always done wholesome roles, albeit smaller ones than this, and her clean, positive image was what all the reporters had capitalized on in their recent stories about her.

"I did not sleep with Terrence Green," Jasmine told him, then shot to her feet.

"Then why are you getting so angry?"

"Because I can't believe that at a time like this, you would even dare to bring that up! Allan, a sex tape has just surfaced that could ruin my career!"

Allan studied Jasmine for a moment, then his expression softened. "You know I would never cheat on you," Jasmine told him as he started to rise.

"I'm sorry," he said, and swept her into his arms. "I'm so sorry."

"We're gonna have to go. It won't take the media long to track us down here."

"You don't want to turn on the news? See what's being said?"

"We can do that at my place. Or better yet, yours. The paparazzi will no doubt stake out my place. Oh God."

Allan rubbed Jasmine's arms, then gave her a kiss on her forehead. "All right. We'll get our stuff and leave. I think you're right. My place is the better choice. When we get there, we'll watch the news. See if this thing is as bad as we're fearing."

Jasmine nodded absently. She was no longer

hearing what Allan was saying. Instead her gaze fixed on the raindrops clinging to the window. She walked toward the floor-to-ceiling window she had stood in front of only a short while before.

Now, when she looked outside, she didn't feel on top of the world. In fact, she felt the distinct sensation of someone falling....

As surely as if someone had pushed her from the thirty-fifth floor, she was falling, tumbling into darkness like a star falling in the black sky. And in some bizarre way, she could see it all, like a spectator watching the event in horror. She could see herself plummeting to the earth, feet over hands, hands over feet. Her body losing the fight to gravity.

Losing everything...

Jasmine shivered. For the good girl who refused to show any skin in any of her movie roles, she knew that no matter how explicit this sex tape, it was going to be her downfall.

For the past seven years, she'd worked immensely hard to succeed in this field. And on the night that she'd seen her biggest dream come true, she was also seeing it crash and burn.

Chapter 2

Shortly after Jasmine entered Allan's North Hollywood apartment, her worst fears were confirmed.
All the major news networks—CNN, MSNBC, Fox
News and of course the local news stations—were
reporting on the latest scandal to rock Tinsel Town.

The tag lines were salacious:

Good girl gone bad, Jasmine St. Clair...

*Jasmine St. Clair stars in the new hit film The
Game, and also stars in a film that could be called
Bedroom Games.*

*It appears Jasmine St. Clair got some ideas on
how to use handcuffs from her latest film....*

Jasmine couldn't stomach listening to the news-
casters, much less watch the portion of the tape the

networks could show on TV. Allan, if he still doubted her, had his mind put to rest—at least in terms of the fact that it was indeed him on the film with Jasmine. The news stations showed them passionately kissing before Allan's head went lower—and it was at that point that they stopped the tape, claiming the rest was too explicit to show on television.

To get through the night, Jasmine had taken two sleeping pills, and even then, she'd barely slept. By the next morning, she was utterly devastated and didn't even want to get out of bed.

She felt Allan slip his arms around her waist before his mouth pressed against her cheek. "Baby," he said.

Jasmine didn't answer.

"Baby," he repeated. "It's almost noon. You've got to get up. Eat something."

"I'm not hungry," she mumbled.

Allan eased his body over hers so that he was facing her. With the pads of his thumbs, he wiped tears from Jasmine's eyes. She was so numb, she didn't even realize she was crying.

"Maybe it's not so bad," Allan whispered. "Maybe, just maybe, this publicity will help your career, not hurt it."

Jasmine knew Allan was trying to help, but he wasn't. For him to think this sex tape could do anything but make her career plummet was outrageous. She wanted to tell him that, but she didn't have the energy.

"Fine," Allan said, clearly testy. "Shut me out.

I'm only trying to make you feel better." Allan stood and quietly left the room.

With him gone, Jasmine snatched up a pillow and whipped it across the room. What was wrong with him? How could he say that perhaps it wasn't so bad? Was he out of his mind? Perhaps if she was known in the industry as some sort of sex vixen, like Pamela Anderson, this tape wouldn't be so devastating. But Jasmine had honed her good-girl image. She'd talked at high schools and preached abstinence. She was a role model for young women, and they would all see her as a hypocrite.

Even the snippets of newscasts that Jasmine had seen had not-so-subtly shown her demise. First, they showed footage of her at her best—on the red carpet, absolutely glowing at the premiere of *The Game*. Immediately followed by that was footage of her face with her eyes closed, in the throes of passion as Allan's mouth moved over her neck.

The second video canceled out any of the positives of the first one.

The reality was so depressing, Jasmine could hardly stand it.

Sometime later—Jasmine wasn't sure how long—Allan appeared in the bedroom with a mug of coffee and a toasted bagel. He placed the plate and mug on the night table beside the bed, but Jasmine didn't even move.

"Come on, sweetheart," Allan pleaded. "You have to eat."

"I'm not hungry," was all Jasmine said. And she

wasn't. Her stomach was so nauseous, the last thing in the world she wanted to do was to eat. She would probably vomit immediately afterward.

"What are you going to do?" Allan asked her. "Lie here and wither away?"

Jasmine cut her eyes at him, but didn't have the strength for a comeback. It was just as well. She didn't want to argue with Allan on top of everything else.

How was it that he didn't understand that what she needed from him now was silent support? She needed him to lie with her, hold her, curse the madman who'd done this on her behalf. It wouldn't change anything, she knew, but at least she wouldn't feel so alone.

Allan was leaving the room again when the house phone rang. Though the phone was beside her on the night table, Jasmine didn't even lift her head. Allan hurried to it and scooped it up.

"Hey, Victoria," he said after a moment. "Yeah, she's here. Well, she's definitely upset. Doesn't even want to get out of bed. Maybe you can talk to her, help her snap out of this depression."

Jasmine was about to protest, but Allan was already handing her the phone. She sighed softly and resigned herself to the fact that she couldn't disappear from the world just because she wanted to.

Accepting the cordless handset, Jasmine said, "Hey, Victoria."

"Oh, sweetie. You sound like hell."

She cleared her throat. "I feel a lot worse than that."

"You've seen the news?"

"What I could stomach of it. I...I still don't understand. How did someone get that footage?"

"People are very resourceful these days. And cameras can be the size of a small button."

"All I know is, I want to get to the bottom of this. One way or another, I have to."

"Allan told me you're still in bed."

"Yeah."

"Sweetie, I know you're having a tough time, and I hate to be the bearer of even more bad news. But I didn't think I should keep anything from you."

"How could there be more bad news?" It seemed impossible.

"Well...I heard from Revlon today. They said that in light of this tape, they've decided to choose someone else for their new ad campaign."

"No!"

"And—brace yourself—I also heard from Norman Judd."

Jasmine's eyelids fluttered shut as her stomach spasmed with pain. Though she knew what her agent was going to tell her, she couldn't muster a cry. "Norman doesn't want to cast me in his feature anymore?"

"I'm sorry," Victoria said.

Jasmine finally sat up. "I can't be here," she said. "Everyone is turning on me. One minute I was Hollywood's darling, now it's like I'm the Antichrist."

"I debated giving you this news. But I decided I should tell you right away. First, I didn't want you to hear it on the news if Norman or Revlon decided to send out press releases. And I also think that the best way to handle this is to come out swinging. Let the world know that you were the victim in this. That someone violated *your* rights."

It sounded like a good idea, but the devastation of what had happened had zapped all of Jasmine's strength. "I don't know, Victoria. I know there's a time to fight back, but I don't think I can do that yet. Maybe I need to let this whole thing blow over."

Jasmine said the words, but she didn't believe them. Already, two gigs she'd had lined up had fallen apart because of the sex tape that had surfaced. What was next—calls from porn directors who thought she'd be great in their films? Jasmine would have a complete breakdown if that ever happened.

"I realize that you might not be ready for this, but there's only one way to move forward. I'll start making calls, see which reporters want to give you air time. I'm sure I can book you on *Larry King Live*."

"Victoria, please. Not yet." This was all too overwhelming. "Can I talk to you later? I've got an awful headache."

"Sure," Victoria said. "But please get out of bed, do something. Eat something. I don't want you thinking this is the end of the world, okay?"

"I'll try."

"I know it's easier said than done, but you have to hang in there."

"Yeah," Jasmine said. Then she ended the call and placed the receiver back on its cradle.

For the first time since the night before, her stomach grumbled. She eyed the bagel for several moments before reaching for it.

Eating the bagel was like eating cardboard, but she finished it and washed it down with some coffee. Allan lowered himself beside her on the bed and kissed her temple.

"There. That wasn't so bad, was it?"

Jasmine ignored the question. "Baby, I think I need to call a lawyer. See if there's some kind of injunction we can get to stop that tape from being aired. Maybe it's too little too late, but it will make me feel better. It was recorded without our knowledge, and if we can find out who did it, I'm sure they can get jail time. Or at the very least, be slapped with a lawsuit." As Jasmine said the words, anger came over her. This was good. An important first step. Feeling angry was so much better than being numb.

"Maybe you want to call your parents first," Allan suggested.

Jasmine's heart slammed against her chest. "Have they called? God have mercy. I didn't even think about them seeing the news footage…and the media." She cringed. A horrible thought struck her, one she couldn't believe she hadn't already considered. What if the media had gone to her family, questioned them about their reaction to the tape?

She snatched up the phone. Then took a long, deep breath. She started to punch in the digits to her parents' home in Miami when she realized that Allan was staring at her.

"Hey," she began quietly, "do you mind giving me some privacy?"

"Of course. I think I'll head out and pick up some groceries. I won't be gone long."

Jasmine nodded. When Allan left the bedroom, she resumed calling her parents.

Her father answered on the first ring, sounding somewhat harried, as though he'd been waiting by the phone. "Hello?"

"Daddy?" she croaked.

"Oh, thank God," he replied, sounding completely relieved. Then he called out, "Martha, it's Jasmine. Pick up the phone!"

Jasmine was silent as she waited to hear the click of another phone being lifted off its cradle, and before her mother even spoke, she felt tears fill her eyes.

"Baby," her mother said. "We've been out of our minds with worry. You weren't answering your home phone, nor your cell."

"I…" Jasmine began, then brushed at her tears. "I'm sorry. I turned my cell phone off. I was scared of being hounded by the media, and I didn't want to talk to anyone."

"They've called here," her father said. "They've come to our door…."

"Oh God. I'm so sorry," Jasmine said.

"Where are you now?" her mother asked.

"I'm at Allan's," Jasmine answered. Her parents had never met her boyfriend, but they had talked to him on the phone. "I figured the media would camp out outside my door, so the last place I wanted to go was home."

"As long as you're safe," her father said.

"For now," Jasmine said. "But I can't avoid the world forever."

"That wasn't you on the tape, was it?" Jasmine's mother asked. "Someone used your face and made that disgusting movie, didn't they?"

A lump lodged in Jasmine's throat. She should have known that her parents would support her, no questions asked. And that's what made this whole situation a lot harder. Having to tell them the truth.

"No, Mom," she admitted quietly. "That wasn't someone else. It was…it was me."

"What?" her father exclaimed.

Before he could go on, she quickly said, "I had no idea I was being taped. Never in my life would I want to videotape what is a such a private, intimate experience between two people. Clearly some pervert gained access to my hotel room when I was on location shooting *The Game*."

Her mother snorted in disgust. "I read a story once. About hotel staff putting hidden cameras in rooms to tape people during their most private moments. Taking a shower, or in bed with their spouses. I wonder if that's what happened to you."

"You could be right," Jasmine said in a horrified whisper. "I figured it had to be some obsessed fan, or a reporter wanting to make a name for himself. But what if it was someone from the hotel?"

"There must be a way to find out," her father said.

"Then you sue the bastards who had the audacity to do this to you."

"You'd better believe I'm going to sue!" Again, Jasmine felt anger. It spread through her like liquid fire. But almost immediately, the feeling was replaced by depression. "I can sue whoever did this," she continued, "but the damage is done. I've worked hard to succeed. I carefully honed my Hollywood image. Right from the beginning, I said I'd never do any nudity or racy sex scenes. I've stuck by my morals and never compromised that position. As a result I've become a role model to young girls. Now this has happened? People are going to say I'm a hypocrite."

"This will all die down," Jasmine's mother said. "Tomorrow, it will be some other scandal, and people will forget this."

"I'm not so sure," Jasmine said.

"All the more reason for you to find out who did this," her mother went on. "Ask the news stations for the footage, see if you can recognize the room."

"And then I can figure out which hotel it was!" Jasmine said, excited. "That is a *great* idea. I'll be damned if I let whomever did this get away with trying to ruin my life."

As the bedroom door opened, Jasmine's eyes flew to Allan's. He hadn't been gone nearly long enough to have finished shopping. Heck, he probably barely made it downstairs before heading back up.

"…support you, no matter what," her father was saying.

"Thank you, Dad," Jasmine said. "And Mom." It

wasn't like they hadn't suffered enough tragedy in their lives. They certainly didn't need this.

"We love you," her mother said.

"I love you, too," Jasmine replied, her eyes misting. Ever since Rickey's death, her mother had rarely said that she loved her. Nor her father. She figured it was because on some level, they blamed her for what had happened to her brother. To say it now meant the world. "Look, can I call you later?"

"Absolutely," her father said.

As Jasmine ended the call, Allan slowly walked into the room. The expression he wore made Jasmine hold her breath.

"What?" she asked.

"I couldn't even make it out of here," Allan said. "The media…they're blocking the parking lot."

"Damn!" But Jasmine should have known that they would find Allan's place. While Allan wasn't a movie star, he was a screenwriter with a few television movie credits under his belt. He was still hoping to sell a feature screenplay, and was working hard to accomplish that goal. The point was, he was also known in the business, and easily tracked down by the paparazzi.

"This is turning into a bigger circus than I ever thought it'd be," Allan said.

At that moment, it dawned on Jasmine that she wasn't the only one who could lose her career over this. Allan was also in the video. Though he wasn't a big-name screenwriter, he could suffer just as badly as she would, losing gigs he might have landed if not for this tape.

Jasmine moved toward him and gave him a long, hard hug. "We'll get through this," she told him. "And my parents got me thinking about something. If I can take a look at the tape—not something I particularly want to do, but it's not like I have a choice— then I can figure out where it was filmed. My mother pointed out that there have been stories about hotel staff hiding cameras in guest rooms, and I'll bet anything that's what happened here. Once we figure out which hotel, we sue for millions. Hell, we sue for the hotel chain."

"The footage on the news was pretty dark. And a short clip. It might not tell us much."

"That was just what they aired. If we call the networks—or better yet, a lawyer—I'm sure they'll have to release the tape to us. Once we view the entire thing…" Jasmine's voice trailed off, and she stepped away from Allan. "In fact, I'll call Victoria right now. And right after that, I'll call the police."

She was punching in the digits to Victoria's office phone when Allan approached her and took the receiver from her hands. She looked up at him in confusion.

"I think that maybe you should just stop and take a breath," Allan said in reply to her unspoken question.

"Why?" Jasmine asked.

"Because you can't…you can't let this thing eat you alive. If you start making calls, obsessing over this…what good is that going to do?"

"I appreciate that you want to protect me."

Jasmine placed her hand on Allan's chest. "I really do. But the sooner we get on this, the sooner we talk to the cops, the better."

"The cops?" Allan dragged a hand over his face.

"Of course. I'm sure whoever did this can be brought up on charges. This kind of behavior *must* be illegal."

Allan groaned.

"What's the matter?" Jasmine asked him.

Allan drew in a deep breath. "Look, there's something I need to say."

Jasmine studied the serious set of his jaw, the concern in his eyes. "What is it, sweetie?"

Allan dropped the phone onto the bed and took Jasmine's hands in his. "I don't know how to tell you this."

As Jasmine looked at their joined hands, she suddenly understood what he must have been afraid to say. Her heart racing, she asked, "You're breaking up with me?"

"No. No, baby. Of course not."

"Then why do you look so serious?" Jasmine asked him.

"Because…because you're upset, and I'm sorry about that."

"This isn't your fault."

"Please," Allan said. "I need to say this." Once again, he blew out a ragged breath. "I just want you to know, I thought it was a good idea at the time."

"Thought what was a good idea?"

Now Allan closed his eyes and kept them closed

for a long moment. And that's when the hairs on the back of Jasmine's neck stood on end.

"Allan?"

"I made the tape," he confessed. "Right here, in this bedroom."

"You *what?*" Jasmine shrieked, stepping backward.

"Look at how Paris Hilton's career took off after that sex tape of her came out."

Jasmine gaped at Allan. "You have got to be kidding me."

"Think about it. At first, the media is in a frenzy. They're clamoring for more information—and let's face it, they're all turned on at the idea of seeing some hot starlet in action. That's only natural. But once the attention dies down, when everyone's attention is on the next big scandal, everyone will know your name and you'll have offers all over the place."

Unable to believe what she was hearing, Jasmine began to pace. "You did this."

"I just told you why. Your star was already rising. It's going to skyrocket now."

Those words made Jasmine halt. She stared at Allan and said, "This story isn't even twelve hours old and I've already lost two gigs. Two *major* gigs."

"For now. But Revlon will call back. And mark my word, you'll work for Norman Judd. Probably sooner than you think. I know you're upset right now, and embarrassed, too, but I still believe this will help your career, not hurt it."

"Help?" Jasmine's eyes narrowed into a glare. "How on earth did you think this would help?"

"I just told you—"

"My career was already taking off! I landed a huge role in a blockbuster film. I was on the cover of *four* magazines! You tell me how a video showing me to be some kind of slut is going to help my career!"

"Like I said, I'm sorry."

Now Jasmine retrieved the pillow she'd tossed and whipped it at Allan's head. "Sorry? You've ruined *everything!*"

"I know you're pissed right now, and you have a right to be, but this isn't the end of your career. And I also know you're concerned about your good-girl image, but people aren't stupid. You're thirty-one years old. They can't expect you to be a virgin."

"You did not just say that. You think this is about people thinking I'm a virgin? I made a decision years ago that I would never show skin on film, and now you release a tape of the two of us in bed? Some *porno?* And you think all I'm concerned about is my image?"

"I'm so—"

"Oh, spare me!" Jasmine spat out.

Now, she marched to the window and peered through the blinds. Sure enough, there was a crowd of reporters at the front of the building.

As Jasmine stared at them, something struck her. An awful realization more devastating that what Allan had already told her. Slowly, she turned to face him.

"This wasn't about me, was it?" she said. "This was about you. *Your* career. *You* getting ahead."

Allan glanced away. The fact that he couldn't meet her eyes told her everything.

"Oh my God."

Or had he wanted to destroy her career because he was jealous of her success? There were subtle things she'd ignored, like Allan not seeming as happy at her announcements of good news, or Allan making jokes about how he had to work harder to become as famous as she was becoming.

"How could you do this to me?" she asked him. "I thought you loved me."

Allan started toward her. "I do love you. Don't ever say that I don't. But how do you think it makes me feel to know that you're the breadwinner in the relationship? That if we ever get a house, you'll be the one to pay for it? And watching you these past months, seeing how excited and happy you are because of your newfound fame... Is it so wrong for me to want my own success, as well?"

Jasmine could stay and argue with Allan, but what was the point? What he'd done was totally and completely unforgivable.

"It's over," she told him. "As of right now, this moment, you and I are through."

"Come on, babe. You don't mean that."

"I have never been more serious in my life."

"For God's sake, I told you that I didn't mean to hurt you. The damage is already done. You may as well forgive me."

Jasmine gaped at Allan, as though seeing him for the first time. "I feel like I don't even know who you are."

"I'm the man who's crazy about you," he said,

slipping his arms around her waist. "You know I would never, ever deliberately hurt you."

Jasmine extricated herself from Allan's arms. "But you did. We're not talking about an accident here, Allan. You planned this. You secretly sent tapes to the media." She shook her head in disbelief. "And the reason why...I can't be with a man who would ever hurt me for his own personal gain."

Allan's jaw flinched as he stared at her. For a few seconds he didn't say anything. When he spoke, his words were slow, pointed. "I forgave your obvious flirtation with Terrence—"

"Do *not* start that Terrence crap again. Because this has nothing to do with Terrence Green."

"I'm only saying that you don't have a right to act like you've been the perfect girlfriend."

Jasmine reminded herself that she was not going to do this. Sometimes, decisions were made in an instant and there was no going back. This was one of those times.

Walking across the room, Jasmine retrieved the silver dress she'd been wearing the night before, then went to the bathroom. She was wearing only one of Allan's T-shirts, and she couldn't very well leave his apartment dressed in that alone.

"Jasmine," Allan called.

Jasmine locked the bathroom door, then pulled the T-shirt over her head and dropped it on the floor.

Allan tried the doorknob. When it didn't open, he pounded on the door. "Jasmine!"

Jasmine slipped into her dress and struggled to

pull the zipper up, which was positioned on the back of her dress. It took her a couple of minutes because her hands were shaking, but she wasn't about to ask Allan for any help.

"I was wrong to bring up Terrence," Allan said through the door. "Maybe I wasn't right to be jealous, but can you blame me? Day in, day out, you were working with him. You were his romantic lead, and everyone knows that when men and women star together, they end up falling in love. Look at Brad Pitt and Angelina Jolie."

Since she spent so much time at Allan's place, Jasmine had a supply of makeup in his bathroom. She pulled open her drawer, withdrew the first lipstick container she saw, and applied a coat of matte brown color to her mouth. She knew that she was going to have to face the media when she left the building, and she may as well look her best. Worse, she didn't have her car here, and would have to call for a taxi.

"I didn't want to lose you," Allan said. He sounded defeated now, almost as though he was about to cry.

Jasmine braced herself and opened the bathroom door. Allan's eyes swept over her. "Baby."

Jasmine ignored him and focused on breathing evenly to calm her nerves.

"Please, baby. Just stay here with me. Let's talk about this."

Jasmine didn't respond. She simply walked to the phone and called for a taxi.

"I love you," Allan said. "I have never loved anyone more than I love you."

At that, Jasmine snorted in derision. But she didn't say a word. She coolly walked to the door and slipped into her Gucci heels.

Allan followed her to the door and flattened his back against it. "You're actually going to leave?"

"I have nothing more to say to you," Jasmine told him. "Please move out of my way."

She saw his eyes fill with tears, but Jasmine wasn't affected by his display of emotion.

She repeated, "Please move out of my way."

Allan stared her down, his chest heaving with every breath. Then he brushed his eyes with the back of his hand. Jasmine didn't even flinch.

After about a minute Allan stepped away from the door. Clearly he realized that he wasn't going to win this battle.

Then, knowing full well that a taxi would take several minutes to arrive—meaning Jasmine would be alone with the media downstairs—she left Allan's apartment.

Facing the paparazzi was far preferable to spending another minute looking at the man she had loved but who had betrayed her in the worst way imaginable.

Chapter 3

The moment Jasmine opened the apartment's front doors and stepped outside, the media swarmed her.

"Ms. St. Clair—tell us how you feel about the release of this tape!" one reporter shouted.

"Jasmine, do you know who leaked this tape to the media?" another asked.

"How do you think this is going to affect your wholesome image?"

Jasmine tried to push her way past the crowd, at first not saying anything. Cameras flashed and microphones danced in front of her face. She held her head high, but didn't say a word. She hoped that these vultures would soon realize she wasn't going to offer them any quotes and let her pass through to the street.

But the questions wouldn't cease and the reporters crowded her even more. So much so that they were beginning to suffocate her.

And scare her.

"I have nothing to say," Jasmine said, fighting her way through the crowd. My Lord, were there that many reporters in this town? Only when Jasmine continued to look around did she realize that gawkers lined the sidewalk, and some even stood on car roofs to get a look at her.

This wasn't just the media, it was a crowd of fans. Or former fans. She wasn't sure which.

"How do you feel about the fact that the video has shown up on the Internet?" a female reporter asked.

"Won't be much longer before it's for sale on eBay," another reporter commented.

That stopped Jasmine cold. But after a few seconds she surveyed the crowd and bravely said, "I had nothing to do with that tape's release. It was made without my knowledge. I can't begin to tell you how disappointed I'll be if people start purchasing copies and capitalizing on the despicable way in which I've been exploited."

There were more questions, one on top of another. Jasmine tuned the reporters out as she continued to push forward. She was forced left and right, and started to panic. Her breathing accelerated, and she wondered if she'd ever make it past this crowd and to the sidewalk, where she could hail a cab or flag down a Good Samaritan if necessary.

"Let her through," a loud male voice bellowed,

and Jasmine turned to see Allan pushing his way toward her. He was the last person she wanted to see, but she couldn't deny that she could use his help right now.

Within seconds, his arms circled around her. Given Allan's six-foot-four-inch height and two-hundred-and-forty-pound body mass, he was able to maneuver his way to the sidewalk without much difficulty.

"Mr. Jackson, do you know who leaked this video to the press?" a reporter asked him.

"I have nothing to say," Allan told them.

At that moment a taxi pulled up to the sidewalk. Jasmine threw her hand in the air to get the driver's attention, in case he was intimidated by the crowd.

"Ms. St. Clair—"

"Jasmine—"

"We're through here," Allan said, his voice authoritative. Shielding Jasmine's body, he led her to the taxi.

She opened the back door and scrambled inside. Only then did she meet Allan's eyes.

"Thank you," she told him.

"I'll call you later," he said, then closed the door.

Jasmine was relieved, because she didn't want Allan to slip into the taxi beside her. She held his gaze though, and easily read his lips when he mouthed the words, *I love you.*

Yeah, right.

As grateful as she was that Allan had gotten her through the crowd, she knew there was no going back to him. He might think her anger would blow over, but Jasmine knew that things between them would never be the same.

She could never be his lover again, and she wasn't sure she could even be his friend.

"Hey," the driver said, craning his neck over his shoulder to look at Jasmine as she settled in the backseat. His eyes grew wide with admiration. "I know who you are. You're that actress. The one who…"

The man's voice trailed off and Jasmine could only assume it was because the expression on her face stopped him cold.

The man turned back to the road. "Where to?" he asked.

"Beverly Hills," Jasmine replied, then gave him her address.

"Wow, this crowd is crazy." The driver moved forward, almost clipping two of the reporters who stood in front of the taxi snapping photos.

"Tell me about it," Jasmine mumbled, wondering if Pamela Anderson and Paris Hilton had been swarmed like this after their sex tapes had been released. A cameraman ran alongside the car, trying to get as much footage of Jasmine as possible.

Then the taxi driver accelerated, losing him and everyone else.

Jasmine blew out a sigh of relief.

Her head hurt and her heart raced, and she had to try to force herself to relax. She failed, and couldn't help wondering if she'd ever be able to relax again.

Jasmine caught the driver staring at her through his rearview mirror. She shuffled across the backseat until she was behind him, then rested her head against the window.

"I'm an actor, too," the driver said after several minutes of silence. "A bit part here, a bit part there. I drive taxi so I can go to auditions when I want, but so far, I haven't had a big break. This business will eat you alive."

"Ain't that the truth," Jasmine said softly, and was happy when the driver didn't say another word. She was in no mood for casual conversation.

Jasmine closed her eyes. Her mind ventured back to twenty-four hours earlier, as she'd been giddy with excitement anticipating the world premiere of *The Game*. It seemed inconceivable that in less than a day, her life could have turned so completely upside down.

But it had. And she wasn't naïve. She knew first-hand that a person's world—and life—could change at the drop of a hat. It had been that way the day Rickey had died. One minute, he'd been laughing while walking along the sidewalk with her. The next, he'd been violently struck by a car, his life instantly taken.

Never would he smile again. It was as though Rickey had been the sunshine in the St. Clair family, and with his death, the sunshine had permanently disappeared.

"Let me guess," the taxi driver said, interrupting her thoughts. "That must be your place right there."

At the driver's words, Jasmine opened her eyes. She was thankful to be pulled from the painful memories about her brother's untimely passing, but seeing the crowd outside her place only reminded her that she had a lot of unpleasantness to deal with yet.

Inwardly she groaned. She wasn't stupid. She had known, of course, that there would be media camped outside of her place, too. But still, the reality that the exterior of her house was swarmed with reporters made her stomach twist into a painful knot.

"Yeah, that's my place," Jasmine answered.

"What do you want me to do? Drive through them?"

"Yes," Jasmine answered without hesitation. "That is my house. My private property. I'll be damned if I have to fight my way through that crowd to get to my own front door."

The taxi driver slowed, and the horde of reporters instantly turned their attention to the car.

"There she is!" someone yelled, and the crowd converged. They swarmed the car like a mass of ants going in for the kill.

"Keep going," Jasmine told the driver. "I need to reach that keypad so I can punch in my security code."

To the driver's credit, he hit the horn in a rapid succession of angry spurts and kept moving forward. After about a minute, the window beside Jasmine came down. She had to push her body forward so that her fingers could reach the keypad. She was aware of several cameras flashing, of the reporters suddenly thrusting microphones into the open window, but she tried to ignore them.

Finished entering her code, Jasmine pressed the

button to raise the window, then crouched in the backseat to hide her face.

She heard the gate start to open, and the taxi picked up its pace. Only after that did Jasmine lift her head. Glancing over her shoulder, she saw the reporters behind her, video cameras catching the taxi's every movement.

"That's some crowd, lady," the taxi driver commented.

"At least they were smart enough to stay off my property." One of the things Jasmine had liked about this house when she'd first seen it was the gate that surrounded the grounds. The house itself wasn't that large, but it was certainly enough for her needs. It was cozy. And the large privacy gate would hopefully protect her from potential stalkers, which was a very real downside to a career as a movie star.

So was having an overly ambitious boyfriend, one who would betray you at the drop of a hat.

Jasmine's phone rang. And rang. She picked up the receiver, then promptly hung it up.

No sooner than the receiver was back on its cradle, it started ringing once again. Again, Jasmine picked up the receiver and hung it up.

Then it started ringing again.

This time, Jasmine grabbed the receiver and put it to her ear. "Hello?"

"Jasmine, I'm Steve Brady from the *Los Angeles Times*."

Jasmine hung up, then took the phone off the hook so no one else could call through.

Slowly, she headed to her front window and peered through the blinds. The media hadn't budged.

Jasmine stepped away from the window and headed into her bedroom. Not bothering to change out of her dress, Jasmine curled up on her bed beneath the covers.

And lay there.

The minutes dragged by and the boredom was too hard to deal with, so Jasmine turned on her television and tried to pretend this was a normal day.

She watched two movies in a row, both comedies, then made herself a quick meal of toast and cereal before watching a thriller with Cuba Gooding Jr.

When dusk covered the sky, she headed back to the front window to look outside.

And saw that the crowd of reporters was still there.

Feeling as though her legs were filled with lead, Jasmine dragged herself back to her bedroom. She finally broke down and had a good, long cry.

Darien Lamont stood at the edge of the cliff, staring down at the idyllic view of the water below. Staring, but not enjoying. Given why he was standing here, enjoyment was the last thing on his mind.

He knew, without a doubt, that it was time to move on.

The dream had forced him out here. The dream

of a woman grinning at him, her smile bright and beautiful.

Darien didn't know who she was, or why she entered his thoughts, but when she visited him in his dreams, he felt a sense of peace.

Not like what he felt right now.

This morning, after dreaming about her again, he got out of bed and immediately snatched the photo of him and Sheila off the night table. Why he had it there, he didn't know. It was a constant reminder of all he had lost.

Maybe that was why. On some level, he didn't *want* to forget.

To forget meant he could make himself vulnerable again at some point in the future.

And that was something Darien Lamont *never* wanted to do again.

But because he'd dreamed of this strange woman again, he had awoken with the very real sense that it was time to put closure on the past. Maybe that's what the dream was about—his subconscious telling him he had to make the effort to move on.

Darien did want to move on, which was why he was standing here, at the edge of the cliff, with the sterling silver picture frame in his hands.

He lifted the frame. Glancing at the photograph it held inside, he felt the same sting of bitter emotion he had every time he'd looked at the picture in the last two months.

He was tired of feeling pain and betrayal. It had gotten him nowhere. And as much as he had tried to understand Sheila's actions, no matter what she said, he never would.

You weren't there for me. What did you expect me to do?

I expected you to love me, to honor your vows before God!

The only vow you honored was to the military.

Darien closed his eyes, trying to block out the memory of the ugly argument he'd had with Sheila when he'd returned from Iraq. "You have to move on," he told himself.

Sheila had.

Darien stared at the picture once more, then held it to his heart. Why, he wasn't sure. The photo taken on his wedding day no longer held any significance.

Certainly not now that his divorce was officially final.

Raising his hand high over his head, Darien tossed the photo into the water below.

He watched it crash into the waves, then disappear into the aqua-blue water.

Gone was the picture. Just like everything else that had mattered to him for the past seven years.

Chapter 4

Jasmine had been hiding out in her house for two days, and for those two days the crowd of reporters and camera crews hadn't budged.

In fact, it had gotten larger.

Her housekeeper was so unnerved, she'd asked for time off. Though Jasmine could have used her help to run errands, she hadn't had the heart to say no.

Life was simply crazy. Jasmine had had to leave her phone unplugged, and ignore her cell as both had been ringing nonstop. The invasion of her privacy was driving her batty.

And she was starving.

Having eaten the supply of food in her house, and

with Fiona on "vacation," Jasmine needed to go shopping. Either that or stay in her house until she starved to death.

That meant she had to venture out.

Jasmine's heart beat rapidly as she slipped into a pair of jeans and a T-shirt. *This is crazy,* she told herself. *I shouldn't have to be nervous leaving my own home.*

Jasmine continued telling herself that even as she left her house to loud questions, screams and general pandemonium. Through her dark glasses, she took one look at the crowd and realized that it was too large to be just reporters. Didn't people have a life? How could "fans" stake out her property like this?

Perhaps Jasmine should have called the police to escort her, but she wasn't thinking of that. Instead she got in her car, drove toward the gate and, when it opened, drove at a steady yet slow pace through the crowd.

And said a silent prayer of thanks when she got through unscathed.

Good grief, people could be vultures! Fine, so there was a sex tape of her floating around. Did people have to lose their minds over the matter? Men and women had sex. There probably wasn't a minute of the day that went by when there wasn't a couple somewhere on the planet making love. It was a natural fact, but by the way the media was dying to get her to tell her side of the story, you'd think she had invented the art of copulation.

Jasmine tried to put the whole ridiculous situation out of her mind as she drove to the grocery store. She drove a little recklessly to lose the car she thought was tailing her, and succeeded. And after twenty minutes, she finally pulled into the parking lot of Gelson's supermarket.

She was en route to the store's front door when she heard, "Jasmine."

The voice wasn't loud, and on instinct, she turned.

That's when she saw a man who appeared to be in his fifties standing about ten feet away from her. His grin morphed into a frown a moment before he screamed, "Whore!"

Jasmine was so shocked, she didn't have time to react. Not even when she saw the man raise a brick above his head and whip it in her direction.

The only thing Jasmine had time to do was think, *I'm going to die.*

Then the world went black.

As fate would have it Jasmine didn't die, but a few days after the vicious attack by a crazed stranger, she found herself debating the merits of being alive versus being dead.

It was one thing for people to lose respect for her because of the video, even if they didn't know how it had come about. But to attack her as though they had the right to impose some sort of morality punishment? That was unacceptable.

Two days spent in hospital because of that creep. Luckily, Jasmine hadn't been seriously hurt. The blow from the brick had caused a concussion and the need for six stitches across her forehead, but she would live.

Not that she had much of a life to look forward to.

Now back home for only thirty-six hours, Jasmine felt defeated. She knew she shouldn't feel that way, but she couldn't help it. And she didn't really want to die, just to somehow escape the madness. She was in no mood to show her face again anywhere, not even outside her front gate to get her mail. Not while it seemed that everyone in Hollywood had turned their backs on her and made her out to be some sort of villain.

Even some of the people she'd considered close friends either hadn't visited her in the hospital or hadn't even called her while she'd been there. It was proof of the fact that everything in Hollywood— even friendship—was fleeting. As fake as the fictional movies filmed every day.

At least her agent hadn't dumped her. Thank God for Victoria Graydon, an exclusive talent manager who represented a select few clients, who was a consistent source of support. Victoria was the one precious gem in this crazy town.

"Thank you, Allan," she muttered under her breath, feeling anger at her ex-boyfriend again. "Thanks for ruining my life."

Groaning, Jasmine threw off her covers. It was well past noon, high time she got out of her bed. Until now, she'd been awake but lying down, her head propped atop three pillows. For the past hour she had passed the time by staring at the wall clock and listening to its rhythmic *tick, tick* as each second passed.

Her brain was numb from the boredom and, quite frankly, the depression. It was hard not to feel a measure of sadness at all she'd been through. One minute, she had been at the top of her career with every reason to believe her place in Tinsel Town was secure. The next, she was at the bottom of a dark pit with no way out.

"What are you gonna do, Jasmine?" she asked herself. "Spend another day feeling sorry for yourself?"

Enough was enough. She'd let this scandal get the better of her and it was time to take charge again. Do something—*anything*—to snap herself out of this funk.

Jasmine forced herself to sit up. She knew what she needed, and that was to get away. The idea had come to her when, to protect her privacy, Victoria had hired a driver to take her home from the hospital in a Hummer with tinted windows. All this so that the paparazzi couldn't get a photo of her with the bandage on her forehead, because God only knew how they'd spin the story accompanying that image.

There was only one way to truly escape the paparazzi, and that was to go somewhere they couldn't find her.

Jasmine was tired of living like a depressed hermit. For her, all life's simple pleasures were gone—and she wanted them back. It seemed like eons since she had enjoyed jogging through the neighborhood in the morning as the sun rose. Or longer still since she'd been able to sit outside and simply enjoy nature. She had a million-dollar view overlooking the Pacific, and yet she didn't feel safe heading to her back patio to watch the sunset.

Victoria had told her to remember the fabulous reviews of her performance in *The Game,* but Jasmine doubted the general public remembered them. She was certain that when people thought of the name Jasmine St. Clair now, they thought of that sleazy sex tape.

"Stop thinking about this," she told herself, swinging her legs over the side of the bed. The hardwood floor was cool beneath her feet and felt almost foreign—yet oddly refreshing. Another forgotten pleasure.

Bracing both hands at her sides, Jasmine slowly eased her body off the bed. Instantly her head swam, so she sat back down. The doctor had told her that she might feel light-headed from time to time because of her injury, and that was proving to be true.

There was one positive in this whole mess. The man who had attacked her—some freak who said he'd been "told by God" to punish her—had immediately been tackled by two men after the assault. Perhaps because he felt he was justified in doing what he did, the man gave the police a full confession. The police told Jasmine she could expect the guy to get around ten years in prison, which was a relief.

The moment of dizziness passed and Jasmine attempted to stand again. Once on her feet, she slowly walked to her bedroom window and stared out at the distant view of the Pacific Ocean from her hillside home. The sun danced on the water's surface like liquid gold. It would be so nice to go to the beach— not to swim; the enormous waves would only pound her into the sand. But how glorious it would be to just walk along the shore and wet her feet the way she had done on many such occasions before the infamous sex tape had surfaced.

Jasmine went to her night table and found the phone cord. She put the phone jack back into the wall so she could call Victoria. The way her voice mail was set up, she would still be able to retrieve messages even if her phone was off the hook. She was certain that her voice mail was full, so she decided to check it before calling Victoria.

Indeed, it was full. The first three messages were from reporters, asking her if she'd give them an exclusive. Then there was one from Allan.

"Jasmine, this is Allan. I know you're probably still mad. But please call me. We need to talk."

More reporters, then another call from Allan.

"Jasmine, it's me again. I called the hospital and couldn't reach you. I'm so sorry about the attack! I can't imagine what you're going through. Please call me. I still love you. I need to know you're okay. Call me whenever. It doesn't matter how late. I just need to hear from you."

There were more messages from reporters, more from Allan. In each of Allan's messages, he sounded increasingly desperate. He wanted her to call him, wanted her to give him another chance, wanted to know how she was doing.

Jasmine deleted all the messages. Allan might want to hear from her, but she wasn't going to call him. He might have thought his scheme wouldn't hurt anyone, but Jasmine could have been killed because of his stunt.

What he'd done was unforgivable, and getting out of town would allow her to escape Allan, as well.

She dialed Victoria's cell number.

"Jasmine," Victoria said, clearly having seen Jasmine's number on her caller ID. "How're you doing?"

"Not so well."

"'Not well' as in you need a doctor?"

"'Not well' as in I'm losing my mind."

"You're lying low, right? You have enough food?"

"I am, and I do," Jasmine replied. Then sighed. "Victoria, I don't think I can deal with this anymore. It was bad enough when it was just the media hounding me. But then I get attacked by that creep, and I can't even feel like I can relax in my own home and recuperate. This isn't right."

"I know."

"You'd think I was the first person to have a sex tape surface. Good grief. The media is hounding me, watching my every move."

"It will pass," Victoria assured her.

"But not soon enough," Jasmine said. "I can't stay here. I can't live like this. Like a prisoner in my own home. Do you know I haven't opened the blinds since this whole thing happened? Not even since I got back from the hospital. Every time I look outside, I see media camped outside my gate. This is insane."

"I have a house in Aspen," Victoria said. "It's empty now, and it's yours if you want."

"Aspen." Jasmine considered the offer. "That'll certainly be better than Beverly Hills."

"And considering it's not skiing season, the town will be fairly deserted. A good place to lie low."

"But it's not far enough away," Jasmine found herself saying. "People will probably still recognize me, tip the media off that I'm there."

"Where were you thinking of going?"

Jasmine hadn't really considered that. She only knew that she wanted to get out of Los Angeles, and the sooner the better.

"I don't know," she admitted. "But definitely somewhere out of the country. Not Jamaica, as I've got family there. I wouldn't put it past the paparazzi to fly there if they get word I've left the country. As it is, I hope no one has the audacity to go there and harass my extended family."

"So you want to head out of the country, but you're not sure where."

"I can call a travel agent."

"No, don't do that. I have an idea about something," Victoria said thoughtfully.

"What?"

"Let me look into it and call you back."

"Vic—"

"I don't want to get your hopes up if I can't pull

this off," she said. "Give me twenty minutes, half an hour tops."

"Okay," Jasmine conceded, knowing she didn't have a choice.

She ended the call and went to her walk-in closet, where she extracted her largest piece of luggage and a smaller carry-on bag. And then she started to pack.

Forty minutes later, the phone rang. Jasmine dropped the pair of jeans she was stuffing into her carry-on bag and ran to her night table. She snatched up the receiver.

"Hello?" she said, only then realizing that it could be someone other than Victoria on the line.

"Great news," Victoria crooned, and Jasmine's spirits lifted.

"How great?" she asked.

"How does St. Lucia sound?"

"St. Lucia? You're serious?"

"Yep. I have a friend who's got a villa on the island that is empty right now. You can have it for a month, or even two if you need it. He won't be heading there until Christmas."

"Oh my God." Laughter bubbled in Jasmine's throat. "Victoria, you are amazing."

"I'm not finished," Victoria said. "It gets even better."

"Better than a villa in St. Lucia? I can't imagine anything better than that."

"How about not having to get on a commercial flight? My friend said you can use his private plane to get there. And you can leave in the morning."

Now Jasmine squealed. "I don't believe it."

"You'll love it there. It's quiet, isolated, near the water."

"I'd love it even if it didn't have modern plumbing," Jasmine joked. "As long as it's far from here." She paused. "It *does* have modern plumbing, right?"

Victoria chuckled, and Jasmine could see the middle-aged woman's strikingly beautiful face as surely as if she were in the room with her. "It's got a lot more than that," Victoria said. "This place is a beautiful two-bedroom villa situated on the hillside, overlooking Labrelotte Bay. The view of the bay is to die for. Lots of palm trees, lush green earth. Certainly more exotic than the view of the Pacific."

"You sound like you've been there," Jasmine said.

"Like I said, you can have the place right up to December if need be, and the best part, you don't have to pay a dime."

"Who would do all this for me? I was sure that everyone in this town hated me. Except for you, of cour—"

Jasmine stopped short as the answer hit her. *Of course.* Victoria *had* been to this tropical getaway— with her ex-husband. That had to be why she could describe it so well.

"You called Stephen, didn't you?" Jasmine asked.

"None of your concern."

"That means you did."

"Yeah, well," Victoria said flippantly. "He always said if I ever needed anything…"

"But you hate dealing with your ex."

"He still wants me back," Victoria explained. "And since he's one of Hollywood's most successful producers, he's got the vacation homes, the private planes. He can come in handy when one of my clients has a sex tape surface and needs to get out of town. That was a joke," Victoria said after a moment. "You were supposed to laugh."

"You've been sleeping with Stephen again," Jasmine went on, ignoring Victoria's banter.

Victoria only hesitated a second. "A woman has needs," she said in reply.

"I hope you know what you're doing. Everything you've said about how he hurt you… I don't know if I should take you up on this offer."

"Are you kidding? You'd be crazy not to take advantage of this. I'm a big girl. Don't you worry about me. You head to St. Lucia and escape the craziness here. Get some rest. Come back rejuvenated. This town hasn't seen the last of you. And when you get back, I'll have it all sorted out and you'll be Hollywood's darling once again."

"I'm not sure that matters to me anymore," Jasmine said softly.

"Nonsense!" Victoria exclaimed. "You told me that you wanted to be an actress for a long time. Don't let what Allan did rob you of your dream. Not many people are able to live a dream like this one. You worked hard for it. Don't you dare talk about giving it up."

"But people hate me now. I read on the Internet that some church group in North Carolina set up a picket line outside the movie theater showing *The Game*."

"And ever since the scandal hit, *The Game* has been number one at the box office."

"You have Terrence Green in a film, and it's going to be number one."

"Stop selling yourself short, Jasmine. Keep this in mind—if people weren't having extreme reactions to this scandal, there'd be something wrong. It would mean they *don't* care. But they do. And in no time, they'll see you as the role model you've always been. That church group will probably invite you to talk to their teens."

"I hope so."

"I know so. Listen, I have to call Stephen back, get all the details, like when you need to be at Van Nuys."

"Okay."

"So I'll call you a bit later. You start packing."

"I already did," Jasmine admitted.

Victoria laughed. "That's my girl."

"I really appreciate this, Victoria. I want you to know that. You've always come through for me." She knew if she continued her voice would crack, so she took a moment to compose herself. "You've been…so good to me. Another agent would have dumped me already."

Victoria chuckled. "Hey, I'm no fool."

Sinking onto her mattress, Jasmine felt a sense of tranquility she hadn't felt since this whole nightmare began. "Thank you. Thank you so much."

"Don't mention it. I'll call you soon."

"Goodbye, Victoria."

"Take care."

Jasmine disconnected the phone, but held the receiver to her chest. Her forehead ached slightly from holding back her tears, but now that she was off the phone, she couldn't hold them back any longer. Slowly, a hot tear trickled down her cheek, followed by a matching one on the other side.

Happiness warming her soul, she smiled. Yes, it was well past time she got past her moping. Despite everything, she was blessed with people who still cared for her. As alone as she felt, she really wasn't.

People suffered far greater heartache than what she was experiencing right now.

That thought made her think of her parents, how they'd never recovered after Rickey's death.

Jasmine pushed the thought from her mind. She wanted nothing to mar her great news.

St. Lucia... She'd never been to the island before but had heard wonderful things about it. She knew some actors had homes there, that they found St. Lucia both beautiful and peaceful. Soon she would experience the magic of the quaint tropical island firsthand.

For the next month or so, it would be her home.

Chapter 5

"You've got to get over the anger, man."

Darien laughed mirthlessly into the phone at his best friend's comment. "Get over it? You think it's that easy?"

"Of course it's not easy," Warren said. "But you can't let this eat you alive."

"You think I'm not trying?" And he was. Every day, he told himself to move on, to put the memory of Sheila and their years together behind him. It was easier said than done. "Sheila and I were married for seven years," Darien went on. "How do you get over that kind of betrayal?"

"I don't know. Start hitting the clubs, find yourself another woman."

Darien scoffed. "Like I need a woman from the club scene."

"Not for anything permanent. But a warm body to help you forget Sheila… It hasn't hurt me any."

"Not yet."

"You just protect yourself, man. No glove, no love."

Darien rolled his eyes, and was glad that his best friend wasn't in the room with him to see. He loved Warren like a brother, but the idea that he pick up some woman in a bar was ludicrous.

"Not gonna happen," Darien said.

"All right. I was just offering a suggestion." Warren paused. "You talked to Rodney?"

The mention of Darien's brother made his stomach lurch. "Nah. I haven't talked to him. And don't tell me to call him, because my answer will be *hell no*."

"Maybe you should."

"Hell no."

"Listen to me—"

"You know what? I've gotta run."

"Hear me out, Darien. Rodney feels awful about the whole thing. He knows he messed up."

"Messed up? I wouldn't call his *sleeping with my wife* messing up. He's my brother. Some things, you just don't do."

"Sheila manipulated him."

"I don't care if she stripped naked and threw herself on top of him. *You don't sleep with your brother's wife.*"

Anger sweeping over him, Darien had to close his eyes and take a breath.

"Look, I didn't mean to get you upset. It's just that I talked to Rodney, and I know how bad he feels."

"I can't talk about this anymore."

"Darien—"

"I'm serious. I'll call you later, okay?"

"All right, man. You take care of yourself."

Darien slammed the receiver onto its cradle. Then buried his face in his hands.

Get over it? Was Warren serious? As if Darien could simply snap his fingers and put the whole incident behind him.

He sat silently for several minutes, his breathing ragged. He didn't like being mad at his friend. Warren wasn't the culprit here. But Warren was a single guy, one who'd never even been seriously in love. He didn't lack for female companionship when he wanted it, but he'd never given anyone his heart.

What Darien hadn't told his friend was that maybe, just maybe, his heart was ready to move on. Even after tossing his wedding photo into the sea, he'd continued having those odd dreams about that beautiful woman.

She definitely wasn't someone he knew, and the dreams weren't of a sexual nature. In his dreams he would see an image of the woman smiling and laughing, or of her walking along a path with pretty flowers.

But he never interacted with her.

She was beautiful, slim, with shoulder-length hair and smooth, dark skin. This woman looked nothing like Sheila, who had a more voluptuous body and light brown skin.

Darien had wanted to tell Warren about the dreams, because while not unpleasant, they left him feeling weird when he woke up. So much so that he was starting to wonder if he was going a little bonkers.

Shooting to his feet, he said, "Forget the dreams, forget Sheila, forget everything."

Then he headed for the front door. Right now, he needed to get out, go someplace where he could lose his thoughts in a beer or two.

It was the best way to block out the pain.

Though she had to do so often, Jasmine hated flying. She hated the moment the plane left the ground and the queasy feeling she experienced looking out at a lopsided world. She hated having to chew gum like a cow on speed just to minimize the pressure in her ears. And she hated the fact that while she might actually feel secure for a short time during a smooth flight, one bout of turbulence sent her stomach plummeting to her knees and her heart scrambling to her throat.

The fact that she was in a small plane, no matter how luxurious, only made her unease more intense. The turbulence felt worse, the smell of gas was worse.

At least the plane was well stocked with alcohol, and all it took was two drinks to calm Jasmine's nerves—and help her make it through hours of flying without dying of fright.

"That, Ms. St. Clair, is St. Lucia on our left," the pilot announced on the loudspeaker.

Jasmine had to leave her seat and cross to the left side, where she saw the island in the distance. She smiled.

"We should be on the ground in twenty minutes," the pilot continued.

Jasmine drew in a deep breath. Several hours of flying, and she was almost there. She hoped this island would give her the peace she so craved.

Her eyes drank in clear blue water below and the stretch of white-sand beach. Victoria was right—this was a far cry from the Pacific. The island was mountainous though, like the west coast in the U.S. But much more green.

Jasmine settled back in her seat, fastened her seat belt when instructed, and said a quick prayer as the plane descended. With only a minor bump, she was back on solid ground.

St. Lucia. Her new home.

She couldn't explain it, but already she knew she had done the right thing by coming here. It was a feeling deep in her soul, a feeling that seemed to whisper, "You'll be happy here."

She should be feeling a sense of fear, or at least anxiety, at the thought of moving to a new country— even if the move wasn't permanent. But she wasn't anxious at all. Jasmine was looking forward to the peace and quiet. The less people who recognized her here, the better.

As the plane's door opened, a rush of humid air enveloped her. She quickly stripped out of her light cardigan, leaving her wearing a tank top and jeans.

She wished she had a pair of shorts in her carry-on bag, but she'd just have to wait until she got to the house to change.

Minutes later, Jasmine had exited the plane and was surveying the lush, green hills. She sniffed the warm island air. Warm climate without the smog. That was a definite bonus.

Her lips curling in a smile, she felt her soul begin to heal.

If there was a place more heavenly than St. Lucia, Jasmine couldn't imagine it. The island was absolutely stunning. The assortment of trees and shrubs was greener than anywhere she'd ever been, the flowers more colorful. If possible, St. Lucia was more attractive than Antigua or Jamaica, two tropical settings that Jasmine adored. St. Lucia was truly a piece of heaven on earth. "Lush" and "paradise" were the two words that best described this small island.

Instantly she fell in love with the country— though the drive to Castries, where the villa was located, left a lot to be desired. The narrow roads and hairpin turns caused her more stress than the flight.

"Um," Jasmine said, glancing around in concern when the driver turned left onto a small, rocky path completely enshrouded in shrubs. She couldn't imagine where he was going. But after several seconds, the path grew wider and the haphazard greenery cleared, leading to a paved driveway and pristine lawn.

And there, in front of her, was an absolutely breathtaking Mediterranean-style villa.

Instantly the harrowing drive became a distant memory.

"This is it?" Jasmine asked, though there were no other houses in the area. This was the only villa on this stretch of land.

"Yes," the driver replied.

"Amazing," Jasmine said. She opened the car door and got out. She walked several steps toward the house, taking everything in. The stunning one-story house was perched on a hill that overlooked the water. The exterior was stucco, painted a combination of pale pink and beige, with myriad colorful flowers below the two front windows. The large front porch had a hammock tied to two posts, a perfect spot for relaxing.

It was far more than she ever would have hoped for.

Jasmine inhaled a deep breath. The smell of the sea made her sigh with pleasure. Already, she felt so much better.

Swirling around, she saw that the driver was taking her bags from the trunk. She hurried back to the car and retrieved her purse, then took out the money to pay him.

As he placed the last of her bags on the front step, Jasmine handed him twenty dollars more than the price they'd agreed upon.

"Enjoy your stay on the island," the driver said, his accent light. In ways it was similar to the Jamaican accent, but with a bit of a French flavor.

"Thank you."

"Here's my card," the man went on, passing her a card with his number on it. "If you don't mind, when your parents arrive at the airport, will you have them call me? I would be happy to bring them here, as well."

"Certainly," Jasmine told the man, whose card said his name was William. Of course, she wouldn't be calling him. Telling him that her parents were coming had been a little white lie. She didn't want this man— seemingly nice, but still a stranger—knowing that she would be staying in a private house alone.

You couldn't be too careful.

William got back into the car and did a U-turn in the driveway. As he drove off, Jasmine waved at him. She waited until he was gone to dig the key to the house out of her purse.

The house had a pleasant smell, somewhat floral, and Jasmine took a good, long whiff. Placing her hands on her hips, she scanned the large living room to the right, the glimpse of kitchen behind that and the doors on the left. The living room had floor-to-ceiling windows, allowing light to bathe the room. The place was spacious yet cozy, with attractive wicker furniture.

Well, there was no time like the present to get settled into her temporary home. One by one, she brought her three pieces of luggage inside and settled them in the foyer. Then she went off in search of the bedroom.

The first door she opened was the bathroom, which was very large and boasted a tub in the center

of the room. It was the kind of tub that graced the
pages of home and style magazines. Jasmine could
easily picture herself in the tub, luxuriating in a sea
of thick bubbles. As soon as she unpacked, that
would be the first order of business.

The next door Jasmine opened was indeed a
bedroom, and her first impression of the room left
her awestruck. It was extremely large, painted a
vibrant peach color. The room definitely had a
female feel—not just because of the color, but
because of the canopy bed and netting around it.
Stepping into the room, Jasmine gasped at the
stunning view of the bay. This room didn't just have
windows—it had two glass doors that led to the back
patio.

Jasmine trotted to the glass doors and peered
outside. When she saw Victoria again, she would
definitely kiss her. This place was simply divine.
The backyard was immaculately landscaped, with
four massive palm trees surrounding the perimeter.
There was a pea-shaped pool and adjoining hot tub,
plus an outdoor bar area. This was going to be the
perfect place for Jasmine to unwind and pass the
days before she was ready to head back to the U.S.

Jasmine decided this bedroom would be hers, but
continued to check out the rest of the villa. The second
bedroom was about the same size as the first one, but
instead of being painted in peach, it was a sky-blue.
Oddly enough, the bed was unmade, and Jasmine was
certain she could smell the faint scent of male
cologne.

She padded into the room, toward the open door on the right. It was an en suite bathroom, smaller than the main one. Jasmine narrowed her eyes. There was deodorant on the counter, as well as cologne. She went to the room's closet and saw men's clothes hanging there.

Heading back out to the living room, Jasmine found the phone. She sat down and called her agent's cell number.

"Victoria Graydon," she said.

"Hey, Victoria. It's me."

"Jasmine," her agent practically sang. "You arrived?"

"Yes, and this place is incredible."

"I knew you'd love it."

"I do. I definitely do. But I have a question for you. Are you sure it's empty? There are men's toiletries in the bathroom, men's clothes in the closet…"

"Not to worry. They must belong to Stephen. He does like to get to his island retreat whenever he can." Victoria paused. "You didn't find any women's clothes there, did you?"

"None that I've seen."

"So maybe it is over with that starlet," Victoria said thoughtfully.

"Pardon me?" Jasmine asked.

"Nothing," Victoria replied. "Sweetie, I have to make some calls—"

"No problem. I'll let you go. I just wanted you to know that I got here safely, and that the place is lovely. Thank you."

"Keep in touch."

With that, Jasmine replaced the phone's receiver. For a moment she sat on the sofa, reveling in the beauty of the villa. She wondered if she'd ever be this successful, to own several homes in different parts of the world.

All she really wanted, however, was to continue working. She didn't care if she had hundreds of millions in the bank, as long as she could pay her bills and help her family financially. To keep working was a blessing.

With work entering her mind for the first time since getting to the island, Jasmine remembered the tape. And wondered if she'd even have a chance to work in the film business again.

Jasmine pushed herself up off the sofa. She had not come here to think about work.

She turned and walked to the kitchen, then opened a patio door and strolled outside. She kept walking until she reached the edge of the hill, then stared down at the world below.

On the other side of the bay, there were a bunch of villas in the hillside, too many of them to be anything other than part of a resort. She remembered the driver telling her that they were passing the Windjammer, one of the island's famous resorts, as they'd neared Stephen's private villa. That had to be it.

But other than that hotel, there was nothing else around her, except lush island foliage. And that resort was a far distance off. Which meant she had plenty of privacy.

Jasmine turned and wandered toward the pool. She did have a bikini in her luggage, but considering no eyes could see her where she was, she obviously didn't need it. So she stripped off her tank top, shimmied her jeans down her hips, then dove into the pool.

The doctor had told her there was no problem getting her bandage and stitching wet, so underwater, she swam the length of the pool before pushing her head through the surface to take a breath. The water was cool and refreshing. She swam on her back in the other direction, again not stopping until she reached the opposite end of the pool.

She continued that routine—one way on her back, the other on her stomach—until she'd done twenty laps. When she was finished, her limbs burned but she felt good. At least she was feeling something other than the despair that had plagued her since the news of her sex tape had hit.

Jasmine held on to the edge of the pool and caught her breath. Then she pushed her body upward until she was sitting on the ledge between the pool and the hot tub. She brushed her hair out of her face, then scanned the area for the controls to start the bubbles.

She saw it about twenty feet away, so got to her feet and headed in that direction. She was about to turn the dial when she heard, "Who the hell are you?"

Jasmine's hands flew to cover her breasts at the same time that she whipped her head around. The next instant, remembering that she was wearing only a thong, she quickly jumped into the hot tub to cover her exposed body. She cried out as the scorching hot water swallowed her whole.

"Who the hell am *I?*" Jasmine shrieked. "Who the hell are *you?*"

For several seconds, they stared each other down.

"I said," the man began as he started toward her, "who the hell are you?"

"Okay, can you stop right there and give me some privacy?" Jasmine asked, totally indignant. "I know you saw that I'm not dressed."

The man stopped, but he was too close for Jasmine's comfort. Even though she was underwater, she pressed her hands harder over her breasts.

"You didn't answer my question," the man said.

"And you didn't answer mine!" Jasmine countered.

"I happen to be the man who's staying in this house."

"Well, I'm the woman who got *permission* to stay in this house. And I know for a fact that no one is supposed to be here."

"Right." The man edged closer.

"Do you mind?" Jasmine snapped.

"Yeah, I do mind. I come home to find a strange woman in my place, frolicking around naked in my backyard like she owns the place. Of course I mind."

"This is not your place," Jasmine protested. "And I'm not *frolicking*. I was swimming."

"On private property," the man pointed out.

Jasmine groaned loudly. They were getting nowhere fast—and she was burning up. Soon, you'd be able to stick a fork in her and pronounce her *done*.

"I will be more than happy to talk to you…once I get out of here and put some clothes on." She deliberately spoke in a more conciliatory tone. "Do you mind getting me a towel?" When the man didn't answer, just continued to stare at her as though he expected her to simply vanish, she added, *"Please."*

"Sure," the man said. "I guess that's the logical next step." Silently he turned and headed toward the house at a brisk pace.

Jasmine watched him stalk off, wondering why he was so angry when she knew she was the one in the right. Victoria had specifically gotten permission for her to be here. Heck, the woman had given her a key and even flown her here on a private jet. So she knew for a fact that this man, whoever he was, shouldn't be in this house. She would do everything she had to not to anger him until she was able to dry off and get her clothes on. Then she would call the police and have him arrested for trespassing.

In less than two minutes, the man returned with an oversized white towel. He placed it on a chair near the hot tub.

But he didn't move.

"You're not going to stand there and watch me while I get out?" Jasmine asked, her tone revealing just how annoyed she was.

The man crossed his arms over his chest and turned.

Anger rose within Jasmine. She had had enough of this stranger. How dare he act as though he had a right to be mad at her, when she'd found *him* trespassing on private property?

But she wasn't about to beg and plead with him to go inside while she got decent. By now, most of the world had seen far worse of her than her naked flesh.

Cautiously, Jasmine stepped out of the hot tub, then quickly wrapped the thick towel around her body. "I'm decent," she said. "But I'd prefer that you give me a moment to get dried off and put my clothes on. That's a reasonable request, isn't it?"

The man turned to face her. And suddenly his eyes narrowed. Not in anger, but in question. It was almost as though he was seeing her for the first time.

"What happened to your head?" he asked, staring at her oddly.

Instinctively, Jasmine touched the gauze bandage on her forehead. "I got hurt," she said, not really answering his question. No wonder he hadn't figured out who she was sooner. But this close to her, he was getting a better look at her face. Any second now, his eyes would widen with recognition.

He'd think of the recent news about her, how she had been painted as the world's biggest tramp. And here she was, standing half-naked in front of him.

Please, Lord—don't let this man jump to any conclusions about my being naked in the pool....

Instead, still looking confused, he suddenly turned away.

What was that about? Did he recognize her and was so disgusted he could no longer look at her?

Well, she'd been there, done that, and had the stitches on her forehead to prove it. As long as this man wasn't hell-bent on punishing her for her sinful ways, she could deal with his scorn.

"If it's okay with you," Jasmine began, "I'd prefer to head inside and put some new clothes on."

"Sure," the man said, his voice sounding sort of distant.

Jasmine scooped up her jeans and tank top, then scooted toward the open kitchen door. Inside, she all but ran to get her larger suitcase. She took it to the unoccupied bedroom, shut the door, then leaned against it as she exhaled loudly.

She found herself remembering the attack at the grocery store. The anger in that man's eyes as he'd whipped that brick at her...she'd never seen anything quite like it. At least this stranger hadn't looked at her with pure, unadulterated hatred. She couldn't be sure, but she didn't expect violence from him.

Jasmine was about to drop her towel when she realized the shutters were open. Considering this man seemed to think she was some kind of trespassing freak, the last thing she wanted to do was to give him a free peep show, so she walked across the room and closed them.

But not before stealing a glance at the man outside. He was still standing near the hot tub, still wearing an odd expression on his face.

He must have recognized her, Jasmine figured. Recognized her and wasn't happy to have a reputed porn star in the same space with him. That was the only thing that could explain the look.

Frowning, Jasmine stepped away from the window. Then she opened her suitcase and pulled out a white T-shirt and white skirt.

Five minutes later, she was dressed and her hair brushed. She was ready to head back outside.

There was no point in putting off the inevitable ugly scene with this stranger.

Jasmine took a deep breath and opened the bedroom door.

Chapter 6

Maybe it was fate. Maybe it was madness. Or maybe it was a combination of both.

How else could Darien explain the fact that the woman from his dreams was here, in the very house he'd been occupying and dreaming of her for the past three weeks?

At first, he hadn't recognized her. Partly because he'd been so shocked to find someone in the pool, and then because that bandage on her forehead had obstructed a good view of her face. But as he'd moved closer to her, seen the face up close and personal that he'd been dreaming of for the past few weeks, it was as if he'd been pounded over the head with a sledgehammer.

He felt…odd. Like he was in the middle of another dream, only he knew he was very much awake.

Who was this woman, and what had brought her here?

"Excuse me?"

Darien turned at the sound of the woman's voice. She was standing near the kitchen door. Darien's stomach instantly tightened with the pull of attraction. Even with a bandage on her head, the woman was a vision of ebony perfection.

He swallowed, tried to push those thoughts aside. The reality was, she shouldn't be here. She was trespassing. He couldn't let the fact that she was a pretty woman—even if he had dreamed of her—cloud his judgment.

"If you want to come inside, we can talk."

Darien nodded, and the woman turned. She went back inside, and he did the same, following her into the living room.

"So," Darien began as he sat on the armchair. "Want to tell me what you're doing here?"

It was strange, but he was no longer angry. If anything, he was curious. Curious to know what had brought this woman from his dreams into his reality. There had to be an explanation for it—something logical, tangible.

"We're still going to play this game?" Jasmine asked. "I was hoping you would just get to the truth."

"I already told you the truth."

Though Jasmine was fully dressed, she couldn't

meet the stranger's eyes. The fact that he'd seen her almost completely naked embarrassed the heck out of her. That and the reality that with her sex tape scandal, he probably thought very lowly of her character.

Still, she wasn't about to back down and be intimidated. Jasmine was the one with the right to be here.

"I'm not playing any game," the man said, and sounded entirely believable.

But he had to be lying. Whether he sounded honest, or looked sexy as hell, Jasmine knew what the deal was. "Then how on earth are you here when I know you're not supposed to be?"

"I was told I could stay here," the man said.

"Which is a lie," Jasmine couldn't help retorting.

"I've been here for three weeks," the man went on, as if that meant he had permission to be occupying this stunning villa.

Finally, Jasmine met his gaze dead-on. "Look, I don't know how you found out about this place, but for your own best interests, you need to pack your stuff and leave."

"Really?"

"You've been here three weeks without detection, so consider yourself lucky. If you leave now, I won't call the authorities."

Chuckling, the man rose from the wicker armchair where he'd been sitting, and Jasmine found herself fully taking note of him. There was something about him that intrigued her, something oddly warm.

It was his voice, she realized. Now that he was no

longer angry, she realized that he had a gentle voice. Not a wimpy one by any stretch of the imagination, just one that was gentle and warm. Even when he'd found her at the pool, he hadn't yelled to convey his irritation. He'd spoken with authority, yes, but there had been a sort of respectful nature about him that Jasmine was just now realizing.

It was a romantic voice, really. The kind that would have a woman's knees growing weak—if the setting was right.

This wasn't the right setting, of course, but still Jasmine's eyes wandered over the man's body. He was tall, around six foot one, with close-cropped hair. And despite his mellow voice, he was clearly strong. He was wearing a loose-fitting silk shirt, and it was easy to see his hard pecs and large biceps. The man obviously worked out. His skin was the color of milk chocolate and, Jasmine had to admit, he looked as delicious.

It was a thought that shouldn't have entered her mind, considering the circumstances. That reality was brought home to her when the man started toward her, and she was reminded of the fact that she didn't know him. She stiffened her back. Not out of fright, because the man didn't scare her. But his presence in what was supposed to be her place of solace unnerved her.

He stood before her, his hands on his hips. "So you figure you show up here, you call the shots, and I just leave?"

From any other man that statement would have

been a booming proclamation meant to intimidate. From this one, with that sexy-mellow voice, Jasmine found her heart suddenly beating harder in her chest.

This is ridiculous, she told herself. *Pull yourself together!*

"We both know you're not supposed to be here," she said calmly, though she felt anything but calm.

"My name's Darien," the man said, as though he were introducing himself to her at a cocktail party. "And yours?"

"Don't come any closer," she warned, wondering if the man actually thought he could suddenly play nice and she'd change her mind about calling the police. Maybe he was deliberately using a bedroom voice to try to make her lower her guard. It wasn't going to work.

Darien's eyes widened. "What—you think I'm going to hurt you?"

Jasmine scooted across the sofa to the end beside the table that held the phone. She quickly grabbed the receiver.

"What are you doing?" Darien asked.

"What I should have done before I got dressed. I'm calling the police to have you escorted off this property."

"Just wait a second," Darien said, and despite herself, Jasmine lowered the phone. "Do I look like some sort of crazy person to you?" he went on.

Jasmine didn't respond. If he was a crazy person, he was the most attractive one she had ever seen....

"Okay, let me pose another question to you. Do I sound like I'm from this island? Do I have an accent?"

Jasmine hesitated. "No."

"Okay."

"But that doesn't mean—"

"That I'm not a creep? I'm an American, just like you are. How do you think I came to be here? By accident? I just stumbled upon this remote property?"

"Well…" Jasmine began, but couldn't think of another thing to say. Score one for Darien. But still, her agent had specifically told her that this place would be empty when she got here. Which is why she was confident that Darien had to be lying.

"Finally I've gotten through to you," he said.

"Not exactly," Jasmine responded. "Look, I don't know what you're doing here. Maybe you overheard a conversation somewhere, learned this place was empty, and flew here figuring no one would ever be the wiser."

"Overheard a conversation." Darien threw his head back and roared with laughter. "That's a good one."

"What I do know," Jasmine went on, trying to ignore the warmth of his laugh, "is that you're lying. Because I happen to know the woman whose husband owns this place," Jasmine told him, jutting her chin forward confidently. "And she gave me a key to the place and told me it as mine for as long as I wanted. That's how I know for a fact that you're not supposed to be here."

"And I'm a friend of the guy whose brother owns this place," Darien replied. He crossed his arms over his brawny chest, clearly as determined as Jasmine to stand his ground.

"I'll bet you are," Jasmine mumbled.

"Why don't you make a phone call?" Darien challenged, passing her the phone. "And not to the police," he added, pulling the receiver back and eyeing her with suspicion.

"Fine," Jasmine said. "A phone call will easily clear this situation up."

"My name is Darien Lamont," he went on. "And I'm a friend of Bruce Beck."

Hearing the name gave Jasmine pause, since Beck was the surname of Victoria's ex. Still, that didn't mean anything. If this guy kept up on pop culture, that wouldn't be hard to find out. Stephen Beck was a well-recognized name in Hollywood and beyond.

Or—Jasmine's stomach instantly sank—what if this guy was someone from the media pretending to be an average Joe? Someone who had somehow figured out she would be coming here, and this was all a plan of his to get the inside scoop on Hollywood's latest scandal?

"Take your time," Darien said, and started for the kitchen.

His words pulled Jasmine from her thoughts. "Hey, where are you going?"

"To make a pot of peppermint tea. Is that okay?"

"Do what you want," Jasmine mumbled.

As soon as he started to walk away again, she

made a face behind his back. Then she called Victoria's BlackBerry.

"Victoria Graydon," her agent answered.

"Victoria, it's me."

"Hey, Jasmine. I didn't think I'd hear from you again so soon."

"Well, I didn't expect to be calling yet, but there's a slight problem."

"Oh?"

"Yeah." She lowered her voice. "There's a guy here. A Darien Lamont?"

"What?"

"My thought exactly. But he claims that he knows Bruce. Your ex-husband's brother?"

"Yeah, Stephen does have a brother named Bruce," Victoria said, a question in her voice. "But Stephen specifically told me that the villa was empty."

"Which is what you told me. Maybe this guy knows about the villa because of Bruce and decided to come out here?" Jasmine offered. "Maybe if he hears the word from Stephen that I'm the one who's supposed to be here, he'll leave."

"Look, let me call him and I'll call you right back."

"Thanks."

Jasmine replaced the receiver and sighed with satisfaction. Darien ventured back into the living room.

"What's with the smug look?" he asked her.

"Because this whole situation is being sorted out. And as soon as the phone rings, you're going to have to pack your bags."

"We'll see about that."

"Yeah, we'll see."

Darien started for the kitchen again. "You want sugar in your tea?"

"Who said I wanted tea?"

"What kind of host would I be if I didn't offer my guest a hot beverage?"

"Your guest?" Jasmine guffawed. "You must be some kind of comedian—"

The phone rang, interrupting her, and Jasmine quickly grabbed the receiver. "So, Victoria. Can I call the police already?" She cut her eyes at Darien.

"Not quite," Victoria said.

Jasmine's stomach dropped. "Victoria?"

"Who knew?" She chuckled mirthlessly. "As you know, Stephen shares the place with friends and relatives, but normally he knows exactly who is there and when. Apparently, Bruce knew the place would be empty so he gave a friend of his the key."

"So he's…he's *allowed* to be here?" Jasmine asked in a horrified whisper.

"Afraid so. What, you think he's a creep or something? Stephen assured me that he's a nice guy."

At that moment Darien appeared, holding a tray, a teapot and two teacups. "Yeah, he's a regular Mr. Wonderful," Jasmine mumbled.

"Pardon me?" Victoria asked.

"Nothing," Jasmine said.

"Stephen said he recently came back from a tour in Iraq. I can't say enough good things about the men and women who fight for our freedom."

"Thanks," Jasmine said absently. "I'll call you later."

"Wait, there's something I forgot to tell you."

"More great news?" Jasmine said sarcastically.

"There's a huge resort practically next door to the villa. The Windjammer Landing. Stephen has a club card there, allowing him and his guests access to the property. So, if you want to go there and enjoy the spa, or the restaurants…all you have to do is use that card and explain you're a guest at Stephen Beck's villa."

"All right," Jasmine said, hardly able to muster any enthusiasm at the news.

"Have fun," Victoria told her. "I'm sure you and this guy will get along well."

Jasmine refrained from snorting in derision— barely. "I'll call you soon," she said, and couldn't help frowning as she replaced the receiver.

"Guess that scowl can mean only one thing. You got the cold, hard proof that I'm nothing but an up- standing citizen."

"That remains to be seen," Jasmine retorted, though she didn't believe her words. Still, she wasn't happy about having to share this private paradise with him.

Darien placed the tray on the coffee table, a combi- nation of marble and glass. "It's a beautiful day, and the sun is about to set any moment. You haven't seen anything until you've seen a St. Lucia sunset." He grinned widely. "Let me pour you a cup of tea—"

"You think this is funny?"

"It's at least a little bit amusing, don't you think? And I'll be honest, I haven't laughed in months."

Jasmine sprang to her feet and shot to the window.

What was she supposed to do now? Call a cab and check into a hotel? The appeal of staying here was that she didn't have to use a credit card, since she knew the paparazzi would track her down in a New York minute. If she checked into a hotel, she could kiss peace and tranquility goodbye.

Hearing soft footsteps, Jasmine turned. Darien extended a cup of tea to her.

Jasmine didn't take it.

"Come on. Take it."

"I don't want it."

"It's fresh mint."

Jasmine sighed and accepted the cup. "One minute, you were angry that I was here. Now you seem like you're happy to have the company."

"It's too late in the evening to do anything about our…predicament," Darien responded. "But first thing tomorrow, we'll figure something out."

"You can always go to a hotel," she said, smiling sweetly.

"There are two bedrooms here. Quite frankly, I think we can co-exist without getting in each other's way. As long as you tell me when you plan on going skinny-dipping, we should avoid any future awkward moments."

"Funny. Real funny." Angry, Jasmine turned. And knew instantly that she'd overreacted. Of course, she was still reeling from the fact that by now, probably all of America had seen her naked, because the video of her and Allan making love was already on the Internet. However, she was beginning to wonder if

Darien had any idea about the video or even who
she was. Surely if he did, he would say something
about it.

Still, there was that look by the pool—the one that
said he had recognized her. Was it possible he hadn't?

If that was the case, thank the Lord for small
miracles.

Putting the questions out of her mind, Jasmine
sipped the tea, which was the most flavorful mint
she'd ever tasted. Then she took a calming breath and
turned around.

"Thank you," she said, meaning the sentiment.
"This tea really hit the spot."

Darien nodded.

"And I'm sorry if I've been…a bit testy," she went
on. "The truth is, I came here because…because I
needed to escape some craziness. I didn't expect
anyone here…."

"Like I said, we can deal with this situation
tomorrow. That's the best we can do. But right now,
I want to take you outside."

Darien placed a hand on Jasmine's shoulder, and
to her surprise, she felt her skin tingle.

How was it that she was reacting to this stranger
on such a physical level? It didn't make sense.

"Outside?" Jasmine croaked.

"You want to see the most amazing sunset of
your life?"

Everything this man did left Jasmine with more
questions than answers. Bringing her tea, offering to
watch the sun set with her…he was treating her like

a friend, not a stranger. Wasn't he as rankled as she about this situation?

Or was he simply able to deal with it more maturely?

Jasmine wasn't at all happy about the day's turn of events, but she had to admit that she wasn't in the mood to spend the evening sulking about it. Arriving in St. Lucia had brought a sense of peace she hadn't felt since the story had broken about the sex tape.

"All right," she conceded. "Let's watch the sunset."

Darien led the way, and Jasmine followed. Once outside, she drew in a huge gulp of the sea air. Immediately it refreshed her and helped assuage her concerns.

"There," Darien said, turning.

Jasmine turned in the direction Darien had, and when she did, she saw the most brilliant orange sun reflecting off the rippling waves.

"You're right," she said, taking a step in the sun's direction, as though she would be able to reach out and touch it. "That is absolutely breathtaking."

"I think so."

"I'm in awe," Jasmine went on. "I thought sunsets in Los Angeles were great, but this…"

"I haven't missed watching the sun go down since I came here."

"Three weeks, you said?" Jasmine asked.

"Yes."

"Whereabouts in the U.S. are you from?"

"Originally—Cleveland, Ohio," Darien answered. "But I was stationed at the Wright-Patterson Air Force Base in Dayton, Ohio."

"Yes, my friend mentioned you'd recently come back from Iraq."

"Uh-huh."

"Well, I do appreciate the men and women of our military."

"What about you?" Darien asked. "Where are you from?"

"Born and raised in South Florida. But I live in L.A. now."

Darien's eyes narrowed thoughtfully, and Jasmine's stomach lurched. Man, she shouldn't have mentioned Los Angeles. She had no doubt that Darien had finally recognized her.

So she was surprised when he said, "You're certainly beautiful enough. You're an actress, right?"

Jasmine hesitated a moment, then said, "Yeah. That's right."

"I should have realized that when you made your call. How else would you know Bruce's brother?"

Was he for real? Jasmine knew she wasn't the hugest star around, but with all the press over her latest flick, she'd been on many magazine covers and interviewed by dozens of television stations. For this guy not to know who she was meant he never watched TV or movies, which was shocking in itself.

"You had a big break yet, or do you make a living doing what every aspiring actor in Los Angeles does?"

"What's that?"

"Waiting tables."

"Right. Yeah, well, you certainly know a lot

about the business. What's it like being in the military?" she asked, hoping to steer the conversation away from herself.

"About as pleasant as you can imagine. I'm retired now."

"Retired? You hardly look old enough."

Darien didn't respond. Just looked toward the setting sun.

Clearly, he didn't want to talk about what he'd been through. Not that she could blame him. She couldn't imagine the horror of living day in and day out in a war zone.

"Are you here on vacation?" she asked.

"Not exactly."

Again, Jasmine waited. But again, Darien didn't elaborate.

"Well?" she prompted.

"I don't want to talk about it right now," Darien said.

Jasmine nodded. "All right." It was probably just as well. She didn't want to talk about what had brought her here, either.

"What I will say," he began slowly, "is that when I'm standing here, looking out at the setting sun...I feel something blissful. Something magical."

Jasmine turned toward the sun. "I feel it, too," she said.

And she did.

Chapter 7

After watching the sunset with Darien, Jasmine retired to the bedroom. She was surprised in the morning that she'd slept for fourteen hours! But with the jet lag, and the fact that she hadn't slept well since the release of that sex tape, she certainly needed the rest.

Jasmine dressed simply in shorts and a T-shirt, then headed out of the bedroom to meet Darien.

She found him sitting at the kitchen table, working on a laptop. When she approached, he quickly closed it.

"Morning," she said.

"Morning," he replied. "I made some coffee. And I've got eggs, cheese, bacon in the fridge. Bread, too. Enough for a decent breakfast."

"Thanks," she said absently. She continued toward him. "What are you working on?"

"Nothing."

"Nothing?" She arched an eyebrow. "Is that why you made sure to shut your laptop the moment you saw me?"

Darien didn't answer, just rose and headed toward the countertop, where he filled his coffee mug. As he took a sip of the black brew, Jasmine studied him. He didn't seem like the same, friendly person he'd been the night before.

"So," he began. "Figured out where you're going to go?"

His words hit her like a slap in the face. Just the night before he'd been showing her the sunset. Now it seemed like he couldn't get rid of her fast enough.

"Are you okay?" she asked him.

"I'm fine," he answered in a tone the exact opposite of his words.

Flummoxed, Jasmine stood there, not knowing what else to say. Maybe this guy was bi-polar or something—which meant his behavior would be unpredictable.

He blew out a ragged breath. "Sorry. That was… an unfriendly way to greet you. It's just…"

He didn't finish his statement, leaving Jasmine more confused. "Just what?"

"Just that I have some things on my mind," he responded.

Jasmine opened cupboards until she found a mug,

then poured herself a cup of coffee. She found milk in the fridge and added some to the cup.

"No Sweet'n Low?" she asked.

"You mean that fake sugar?" He shook his head. "No, but there is brown sugar."

"I'll do without." Jasmine lifted her mug from the counter and brought it to the table where Darien was sitting. "I'll go first, okay?"

He glanced at her oddly. "Excuse me?"

"Spill my dirty laundry. The reason I'm here." Of course, she wouldn't tell him everything. But she needed to do something to break the ice.

"My ex," Jasmine went on, and Darien's eyebrows lifted at that. "I was involved with this guy for two years, and…well, he broke my heart."

"Cheated on you?"

"I wish," Jasmine mumbled.

"Excuse me?"

"Worse," she said. "He betrayed my trust, exploited me. Ruined some job opportunities."

"Did he hit you?"

"Why would you say that?"

"The bandage on your forehead."

"Oh. Well, no." She fingered the bandage she had all but forgotten about. "He didn't hit me. Someone else… It was a random attack. All things considered, I needed a break."

"I know what that's like," Darien said.

Jasmine expected him to go on, but he didn't. It suddenly dawned on her that what he was running from might have been the horrors he'd seen in Iraq, and if that was the case, she understood why he didn't want to talk about it.

In fact, her own issues felt horribly superficial compared to what he must have experienced.

Jasmine sipped her coffee before speaking. "I was thinking about our *situation*," she said. "And something you said last night."

"Mmm-hmm?"

"You pointed out that there are two bedrooms here, and that we should be able to co-exist without getting in each other's way." *Of course, you were in a better mood when you said that....*

"Are you suggesting we both stay here together— long-term?"

"Is that so awful?" she said, feeling a smidgen of disappointment that he didn't seem to like the idea. "It's not like I'll be cooped up inside twenty-four- seven. I'll head out to the beach, to the market, to eat.... It's not like we'll both be here all the time and suffocating each other."

Darien didn't respond.

"And," Jasmine continued when he remained silent, "the truth is, I can't afford to go anywhere else. I— My credit cards are maxed out," she added. That was a little white lie, but considering he didn't know who she really was, she didn't want to tell him the real reason she didn't want to use her credit cards was the fear that the paparazzi would track her down. "And I really don't want to head back home." She paused. "What about you? Are you prepared to go to a hotel?"

Darien dragged his hand over his face. "Not right now, no."

"Then we have to do what you said. Find a way to co-exist." Jasmine couldn't believe the words spilling from her mouth, but she'd woken up accepting the situation. Besides, there was something about him she trusted, and the idea of not being here completely alone was more appealing than she expected.

Because you think he's hot, was the thought that popped into her mind.

She pushed that thought from her mind and said, "Besides, we won't be completely alone. I'm told there's housekeeping staff that comes by three times a week."

"Not anymore."

"Oh?"

"I sent them away. Told them not to come back for two months—unless I call them."

"I see."

"So, if you're one of those gals who needs a maid to fluff her pillows in the morning and leave a chocolate mint on the bed in the evenings, a hotel would be the best bet."

"I'm perfectly capable of making my own bed, thank you. And I'm not a big fan of mint chocolate. Fresh fruit is a healthier option."

Darien simply shrugged.

"So what do you say?" Jasmine asked. "Think we can both act like adults and get along?"

"Sure."

He couldn't have sounded less enthusiastic. Jasmine drank more of her coffee, then pushed her chair back and stood.

"To show you that this can work, I'll head out right now. Give you space to keep working on whatever you were doing on your laptop."

Darien's mouth parted slightly, as though he wanted to say something, but then his lips closed.

"I'll just, um, go check out the beach," she told him, taking a few steps backward.

Darien didn't say a word, and Jasmine found herself frowning as she turned around. She couldn't get over the change in him. Last night, he had been warm and inviting. Now, he was cold and remote.

My God, she thought, halting as she reached her bedroom door. What if he *knew*—realized sometime during the night exactly who she was?

Jasmine swallowed at the painful reality. She didn't know why it mattered, but she didn't want Darien to think badly of her.

And she'd far prefer that he confront her with the knowledge as opposed to sulk.

Well, Jasmine was determined *not* to sulk about the fact that Darien's attitude toward her had completely changed. She went into her room, slipped into a bikini, applied sunscreen to her body, then put her clothes over her swimsuit. When she left the room, Darien was at the table, his laptop open. He didn't even turn to look at her.

So much for that, Jasmine thought. She slipped on her sunglasses, then opened the door and quietly left.

* * *

The moment the door clicked shut, Darien closed his eyes and groaned. What was wrong with him? Even though he'd tried to find the strength to be pleasant to Jasmine, he hadn't succeeded. Now she'd think he was mad at her—or worse, emotionally unstable.

It was the news he'd gotten less than an hour before when he'd called his best friend that had shaken him to the core. The ink was barely dry on their divorce papers, yet Sheila was getting married again.

To his brother.

And to think Darien had entertained the idea of calling Rodney, of trying to take the first tentative steps toward some sort of reconciliation. As far as he was concerned, his brother had just hammered the last nail in the coffin on their friendship.

Sighing, Darien stood. He was angry, yes. Angry enough that he wanted to head to the edge of the cliff and scream at the top of his lungs.

Yet he'd taken his frustration out on Jasmine.

"Jasmine." He said her name out loud, thinking again that her being here had to be fate. Maybe God had sent her here as a sign, knowing how his brother and ex would betray him. A sign that it was time to put Sheila fully in the past and move on.

Being here with someone, even a stranger, would help take his mind off his brother and ex-wife. That was something he desperately needed, because the anger had consumed him for months.

Darien glanced down at his laptop. On the screen

was something he was writing, his attempt at purging the demons inside him. One of his friends in the military had told him doing that was helpful, and it had helped—somewhat.

He could stay here and keep reliving his pain…. Or he could head outside and try to find Jasmine at the beach.

Darien closed the laptop.

In five long strides, he was at the front door. When he opened it, however, he jerked backward in surprise.

Jasmine was standing there.

"Jasmine," he said. "I thought…"

She held out a hand, palm up. "It's starting to rain."

"Oh," he said, feeling somewhat winded at her being there when he didn't expect it, as though he'd gotten an electric jolt to his system.

"No point heading to the beach now."

"Right." He looked past her and saw the rain-drops. They weren't heavy yet, but on the island, a downpour could start out of the blue. He stepped backward. "Well, come on back in."

Jasmine scurried past him, pulling her damp T-shirt over her head as she did. His eyes bulged at her actions—and his groin tightened—and then he saw that she was wearing a sparkly silver bikini top beneath the shirt.

Darien allowed his eyes to wander down the length of her back. He took a good, long look at her body, and found himself swallowing. Though he'd seen her almost naked at the pool the day before, it was as though he were seeing her for the first time.

That smooth, dark skin. The slim waist that flared out at her hips. Her full bottom…

She turned fully around, and Darien quickly looked away. "So, uh, the rain showers here can come down hard, but, uh, they, uh, usually they're over quickly," he stammered, feeling like an idiot.

"Like summer showers in Florida," Jasmine said. "One minute the sun is shining brightly and the next, there's a torrential downpour."

Damn, he was trying *not* to look at her, but he kept glimpsing her bust in that sexy bikini of hers—and Lord have mercy, it was hard to think.

"Why are you looking at me like that?" Jasmine asked.

"Like what?" he answered quickly, defensively. He hoped she hadn't caught him inadvertently checking out her breasts.

She put her hands on her hips and stared directly into his eyes. "Do you have something to ask me?"

"Ask you? Like what?"

She studied him for a moment, and Darien had no idea what she was trying to figure out.

"Like what?" he repeated.

"Like something you're curious about," she offered, leaving him completely clueless.

And then he *got* it. His face grew warm. She couldn't be talking about her breasts, could she—and whether or not he wanted to know if they were real?

She arched an eyebrow, as if hoping her stare could break him.

"You're not alluding to…" Darien hesitated,

unsure. "To…a cosmetic enhancement?" he finished in a whisper.

Jasmine's eyes grew wide in horror. "You think I had my breasts done?"

"No!" Darien exclaimed, knowing that no matter what he said next, he was screwed.

"These are one hundred percent real, thank you very much. Just because I live in Hollywood doesn't mean I went all crazy and—"

"Hey, you don't have to convince me. They look real."

Jasmine's mouth fell open as she gaped at him. She quickly crossed her arms over her chest.

Darien quickly directed his gaze at the ceiling, the only place he figured was safe. "You were the one who kept asking if I was curious about something. It was the only thing I could think of."

"I was thinking of something else," she said softly.

Cautiously, Darien lowered his eyes. He made sure they remained steadfast on Jasmine's face. "I don't understand."

"Maybe you don't," she said after a moment.

"Pardon me?"

"Nothing."

"What did you mean by that?"

"Nothing," she repeated.

This had to be one of the oddest conversations Darien had ever had. One of the oddest moments in his life, really. And not just because of the subject matter and how he'd stuck his foot in his mouth. But to be having a real, live conversation with a woman he had dreamed about nearly every night for three weeks… He was still trying to wrap his mind around that one.

"Feel like going snorkeling?" he suddenly asked, and was a little surprised to hear the words come from his mouth. But it was as good a way as any to change the subject.

"It's raining."

Darien turned, opened the door and stared outside for a long moment. "Looks like it stopped. Besides, the water's wet…so is the rain."

"This is true."

"Or, I could take you around. Show you the island. At least what's here in Castries. It's quite a neat little town. There's a great market not too far from here, with fruits and vegetables in one part, and clothes and knickknacks in another."

"Actually, I'd love to go to the beach. Seeing the water from the plane, it was such a beautiful shade of blue, and so clear…."

"Then let's snorkel."

"Or, we can just hang out on the beach," Jasmine suggested. "You need all kinds of equipment for that—"

"No need to worry," Darien said. "There's gear here. All I have to do is change."

"Right," Jasmine said, stretching the word.

Darien headed to the bedroom, where he quickly changed into his swimming trunks. When he returned to Jasmine, he found her standing where he'd left her. Gnawing on her bottom lip, she looked a little uneasy.

"What's the matter?" he asked her.

"It's not hard, is it? Snorkeling?"

"You've never been?"

"No."

Her answer surprised him, especially since she said she'd grown up in Florida. "Well, no worries. It's a piece of cake."

His answer didn't seem to satisfy her. "Don't you need professional instruction for that?" she asked. "Just wondering."

"I'll guide you."

"Because I don't want to get the bends or anything. I've heard they're brutal."

"I guarantee you, you won't get the bends from snorkeling. That only happens when you go scuba diving." He paused. "Didn't you say you were from Florida?"

"Yeah, but I didn't get to the water much. And in L.A., you can't do much more than frolic along the shore because those waves will swallow you whole."

"Don't worry, Jasmine. I'll teach you."

"And you'll bring me back alive?" she asked.

Darien grinned. "Of course."

"Help!" Jasmine cried, the water enveloping her entire body. She flailed her arms helplessly, gasping for air as she went down. Lord help her, she was going to die. *"Darien!"*

Darien wrapped a strong arm around her torso and pulled her body upright. "Jasmine?"

She drew in several deep breaths to fill her lungs before speaking. "Yeah?"

"Feel that?"

"What? And why are you...*smirking* at me? I could have drowned and you think it's a joke?"

Darien started laughing. "Are all actresses drama queens?"

"Excuse me?"

"Do you feel what's beneath your feet?" Darien asked her, still smiling. "It should feel like wet sand."

At Darien's words, Jasmine looked down. My God, she *was* standing on sand. In fact, only from the waist down was she submerged in water.

She immediately felt stupid. The fear that she would be carried away by the tide had overwhelmed her, and she'd panicked.

"Can I let you go now?" Darien asked.

Jasmine glanced at his arm, which was secured around her torso. There was a part of her that wanted to tell him no, not to let her go. His arm was strong, and she felt secure with it around her.

But, she had her pride.

"Of course you can let me go," she quipped, hoping he didn't think she was faking her fear to get close to him. She pushed her body backward to prove her point.

Only she stumbled on a rock and her body went down. She screamed, got a mouthful of salt water and reached for Darien's arm as though her life depended on it.

Darien pulled her up and her body landed

against his. He was laughing softly. That warm, sexy laugh of his.

"I can't believe you're laughing at me. I nearly drown, and you think it's the funniest thing ever!"

"You're not going to tell me that you can't swim," Darien said.

"Of course I can swim. I can do several laps in any pool."

"Then what's the problem?"

Jasmine looked past Darien at the vast water that had no end. Her stomach fluttering, she gripped his arm tighter. "I have a fear of the ocean," she admitted.

He tilted his head as he gave her an odd look. "Really?"

"I know it doesn't make sense. Trust me, I know that more than anyone. But…" Her voice trailed off.

"But what?"

"When I was in high school, a guy I had a crush on went swimming in the ocean. He got carried away on a riptide. Drowned."

"Oh my God." Suddenly, Darien wrapped both his arms around her, as though he feared she would suffer the same fate.

"In Florida, you hear those kinds of stories a dozen times a year. There are very real threats to swimming in the ocean. Take me to a pool and I'm entirely confident. But wading past shallow water in the ocean…"

"I'm here," Darien said. "And I won't let anything happen to you."

He said the words softly, but with such conviction that Jasmine absolutely believed him. His teasing smile had disappeared, replaced with a genuine look of concern.

"It's a silly phobia," she said.

"You feel the way you feel. There's no right and wrong to that."

Jasmine gave Darien a soft smile.

He released one of the hands secured around her, and Jasmine inhaled sharply. "I got you," he told her.

She nodded, then forced herself to inhale and exhale slowly. She wished she wasn't so afraid, but life had taught her that one wrong move could mean tragedy. She'd learned that with her brother, and with Clive, the guy from her school who'd been an excellent swimmer yet had lost his life when a riptide had carried him far out into the Atlantic.

"Look," Darien said.

"At what?" Jasmine asked.

"My hand," he said. He was holding his hand steady beneath the water.

"What about your hand?" she asked.

"Look at the water around it. How calm it is."

Jasmine studied the water. It was very calm. Hardly a wave rippled the surface.

"The water here in the bay is very calm," Darien explained. "I've been coming here practically every day since I got here, and it's always been the same."

She nodded, but she was still nervous.

"You know how to swim," he said. "And in the salt water, it's very easy to float."

"So they say," Jasmine commented.

"Want to try?"

Again she nodded. "All right."

"I'm right here," he said gently. "I won't let you float away."

Jasmine swallowed, then suberged her body in the water. She counted to five, then lifted her feet.

"That's it," Darien said. "Just let your body go. Let the water hold your weight."

Even though Jasmine believed him, she was afraid that she would sink. So when she actually floated on the gentle currents, she smiled.

"See. Easy as pie." He took her by the hands and pulled her upright. "About fifty feet away, there's a coral reef. You should see the fish. You feel confident going that far? If you don't, we can stay right here."

There was something inherently trustworthy about Darien. Something that had her willing to confront her fear.

"Let's do it," she said.

Darien smiled brightly, as though he was proud of her, and that gave Jasmine even more confidence.

"Here." He pulled her snorkel mask down onto her face, careful of her bandage, then did the same with his own. "And you put the tube in your mouth like this," he went on, showing her how it was done. "You don't have to fully submerge your head in the water, just your face. Like this."

Darien demonstrated for her, letting his body float.

"Okay," Jasmine said.

Darien stood and took her hand. "I'll lead."

Darien lowered himself into the water, and beside him, Jasmine did the same. He started to swim, and so did Jasmine—never letting go of his hand.

A short while later Darien stopped and started treading water. "You okay?" he asked.

Jasmine's heart beat faster, but she was determined to conquer her fear. "I can tread water in a pool," she said. "I can tread water here."

She released Darien's hand and quickly started to go under.

Darien reached for her, steadied her. "Easy," he said. "I won't let you go, okay?"

"Okay," she said nervously. Then she laughed.

"What's so funny?"

"We sound ridiculous, talking with our noses plugged."

"This is true," Darien agreed, laughing, too.

"Not to mention how funny you look."

"Me? Lady, you need a mirror."

"Oh, do I now?"

As their laughter faded, their eyes met and locked. Despite how comical Darien looked with his snorkeling gear on his face, something hot passed between them—something hot and strong.

Jasmine glanced away. "So. Now what?"

"I'm going to lower my head, just like I showed you before." He did, and quickly lifted his head to face Jasmine. "Oh, you've got to take a look. The fish are so colorful."

Once again Darien dipped his head, and tentatively, Jasmine did the same. When she did, she was immediately rewarded with the beautiful view of a school of clown fish.

Turning to face Darien, she pointed excitedly. But she also opened her mouth, swallowed more salt water, then bolted upright, gasping.

Darien quickly raised his head and pushed his mask up. "You all right?"

Jasmine nodded as she coughed. "I'm fine. More than fine, really. I just saw Nemo!"

Darien chortled. "Yeah, Nemo and all his brothers and sisters."

"I can't believe I'm doing this. I can't believe how beautiful the fish are! And you know what else?"

"What?"

"I'm not even trying to float, yet I am. I'd always heard that it's easy to float in salt water, but until now, I didn't believe it."

"Just maybe not in the Pacific," Darien said.

"Right." She laughed. "Definitely not in the Pacific!"

Excited that she was really doing this, Jasmine was the one to lower her head first. This time, she kept her head down long enough to see more than just the clown fish. She saw fish that were a combination of yellow and neon-blue, striped fish, colors so vibrant, so incredibly stunning, the view took her breath away.

Still holding her hand, Darien started to swim a little. Jasmine swallowed her nervousness and went along with him. *Easy as pie,* she thought.

Darien gazed at her and smiled. She smiled back.

Chapter 8

Hours after their snorkeling excursion, Jasmine was still smiling. She wasn't naive enough to think she'd completely conquered her phobia of wide bodies of water, but she had felt safe with Darien. Safe enough to trust him to guide her through the experience.

He took her into town for a quick stop at the market, where they picked up fresh fruits, vegetables and chicken. And some wine. Now, he was cooking while Jasmine was sitting on the back patio drinking a glass of Chardonnay. Not that she didn't offer to help him, but Darien had given her strict instructions to stay out of the kitchen while he prepared her a feast.

Jasmine took a sip of her wine as she enjoyed the view of the setting sun. Yes, she had taken a big step toward conquering her fear today, but that wasn't the only reason she was smiling.

There was no point denying to herself that she was also smiling because of Darien.

Maybe it was because this island was simply incredible, from its lush mountains to its stunning ocean view, and the island's beauty had her romanticizing to a degree. Or maybe it was because Darien was the one who'd helped assuage her fear earlier. Sure, another man could have done the same thing. But it hadn't been another man. It had been Darien.

Jasmine wasn't entirely certain where her thoughts were heading. She liked Darien. She was enjoying his company. That didn't mean she was attracted to him.

She was still dealing with Allan's betrayal. It was far too soon for her to be interested in another man.

And yet…

And yet her life with Allan seemed like a distant memory. Same with the scandal back home.

Sighing softly, she sipped more wine as her gaze wandered to the brilliant sun. Who was she kidding? She *was* attracted to Darien. How could she not be? She was a flesh-and-blood woman—she reacted to a sexy man the same as any woman did.

And Darien was one sexy man.

Jasmine sensed him rather than heard him. Quickly she turned her head and found Darien was standing at the open back door.

He smiled at her, and butterflies filled her stomach.

"You look relaxed," he commented.

The smell of garlic and chicken wafted into her nose. "And something smells incredible. I thought you were a soldier, not a chef."

"When you join the military, you're trained in two specialties. Military routines and combat, naturally, but also a regular job. Like public relations or law enforcement, or even being a cook. So I was an airman, yes, but also a cook."

"Wow. I didn't know that."

"It worked out well for me. Cooking was always a hobby of mine. Before I joined the military, I'd considered becoming a world-renowned chef." Darien grinned and playfully rolled his eyes, as if to say he was kidding.

"I'm sure you could have been," she said, "if the smell coming from the kitchen is any indication." She paused, then added, "In my books, a man who can cook—and wants to—is as precious as gold. I can't believe some woman let you go."

Darien's smile disappeared and his eyes widened— and Jasmine immediately regretted her words.

"I'm sorry," she quickly said. "It's just that… Well, I saw the ring line on your wedding finger, and since you're here alone, *not* wearing your ring…" She cringed when she saw Darien's blank gaze, wondering if she'd just ruined what had so far been a lovely day.

"And you just assumed that my wife had left me. Not that I, perhaps, had left her. Or that she died."

Jasmine gasped. Threw a hand over her mouth. "Oh my God. I'm so sorry."

"Or," Darien went on, "that I just lost my ring."

Jasmine's eyes narrowed. She was simultaneously embarrassed and perturbed. Would Darien have the audacity to actually joke about his wife having died?

Of course, *she* was the one who had jumped to conclusions when she had no right. But acknowledging that fact didn't make Jasmine feel much better. In an instant, she knew why—for some reason, Darien's last comment stung.

Were his last words the truth? That he was very much married but had only misplaced his wedding band?

If so, Jasmine felt even more foolish for feeling any sort of attraction to him.

"Please forgive me," she said, unable to meet his eyes. "I shouldn't have assumed anything."

"Don't worry about it."

Jasmine waited several seconds, wondering if Darien was going to clarify the matter. Tell her one way or another that he was married or he wasn't.

As even more seconds passed she realized that he had no intention of setting the record straight.

Disappointed, Jasmine turned back toward the sunset. Maybe she had read him wrong. Until now, she assumed he wasn't wearing a ring because he had endured a recent breakup, as she had. There was sadness in his eyes. She saw it as surely as he must be able to see the same emotion when looking at her.

After the wonderful time they'd spent at the beach today, Jasmine was hoping that the sadness was because of a breakup. Breakups were often bitter and people wanted to move on and find love again, if only to firmly close the door on the past. But a deceased wife? Darien could have loved her with every fiber of his being, and be the type to remain faithful to her until the day he died.

What is wrong with me? she asked. Whether Darien was grieving the death of a wife, or whether he was newly divorced or whether he'd taken his ring off deliberately because he was a player, it shouldn't matter one iota to her.

She had only met the man, for goodness' sake, and attractive as he was, she didn't have anything invested in a relationship with him. If he *was* married, this was the time to learn that fact, before she got carried away on this romantic island and ended up with a full-blown crush on him.

"I must say, you have good instincts," Darien said, and Jasmine was surprised to realize that he was standing only inches behind her. The deep timbre of his voice snaked down her spine like a caress. Jasmine closed her eyes and swallowed.

"I am divorced," Darien went on. "It's been a recent development, and yeah, she did leave me."

Slowly, Jasmine turned. She did her best to act unaffected by the nearness of him, by his sexy, gentle voice. "You could have mentioned that to me when I told you about my ex."

"It hasn't been easy to deal with," Darien said. "I was married to this woman, not just dating her."

"I can assure you that what I just went through with my boyfriend will rival even the worst marital betrayals." Just thinking of Allan's betrayal, and hence, what the media back home was saying about her, had Jasmine feeling nauseous. She whirled around to gaze at the ocean.

Two strong hands rested softly on her shoulders. "It's a beautiful evening. Dinner is ready. There's no need to spoil the mood with talk of the past."

A smile lifted Jasmine's lips. Darien was absolutely right. She was on this island to forget the past, not to dwell on it. Staring at the water, Jasmine absorbed the stunning view and allowed peace to wash over her like the gentle waves of the bay.

"You ready to eat?" Darien asked.

Facing him, Jasmine smiled. "You bet."

"This chicken is divine!" Jasmine exclaimed as she swallowed the first mouthful. "So succulent, so tasty."

"Thank you," Darien replied.

They had considered eating outside, but with dusk had come the mosquitoes, so inside was a better choice. The view from the formal dining room was magnificent, as they could see not only the water but the lights from the resort below, so they sat there instead of at the small dinette in the kitchen. Jasmine even lit a couple candles for ambience.

Jasmine ate a tasty potato, then commented, "I thought you were from Cleveland."

"I am."

"So someone taught you how to make Caribbean-style chicken since you got here—or did you learn that in the air force?"

"When I was a teenager, I worked at a Jamaican restaurant," Darien replied after swallowing his mouthful of food. "But what do you know about Caribbean-style chicken?"

"First of all, I lived in Miramar—the part of South Florida where there are a lot of Jamaican families. Second, I am Jamaican, so my mother cooked this chicken all the time, with rice and peas, some yam on the side…"

Darien looked at her with interest. "You're Jamaican?"

"Well, by way of my parents. I was born in Florida."

"So you'll be able to share some cooking secrets with me, then."

"Uh…" Jasmine smiled sheepishly. "Not exactly. I used to watch my mother make meals like this, see the way she seasoned the meat, added the browning sauce for color, sometimes some tomatoes, then fry it in the pot before making a sort of stew of it—but can I do it myself? Shamefully, I have to admit that I can't."

"You've described the process to a T. I find it hard to believe you can't make this."

"I could never get the seasoning right. I'd add too much salt or not enough paprika." Jasmine shrugged. "Pathetic, I know."

Darien ate more food before responding. "I guess I'll just have to give you a cooking lesson. But you certainly seem to know the basics."

"For me, I really think it's mind over matter. Every time I set out to cook a Jamaican dish, I'd think, 'You're gonna screw this up.' And then I somehow did screw it up. Maybe because I wanted to impress my parents so badly."

"Okay, then before we leave here, we'll definitely spend some time in the kitchen."

Jasmine drank some wine. "Now, don't get me wrong. I'm not an invalid in the kitchen. I'm great at cooking pasta, which I love."

"Macaroni and cheese?" Darien asked, smiling as he said the words.

"Hey, don't tease me. And no, I can do better than that. Fettuccini Alfredo, lasagna. And I can make a mean salad," she added, smiling to show Darien that she could laugh at herself, as well.

Silence settled over them. For several minutes they ate without speaking. In a way it was odd for them to be here enjoying a meal like this, given that when Jasmine first met Darien, she had wanted nothing to do with him. He had been an unwelcome kink in her relaxation plans.

As if reading her thoughts, Darien asked, "Were you really going to call the police to escort me off the property?"

"Oh, goodness." Jasmine closed her eyes, embarrassed at the memory of their first moments together.

"If it makes you feel any better, I figured I'd have to do the same thing. Because you seemed hell-bent on staying."

"Because I knew I was allowed to be here," Jasmine replied, then chuckled.

"I said the same thing, but you weren't having any of it."

Jasmine liked the way Darien's eyes lit up when he smiled. The truth was, the more time she spent with him, the more she liked about him.

Once again, silence fell between them, and Jasmine drank more wine. Her gaze wandered to the view of the resort lights in the distance, then back to Darien.

"So here we are," she said, "two people fleeing the pain of love. I don't think we could have chosen a more beautiful spot on the planet, do you?"

"This is a piece of paradise. It's going to be hard to return home."

"Is that—" Jasmine strained her ears to hear. "Is that music?"

"Yeah, it's coming from the resort. All the tourists getting their groove on."

Jasmine pushed her chair back, stood, then wandered to the dining room's bay window. "Maybe one of these days we can head over there. Spend an evening enjoying the entertainment, dancing under the stars."

"Sure."

"It just dawned on me, there's not a television in this place."

"In a place like this, who needs television?"

"Good point," Jasmine conceded. And now she understood why Darien didn't know who she was, or at least why he hadn't heard about her scandal. If there was no television in the villa, he wouldn't have seen the news.

Thank God. That was one less headache to deal with.

"But if you want to keep up with what's happening back home, there is a television at the back of the closet in my bedroom. I assume it works."

Jasmine glanced over her shoulder at Darien. "No. That's okay."

Sipping more wine, she walked back to the table, but this time to Darien's side. She pulled out the chair next to him and sat. "The meal was delicious," she told him. "Thank you."

And then she touched him—a feathery stroke of her fingers across his arm. It was a subtle touch, but a deliberate one. Something was happening between her and Darien. Something she couldn't put into words.

With Allan, the attraction had been slow and steady, more like a friendship that grew into something else. With Darien, just looking at him made her very much aware that she was a woman. His smile not only warmed her, it filled her with butterflies.

And it wasn't only the butterflies. It was the way it was hard to look directly into his eyes. At least without trying to find something to say. It was as if they were both afraid that if they stared quietly, truly saw each other, that uncontrollable passion would ignite.

But now...Darien was meeting her eyes and neither was fumbling around for anything to say.

And there it was—that unmistakable heat. It burned Jasmine's insides, made her flush.

"You're welcome," Darien said softly.

"I look forward to that cooking lesson," Jasmine said.

"Anytime."

The skin beneath her bandage started to itch and Jasmine scratched at it.

"So someone attacked you," Darien said.

"Yeah. Entirely random," Jasmine added, hoping he didn't ask her more questions about the assault.

"Have you taken that bandage off yet?"

"No."

"Let me take a look at the stitches."

"According to the doctor, I should be able to take the stitches out in a few more days."

"Here." Darien reached for her head and carefully lifted the edge of the bandage.

"You sure you should do that?" Jasmine asked.

"You're in good hands," Darien assured her. "I've seen plenty worse on the front lines. I'm just going to see how it looks."

He was careful not to hurt her, and several seconds later he had the gauze bandage completely off.

"There you are," he said. "I can see your whole face."

Jasmine wanted to ask if he liked what he saw, but she didn't. She didn't need affirmation of the fact that he was attracted to her.

Lightly, Darien fingered the length of her cut. "Wow. You got hurt good."

"It was a brick," Jasmine told him, sighing softly. "I didn't even have time to react."

"You have a serious bruise," he went on. "But the cut looks like it's healed." He scrunched the bandage in his hand. "You don't need this anymore."

"You sure?"

"I could probably take the stitches out now, but there's no harm waiting another day or two."

Jasmine nodded. For a moment she watched him studying her face. A peculiar look passed over his features. Again, she had the feeling he recognized her.

Maybe he *had* seen her face somewhere, but couldn't pinpoint why she looked familiar.

"I, uh, should clear these plates." Darien moved his chair back and got to his feet.

Jasmine also stood. "Let me help."

They both reached for Darien's plate and got in each other's way. Then they tried to sidestep each other, both blocking one another's path. Simultaneously, they stopped. Chuckled.

Jasmine looked up. Heat sizzled when her eyes met Darien's.

She tilted her head slightly, holding his gaze. She also held her breath, wondering if he would kiss her.

Instead, Darien cleared his throat and stepped backward. "I'll get my plate, you get yours," he said, reaching to lift it off the table.

Jasmine tucked a strand of hair behind her ear. "Okay."

"And how about some dessert? Fresh strawberries and whipped cream sound good?"

"Sure," she said, disappointed that he would no longer look at her. "Sounds wonderful."

Then Darien turned and walked away. And their moment was lost.

Chapter 9

For the next week Darien and Jasmine fell into a routine of sorts. They got up, made coffee and enjoyed a light breakfast of fresh fruit. Around ten they headed to the beach to snorkel or swim, as the sun tended to be bright but not at its hottest, and the water was very clear. After a few days of Jasmine getting comfortable in the water, Darien brought some bread on their snorkeling trips to feed the fish. It had been a highlight for Darien to see Jasmine's excitement when the fish, wanting the food, swarmed them in droves.

She felt comfortable only if by his side, however, but Darien had to give her credit for being brave enough to tackle her fear. He wouldn't mind planning a larger snorkeling trip with a tour guide, but he knew Jasmine wasn't ready for that.

Usually when they came back from the beach, they would do their own thing, and Jasmine tended to hang out by the pool or lounge on a sofa with a book. Darien sometimes headed to a local bar he liked, or retreated to his bedroom to purge more of his thoughts onto the computer screen. Originally he'd planned to send a copy to Sheila and to Rodney, but now he couldn't see what that would accomplish. Warren's bombshell that they were planning their wedding was the cold, hard proof that they didn't give a damn how much they'd hurt him.

Darien found himself missing his brother, but he didn't know how they could ever have a relationship again.

At least spending time with Jasmine had helped keep his mind off of his pain. Things between them were…pleasant. If a little strained. Because despite the fact that they enjoyed each other's company and had some nice conversations, Darien felt the sexual tension between them every time they were in the room together. Especially after he made dinner and they sat at the table, casually drinking wine.

There were the not-so-subtle looks, the not-so-subtle touches. Last night, Jasmine had come up behind him at the kitchen sink and put her hand on his back—and let it linger. Unsure how to react, Darien had all but fled to his bedroom.

Even when he'd taken her stitches out a few days

earlier, she had given him a lingering look. Darien had been sure that she wanted him to kiss her.

He hadn't. Just as he hadn't the first night he got the same feeling from her. Not that he hadn't wanted to, but something had held him back.

Fear.

Every night when he went to sleep, he thought about the obvious attraction between him and Jasmine, how in some respects it was nice, but more so, how complicated it would be to get involved. His mind told him to be cautious while his heart said to take a chance, and mostly, he was left feeling frustrated.

It was that frustration that had him waking up in a foul mood this morning.

If a casual observer were to analyze his situation, he wouldn't understand the problem. By all appearances, Darien should be happy. He was no longer married to a cheating wife, and he was in a beautiful villa in a place that could only be described as paradise. Even better, he was sharing the villa with a woman he found extremely attractive.

Not the kind of scenario that had the average guy feeling blue.

But Darien wasn't the average guy.

His very attraction to Jasmine was what had him conflicted. Half the night, he had replayed the previous week's events in his mind. He couldn't pinpoint it, but somewhere along the way, something between them had changed. A spark had ignited.

Was Jasmine attracted to him only because he'd been helping her in the water? Women had fallen for men over a lot less. Hell, Sheila had fallen for his brother because he had "been there" for her when he couldn't be. What if Jasmine had developed a sort of hero complex where he was concerned, and that was fueling her desire to get a little closer to him?

"Shut up, man," he told himself. "You know she likes you."

It shouldn't surprise him. Between the snorkeling every morning and having meals together, they were getting along well.

And that was exactly the problem. They were getting along *too* well.

Darien would have to be stupid to have missed the looks Jasmine had been shooting his way. The little smiles, the bashful eyes.

It wasn't all one-sided. Far from it. He'd been subtly—or not so subtly—flirting with Jasmine, as well. After spending so much time together, the flirtation had come easily.

Darien could only imagine Warren's reaction if he told his friend what he was feeling—that the cause for his angst was how well he was getting along with a gorgeous woman.

Warren would probably have him committed.

If only the matter were simple. Darien's problem was that now, after debating the situation in his mind last night, he realized he had to put a stop to whatever was happening between him and Jasmine—despite their mutual attraction.

He had dreamed of her before he'd even met her. There was no doubt about that. And in his heart, he knew that the reality of her being here had to be some sort of cosmic sign.

He *wanted* to entertain the idea of seeing where things could lead between them, especially if fate had brought them together for a reason. But alone in his bed last night, as he'd seriously considered the very idea, tension had formed a huge knot in his stomach.

It was one thing to try to close the door on the past. It was another to think of getting involved with another woman, even on a casual basis as a way to help him move on.

He thought about his best friend's words, that what he needed to do was to find another woman to keep him warm at night, but that wasn't Darien's style. He wasn't the kind of man to love casually. When he'd fallen for Sheila, he'd given himself to her completely, and when he'd promised to love her until death, he had meant every word before God.

It was hard to even consider the idea of being in a relationship with another woman. Rationally, he knew he was moving ahead of himself, because there was no reason he couldn't enjoy time with Jasmine. Emotionally, he knew that the more enjoyable times he spent with her the more likely they'd end up in bed.

Warren would slap him for even thinking this, but the idea of making that kind of emotional and physical connection with another woman was a little overwhelming. He wanted to…and yet there was the pain he'd endured because of Sheila that was so fresh.

So he had to put a stop to it. Emotionally, he couldn't handle the thought of giving himself to another woman.

Because when it ended, the pain was simply too much to bear.

Jasmine was smiling as she cracked eggs into a bowl. She added a pinch of salt and pepper, fresh onion and bits of turkey slices she'd found in the fridge.

"Darien, you are going to love this," she said out loud.

After their first talk about cooking days ago, she must have made herself sound like she had two left hands in the kitchen, but that wasn't the case. And sitting back for the past week and letting Darien cook one culinary delight after another certainly must have reinforced his belief that she couldn't cook to save her life. Now, she wanted to show him that she *could* make a decent meal—one that would have him salivating rather than keeling over.

Breakfast was her favorite meal to cook, and Jasmine was happy to find that Darien was still in his room when she'd gotten out of bed. That had allowed her to head to the kitchen and start the meal she had wanted to surprise him with for the past few days.

The butter was in the fridge and hard as a rock, so Jasmine greased the skillet with some oil. While she turned on the stove and let the pan start to warm, she turned her attention to the coffee machine. Too bad there was no fresh chicory to add to the pot, but maybe she'd pick some up at the market later.

Hearing a door shut, Jasmine's hand stilled on the handle to the cupboard she was about to open to retrieve a couple mugs. "I'm in the kitchen," she called. "There's fresh coffee, so come and get it."

Moments later Darien rounded the corner into the kitchen. Jasmine smiled in greeting, but the smile on her lips soon died when she saw the sour expression on Darien's face.

"Hey," she said. "What's wrong?"

"What are you doing?" he asked, his voice deadpan.

"Making breakfast," she answered, realizing he must be worried that whatever she was going to make would cause him to die a slow and painful death. "After our conversation the first night you made a meal for me, I know you must think I can't even boil water. But the scrumptious omelet I'm going to make for you will prove otherwise."

Jasmine grinned, hoping to elicit even a half smile from Darien, but he only looked at her with narrowed eyes.

"Well, uh, thanks anyway, but I'm gonna head out."

"You are?" she asked, disappointed.

"Yeah," he said curtly. "So you enjoy."

Without another word, Darien turned to leave.

Jasmine *knew* something was wrong—and found herself wondering if *she* was the problem.

So she followed him. "Darien, wait."

"What?" he asked, his tone bordering on rude.

"What's really going on here? Why are you acting like…like you want to get away from *me?*"

Darien glanced down before answering. "What's wrong is that I'm not ready for this."

"Ready for what?"

"Come on," Darien said, his face souring with a half frown. "You know what's going on here."

"No." Jasmine shook her head. "I don't."

"I told you last week that I just went through a divorce. I am not ready for another relationship."

Jasmine guffawed. "Relationship? Because I get up to make breakfast, you think I want a relationship?"

"It's not just the breakfast. It's everything."

"Oh yeah?" One of Jasmine's eyebrows shot up in challenge. "Like what?"

"Like...like how you touched me last night at the sink. The looks. You know."

"The looks?"

"Yeah. You know. How you...you like to bat your eyelashes at me over the dinner table."

"Bat my eyelashes?"

"Whatever you want to call it. Flirting with me. Whatever."

Darien's words stung, but Jasmine swallowed and straightened her spine. "You are insufferable!" she exclaimed. "You've been odd right from the time I got here. For the most part you wake up cranky, but as the day goes on you turn into a decent human being. I figured you just weren't a morning person, but maybe there's more to it. What do you do? Wake up depressed, take your happy pills, then everything's better?"

Jasmine only had to see the look in Darien's eyes to know she'd crossed the line.

"Nice to know you don't like hitting below the belt," he muttered.

"I'm sorry," she quickly said. He had hurt her with his comment about batting eyelashes and she'd wanted to hurt him in return. "It's just that you can be so hot and cold, so up and down, and I…I don't know what's going on here."

"Maybe you'd have to take happy pills if you'd been through what I've been through."

Jasmine's eyes widened. "You…you *are* on medication?" she asked tentatively.

"No," Darien said, shaking his head slightly.

"You wouldn't be the first person in the world to take antidepressants," she went on, her voice suddenly gentle and encouraging. "I think probably ninety percent of the people in Hollywood do. If you've got some sort of chemical imbalance—"

"Slow down, will you?" Darien scowled. "I do *not* take any sort of medication. No antidepressants, no sleeping pills. Only a beer or two if I need one."

"What are we doing?" Jasmine asked. "Please tell me, because one minute, we were getting along, the next—"

She stopped talking when the smell of smoke assaulted her nostrils. Turning, she walked back toward the kitchen—then screamed when she saw that the skillet was on fire.

She charged for the kitchen, her first instinct to reach for the skillet's handle and grab it off the stove.

"Don't touch it!" Darien yelled and, frightened, Jasmine looked over her shoulder at him.

"That pot is pure iron. You touch it with your bare hands, and your skin will melt."

"Right, right," Jasmine said, then whimpered. She hadn't even thought of that.

Darien rushed into the kitchen, opening one cupboard after another. "Where's the damn oven mitt?"

Jasmine turned off the stove, then grabbed a dish towel and started to beat at the flames, which seemed to be getting larger by the second.

The smoke alarm began to blare.

"Got it!" Darien exclaimed. Hurriedly, he slipped the oven mitt over his hand, then grabbed the iron skillet's handle. He dragged it to the nearby sink.

Jasmine quickly turned on the faucet, and the pan sizzled angrily as water hit it. A plume of smoke erupted from the sink—but not all the flames died.

"Flour," Darien said, reaching for the bag. "That'll do it."

He dumped flour onto the pot, and just like that, the flames died. But in his panic, he'd emptied more than half the bag. Now, floury smoke mixed with the smoke from the fire.

For several seconds all Jasmine and Darien could do was stare at the mess and cough intermittently.

Finally, Jasmine faced Darien. "I hope you're happy," she said, and stalked off.

Chapter 10

That incorrigible, insufferable man!

Jasmine slammed her bedroom door, then pressed her body against it, as though she feared Darien might push the door open.

But he didn't.

What's his problem? Jasmine wondered, gritting her teeth. The man might not be on medication, but he certainly seemed to have a few screws loose.

It wasn't as if they'd ended up in bed last night. Heck, they hadn't even kissed once since they'd been sharing this romantic villa. So why on earth was he acting as though she'd told him she loved him or something?

Confident that Darien wasn't going to come into

her room, Jasmine heaved her body off the door. Men. She didn't understand them. From the Allans of the world who would hurt a woman for their own personal gain, to the type who thought a look or touch meant a woman wanted to marry them, Jasmine didn't get them.

Now she fully understood the saying that men were from Mars.

Maybe she had to rethink the idea of getting a hotel. How long would it take for the paparazzi to track her down? Maybe a few days. If that was all the time left she could have in this paradise, then so be it.

Because sharing this house with Darien was surely going to make her lose her mind!

For now, however, she would go to the beach. There was only one car here, Darien's rental, and she couldn't very well ask him to borrow it. Even if she wanted to, it was a standard and she wouldn't be able to drive the car. Later, she would deal with calling a taxi to take her to a nearby hotel, but for now, all she wanted was to escape this tense situation.

The way Jasmine saw it, one of them had to leave the house immediately.

And that person was going to be her.

Jasmine changed into a blue one-piece bathing suit and a sarong, filled a tote bag with a couple magazines and a suspense novel, then exited the bedroom.

"Where are you going?" Darien asked when she reached the door.

"To the beach," she replied, her tone clipped.

"You're not gonna help me clean this mess up?" he asked incredulously.

"If I do that, you might think I'm trying to seduce you," Jasmine retorted. "And we can't have that, now, can we?"

"I wouldn't go to the beach by yourself," Darien warned.

"I'm not going to drown. You're the one who proved to me how calm the water is." Just saying the words made a lump of emotion form in Jasmine's throat. Darien would never know how grateful she was to him for helping her try to conquer her phobia. He could be so sweet—but he could also be a big jerk.

"That's not what I meant," Darien said. "It's because you're a beautiful woman. Alone…you might find yourself harassed by the men."

A beautiful woman… Even though she was angry, the compliment made her flush.

Don't get sucked in by his ploy, Jasmine told herself. So she said, "As long as I'm out of your hair—and your space—I wouldn't think it would matter to you."

"That's not true."

"Right," Jasmine mumbled. Then she turned and marched out the door.

Outside, the sun warmed her face, something that would normally help lift her spirits. But now…now, mixed emotions were swirling inside her gut and she felt anything but in a good mood.

She started down the long driveway. There were

two ways to get to the water. One way was to head right once she hit the road, and that was the way she and Darien had gone most often to get to a quieter stretch of the bay for their snorkeling trips. But it was also longer, which is why they'd taken the car. No, Jasmine would go the way she had the very first time she and Darien had gone to the beach, which meant she had to turn left once she hit the base of the driveway, then turn left again along a rugged road that would lead her to the more populated beach. It was about a ten-minute walk.

When Jasmine neared the road, she looked over her shoulder to see if Darien was coming.

He wasn't—and wonder of all wonders—she actually was a bit disappointed. How crazy was that? The fact was, even though she found him attractive, she barely knew the man. And having just ended her relationship with Allan, the last thing she should be considering was a relationship with someone else.

There. She'd thought the thought.

Relationship.

Maybe Darien hadn't been entirely out of line when he'd broached the subject earlier. He'd obviously sensed her attraction to him and wanted to put a stop to anything that could happen between them before it even started.

It was the safest bet, the smartest thing to do. Stop things before they started. Because Jasmine knew that he was exactly the type of man she would pursue. Tall and gorgeous, he also had a special quality she couldn't put her finger on. She knew he was trustworthy—even if he was running from his pain.

Moments later Jasmine reached the main road. There, she turned left. Perhaps she wouldn't bother heading to the beach, just take a long walk to clear her thoughts.

Did anyone in the world have as much bad luck as she did? Seriously, she couldn't understand it. First, Allan had betrayed her, and by now the whole world had likely seen her not only naked but in flagrante delicto. Then, as if she hadn't suffered enough embarrassment, she'd been caught nearly naked by Darien. But even worse, she was attracted to him and he wanted nothing to do with her.

She wasn't sure her ego could handle much more of a beating.

Jasmine was so intent on going where she was going that she didn't notice the car that slowed beside her. When she did, she saw two men. The driver's head was hanging out of the car.

"Hello, beautiful."

Jasmine forced a polite smile, then kept walking.

"What's a pretty girl like you doing walking all alone?"

She didn't answer that, but her heart rate started to pick up. When the car didn't continue on, she wondered if she had been foolish to ignore Darien's advice. She wished she were back at the house with him, rather than on the side of the street alone.

A horn blared, and the car finally sped up. Jasmine blew out a sigh of relief. She walked a bit more before reaching the path going left through the brush, which led to the beach.

Hastily she turned onto the dirt road, thankful to be rid of the men in the car. And thankful that this road was populated. People in bathing suits walked toward her, locals leaving the beach. Were there really that many happy couples out there? They all were holding hands or walking with their arms wrapped around each others' backs.

Jasmine looked away, uncomfortable with all this public display of affection after the fight she'd had with Darien.

Another five minutes and she was at the beach. The brisk walk over uneven terrain had worn her out, so she was more than happy to lay her towel out on the sand and collapse onto it.

She stared at the pristine blue water. Just last week, with Darien by her side, she'd had the courage to tackle her fear. Today, she doubted she'd even touch the water.

It's no big deal, she told herself. She'd just lie on the beach and read her magazines to pass the time. It was a time for her to de-stress and concentrate on herself.

She closed her eyes and allowed herself to feel nothing but the heat of the sun on her skin and the gentle breeze off the ocean.

"Beautiful."

At the word, Jasmine's eyes flew open, and to her horror, she saw standing next to her one of the men who'd been in the car.

He lowered himself to his haunches and said, "You look like you could use some company."

"Actually, I was hoping to sit here alone and enjoy the view."

"Nah, man. A view like this is meant to be enjoyed by a man and a woman."

The back of Jasmine's neck tingled. She knew she had trouble on her hands, trouble she didn't want. At least there were people around, so hopefully someone would come to her aid if need be.

"I'm enjoying the view quite nicely," she said. "I really would like to be alone," she added, not leaving any room for doubt.

"Where you from?" he asked, a grin on his face.

Maybe this man was harmless, but he knew nothing about respecting personal space. "Seriously," she said, and pulled a magazine from her tote bag.

"C'mon, tell me where you from. The States, nuh?"

If he wasn't going to leave her alone, then she would leave. Jasmine got to her feet, then bent to scoop up her tote bag.

But the man got to her towel before she could.

He folded it nicely, then handed it to her. Sure, he wasn't threatening her, but still. Jasmine didn't like guys who didn't leave you alone when you asked them to.

"Thank you," she said as she stuffed the towel into her beach bag.

"Why don't I tek you to another part of the island? Not far, but the water is—"

"Please," Jasmine said, cutting him off. "I don't mean to be rude, but I came out here for some peace and quiet."

"You can have even more peace an' quiet at the spot I wanna tek you."

Jasmine shifted her weight from one foot to the other, wondering what to say or if she should scream for help.

It was that moment that she felt a hand on her arm, and she spun around. Standing behind her on the sand was a young boy, not more than eleven years old. Jasmine had never been so happy to see another person in her life.

The boy looked from her to the man. "Is Johnny here bothering you?" he asked Jasmine.

"I believe Johnny was just leaving," Jasmine said, and dragged a hand across the back of her neck.

"Johnny, this is mi auntie." The boy slipped his arm around Jasmine's waist.

Johnny narrowed his eyes with suspicion as he looked at the boy. "Your auntie?"

"Mmm-hmm. Came from the States to visit me. And if mi fatha find out you been bothering her…"

"Nah, mi not bothering this pretty lady." Johnny started to back away from Jasmine.

Jasmine glanced at the child beside her and smiled. Then she draped her arm across his shoulder and snuggled him close.

Whoever this kid's father was, he clearly intimidated Johnny. Because he said, "All right. You have a good day, miss."

When Johnny was gone, Jasmine looked down at her new friend and said, "Thank you."

"No problem. Johnny likes to talk to all de pretty girls."

"I think I should be fine now," Jasmine told him. "Johnny's gone."

"Where you from?" the boy asked.

Jasmine hesitated. "The States," she replied. "Just like you said."

"But where?"

"Florida."

"Maybe you'll tek me one day."

"Thank you again," Jasmine said. She withdrew her towel from the bag and placed it on the sand once again. But by the time she sat down, the boy was sitting beside her.

Jasmine's eyes ventured over his feet first, clad in well-worn sneakers, and then his jean shorts and AC/DC T-shirt. *An odd shirt,* she thought, wondering where he'd gotten that.

He offered her his hand. "I'm Luc."

Clearly, Jasmine had traded one stalker for another. Reluctantly she shook his hand. "I'm Jasmine."

"Nice to meet you, Miss Jasmine."

Jasmine nodded, then opened the copy of *Vogue* she'd brought to the island with her. Hopefully this kid would get the hint and be on his merry way.

"You a model?" he asked. "Cuz you beautiful enough to be one."

"I'm not a model, no."

She flipped more pages, and still this kid didn't get up.

"What happened to your head?" he asked.

Jasmine's hand went to her forehead. The stitches were gone, but now she had a noticeable scar. "I got hurt."

"A man?"

"Why would you say that?" she asked. Either the kid was amazingly perceptive or it had been a lucky guess.

He shrugged, but didn't answer.

Jasmine went back to her magazine, but she couldn't concentrate with Luc sitting beside her, staring at her.

"You hungry?" he asked after several moments.

A little annoyed, Jasmine closed her magazine and dropped it onto the towel beside her. "Do you think you can go back to doing whatever it is you were doing before you came over to me?" she asked Luc.

"But mi wasn't doing nothing."

"Well, what were you *planning* on doing?"

"Nothing."

Great.

"But now I can protect you. No one will bother you with me aroun'."

Jasmine was trying to think of a comeback when the sky opened up and it started to rain, the drops thick, heavy and hard. She shot to her feet, grabbing her towel as she did.

"No, no, no! Oh God."

She stuffed the towel into her bag, then grabbed her copy of *Vogue* to use as an impromptu umbrella. "See you later, kid," she said, then started to run.

Luc started to run alongside her.

"What are you doing?" Jasmine asked.

"Making sure you get to your car!" Luc answered.

"I don't have a car," Jasmine answered.

She kept running and the kid kept running with her.

When they reached the main road, Jasmine turned to the kid. She was soaked to the bone. "I'll be okay from here," she told him. "My house is just up the hill."

"Then come on." Luc grabbed her hand and urged Jasmine to run with him.

It was obvious she wasn't going to get rid of him, so she accepted her fate.

Chapter 11

At the sound of the front door opening, Darien's stomach tightened nervously. He dropped the sponge onto the counter and wandered out of the kitchen, ready to face Jasmine and to tell her that he was sorry for making a fool of himself earlier.

He saw Jasmine enter the foyer, absolutely drenched. But he also saw a kid, a young boy who had to be a local. They were laughing as she pulled a damp towel from her beach bag.

"Hello," Darien said.

Either Jasmine didn't hear him or she deliberately ignored him. To the kid she said, "This towel will be of no use. Let me get some fresh ones."

"Hey," Darien said, and Jasmine glanced his way.

The look of shock in her eyes said she was seeing him for the first time.

"Oh. I didn't see you."

Darien crossed the living room floor toward them. "Who's this?" he asked.

"Darien, meet Luc. Luc, this is Darien."

Luc headed straight for Darien and offered him his hand. This kid wasn't shy at all.

"Nice to meet you, sir," Luc said.

"Likewise," Darien responded, eyeing the kid curiously.

Luc looked at Jasmine. "This your husband?"

Jasmine chuckled, as though the idea were completely absurd. "No, no," she replied. "He's definitely not my husband."

The way she so quickly and emphatically said that rankled Darien, but he wasn't sure why. He was the one who'd told Jasmine that he wasn't ready for a relationship.

"Your boyfriend?" Luc pressed.

"He's a friend."

Luc glanced at her left hand. "No ring." He shook his head and tsked. "Pretty girl like you—an' you not married?"

Jasmine placed her hands on her hips as she stared at him. "For a kid, you're asking a lot of grown-up questions."

Luc shrugged, then glanced around. "I never been in here before. This is real nice, mon. Real nice."

"I'll get the towels," Jasmine said, and headed off in the direction of the linen closet.

Luc's mouth hanging open in awe, he hurried to the dining room. "Wow." He pressed his hands to the window and looked outside. "Really nice, mon. Expensive."

Darien sighed, impatient. "Hey, be careful around that furniture. You need to get dried off."

"Here are the towels," Jasmine announced, and Darien looked her way. She was holding two thick towels. Seeing her, Luc trotted back to the foyer, where he happily took one from her hand and started to dry his body.

"Me feel a little cold," Luc said. "You got some tea?"

"That's a great idea," Jasmine said. "Darien, do you mind?"

Yeah, he did mind—though he couldn't exactly say that. The thing was, Darien wanted to talk to Jasmine, make amends for earlier, and he couldn't do that with this kid around.

So he did the only thing he could. Turned and started back toward the kitchen. "Sure. I can boil some water."

Five minutes later Jasmine and Luc were sitting at the small kitchen table, drinking fresh mint tea and chatting up a storm. Darien lingered in the background watching them.

He knew Jasmine had to have just met the kid, and yet there she was, chatting and laughing as though they were old friends.

Darien would bet a million dollars that she was being extra chatty with Luc so she could avoid talking to him.

He had no choice but to wait, however, and went back to the kitchen sink. There, he got back to work trying to scrub the burned oil out of the skillet.

After another five minutes—and more laughter than he could stomach—Darien looked out the kitchen window. "Good news," he said. "It stopped raining."

Both Jasmine and Luc looked to him.

"Which means Luc can go back to playing with his friends."

"Nah, mon. I have time."

"But Jasmine and I don't have time," Darien said, and when he glanced at Jasmine, he saw her staring at him in confusion. "We were just heading out."

"I can come?" The kid's eyes lit up.

"No, you can't," Darien said matter-of-factly. "Jasmine and I have some things to discuss. Adult business," he added before Luc decided to interject an objection.

Luc looked up at Darien and studied him with intelligent eyes. After a moment, his lips curled into a sly grin. "You like her," he said, not a question. "You want her to be your wife."

Darien placed his hand on the kid's shoulder. "Okay, Luc. Time to go."

"If you like her, you shouldn't let her walk around alone, ya know," Luc said. "Bad men out dere will try an' take advantage."

Now Darien's eyes flew to Jasmine's. Alarm shot down his spine in the form of an icy chill. "Did something happen?"

"Not really," she answered.

"Cuz I was dere," Luc quickly said, pushing his chair back to stand. He skipped toward the front door. "Miss Jasmine, come visit me again, okay?"

"Sure." Jasmine got up and walked to the front door. She gave Luc a hug. "Thank you for walking me home."

With that, Luc darted through the door. As soon as he was gone, Darien approached Jasmine and put his hands on her shoulders. "What happened?"

"Some guy was bothering me. It didn't get out of hand or anything."

"Because Luc showed up," Darien stated.

"Yes, because Luc showed up. Now, I don't know if this guy was going to do anything crazy—"

"I shouldn't have let you leave." Darien blew out a frustrated breath as he released her.

"What?"

"I shouldn't have let you leave," he repeated, speaking louder this time. "We weren't getting along, you left, and clearly something happened from which you needed protecting."

Just saying the words made Darien sick to his stomach. He couldn't help feeling an awful sense of déjà vu. How he hadn't been there for Sheila that awful day when she had been attacked, and how that had changed the course of his life.

"Luc was there, and I'm perfectly fine."

"Right," Darien said absently, guilt making his stomach clench.

"Did you really want to talk to me?" Jasmine asked. "Or did you just say that to get rid of Luc?"

"I do want us to talk," Darien said.

Jasmine's lips pulled into a tight line. "I think I know why. You want me out of here. I could push the issue, but I've decided I'm not going to fight you."

"Jasmine."

"If it hadn't started to rain, I was going to try walking to that resort next door, see if they have space."

"That's not necessary."

"I think it is."

"Trust me, it's not."

"Why not?" Jasmine asked, meeting his gaze. "Have you made arrangements to leave?"

"No." Darien swallowed. He found it hard to stare at Jasmine without feeling like a big jerk. "Look, I'm sorry about earlier. I was wrong. I promise not to start any more stupid fights."

Darien offered Jasmine a small smile, but she didn't react the way he had hoped she would. She turned away from him.

"Jasmine?"

She turned back to face him, her expression weary. "I don't know. Maybe it is better if I go my own way."

"I said I was sorry."

"I know, but—"

"And Luc had a good point," Darien quickly went on. "I shouldn't be letting you wander around on the island alone."

"You're not responsible for me."

He didn't know why, but it was important to him

that she didn't leave. Even if they didn't make a romantic connection, he would miss her company.

"I couldn't live with myself if something bad happened to you because you felt you had to leave over a stupid argument," Darien told her. "We've been getting along reasonably well. There's no reason one fight should change that."

His words made sense, but it wasn't just the fight. It was that for the past several days she had been falling for him—and if he had no interest in her whatsoever, she wasn't sure she could continue to stay here with him. It would hurt too much.

Darien blew out a hurried breath. "I have an idea. Maybe we can do something different tonight to change up the monotony."

"You think we're bored with each other?"

"I'm not saying that. But...I was thinking that we could go out tonight, get a bite to eat, maybe dance a little."

"You want to go dancing with me?"

"There are a lot of hot spots on the island. I think it's time we check one out together."

One minute Darien was telling her that he didn't want to get involved with her. The next he was asking her out on a date? Jasmine wasn't sure what to make of this.

"You'll like it," he assured her. "What do you feel like—casual or a place that's a bit more upscale?"

"Casual upscale," she answered, thinking of the cute outfits she'd brought but had yet to wear.

Then she eyed him cautiously. "Are you sure about this?"

"Yes," Darien said, no reservations.

Slowly she nodded. "All right then. Sounds like a plan."

Chapter 12

Allan Jackson slammed down the receiver, then cussed a blue streak loud enough to be heard through the walls. He didn't give a damn who heard him. His fairweather neighbors had treated him with nothing but scorn since the sex tape of him and Jasmine had been released, as though he were some sick and depraved individual.

There was the occasional guy at Starbucks who gave him a slap on the back and congratulated him on banging such a hot babe. Allan had no patience for such idiots, since they acted like he'd "scored," when the truth was, he had been in a relationship with Jasmine.

Had been. It hurt more than he ever thought

possible to think of his relationship with Jasmine in past tense. Two years down the drain, just like that. How could it be possible?

Clearly he'd made a mistake with the tape. Its existence had angered Jasmine beyond reason, and with the way people were treating him with such disdain, Allan could understand her ire. But did that erase the love they were supposed to share? What ever happened to forgiveness and second chances?

Allan tried Jasmine's number again, and once again got the message that her voice mail was full. Where the hell was she, and why hadn't she thought to call him, even to let him know she was okay?

Bitterly, he wondered what her loyal fans would think of the good girl with the stone-cold heart.

Rising from the bed, Allan strolled to the window. He peered outside. Not one person from the media was there. Just as they were no longer outside Jasmine's house.

He didn't doubt for a minute that they *would* be parked outside Jasmine's house, *if* she were there. Him—well, he wasn't the big box-office name. No one cared one bit about him.

Allan swore again.

Though he knew it was pointless, he retrieved his cordless handset from the bed and punched in the digits to Jasmine's cell number. He got her voice mail, which was, like her home number, full.

He needed to find her. There had to be a way to track her down. She couldn't just write him off the way she had, all because of a lapse in judgment. It wasn't as if he'd altered the tape to make the Virgin Mary look like some nasty whore.

Allan trudged from his bedroom to the kitchen, where he had his laptop set up on the table. He sat down in front of it and glanced at the screen. Currently he was doctoring some other person's script—a pathetic sci-fi thriller that would win awards only in hell. He hated this garbage. He had so much more potential than this. But script doctoring paid the bills, even if he was working on B-list crap that would go straight to video.

Allan opened another file, the one that was really exciting him. Without a doubt, this screenplay could be his big break. He was working on spec, but a friend of a friend knew Will Smith well and thought that Allan's idea would be right up Will's alley.

If only he could write it.

Allan forced himself to pound away on the keys for five minutes, but he produced pure crap and deleted every word.

It was no use. His muse had to be happy in order to create, and with Jasmine off God only knew where, he was far from happy. He was downright miserable.

He needed to find her, make her see reason. He needed to look her in the eyes and tell her he was sorry. She would forgive him, he knew she would. And soon, all this media interest in her would die down and she would be able to hold her head high again.

They would get married, just as he'd always

dreamed. Then they would become one of Hollywood's supercouples, maybe even start their own production company.

One lapse in judgment shouldn't cost him everything that he held dear. Especially not the love of his life.

Allan closed the laptop and stood. He had put off proposing to Jasmine because he wasn't at the place in his career where he wanted to be. He had wanted to have his first major motion-picture script under his belt. In fact, be able to value himself as an equal partner in their relationship.

Now he knew that kind of thinking was superficial. It didn't matter if he had a dollar in the bank or one hundred million—as long as he and Jasmine had love, that was what mattered.

And they did have love.

His mind made up, Allan grabbed his wallet, then headed to the door. He had some shopping to do—ring shopping.

As he made his way downstairs, a thought struck him, so brilliant that he laughed out loud in the elevator.

Of course. Why hadn't he thought of it before?

Jasmine was mad because she felt her image had been ruined—mostly because she was an unmarried woman fornicating in a video.

But if she were engaged—to the very man she was with in the video—certainly her fans and the media would realize that she wasn't a slut, but a woman enjoying physical intimacy with the man who would be her husband. An engagement would cast a whole different light on things. All that mattered was perception, and if he made an honest woman out of Jasmine, that would garner lots of positive press.

Stepping outside, Allan stopped and let the sun shine on his face. He drew in a deep breath of air and chuckled once again at how brilliant his idea was.

Even Jasmine wouldn't be able to deny that his plan was the best way to offset the negative publicity.

Allan headed to his car, excited to buy the perfect engagement ring. And along the way, he'd be sure to call his source at one of Hollywood's biggest tabloids and slip the story….

Chapter 13

Even though Darien had taken steps toward resolving the situation with Jasmine, she stayed in her room for the next couple hours. While he'd continued to clean and air out the kitchen, he had hoped that she would make an appearance.

But she didn't.

He was going a little stir crazy, but tried not to let the silence get to him. He went outside, swam for about an hour—and still Jasmine didn't make an appearance.

He was disappointed, but wasn't going to let that stop his plans for that evening. As he showered, he contemplated where to take her. A place that was more upbeat or more casual?

Casual would give them time to talk—but that

might not be the best idea. They had talked about a whole host of things over the past week—how beautiful the island was, their favorite U.S. cities, their favorite foods, how nice it was to be away from the hustle and bustle, and of course, the weather. Everything *but* the obvious attraction between them. The way Darien saw it, they had talked the neutral topics to death. Besides, if Jasmine continued to be wary of him the way she was now, she might have nothing to say to him over dinner, which would make the night extremely awkward.

No, a place with good music, where they could dance, was the best option. If they ended up at a loss for words, music would fill the gaps.

There was a place called Sunshine in town that played a mix of reggae, R & B and hip-hop. The one time Darien had ventured into the establishment, he'd felt out of place because he'd been surrounded by couples. He and Jasmine would fit in, but it wasn't a quiet, intimate spot—so there wouldn't be pressure for them to snuggle up and get a little closer.

Back in his bedroom, Darien glanced at the clock. It was a little after 4:00 p.m. Darien figured he'd give it another couple hours before he and Jasmine headed out for a night of fun.

She was still as quiet as a mouse in her room, so perhaps she was sleeping. Darien hoped that explained her silence—as opposed to the very real possibility that she had changed her mind about going out with him tonight.

* * *

Promptly at six o'clock there was a light rapping on her door. Jasmine, who had some clothes laid out on her bed in an effort to try to decide what to wear, looked in the door's direction. Her stomach twisted and she had to force herself to take a breath. Why she was so nervous about the idea of going out with Darien tonight, she didn't know.

"Yes?" she called out.

"It's me. Darien."

Of course. Who else would it be?

"Just wondering if you still wanted to head out tonight?" he asked.

"I'm getting ready as we speak," Jasmine answered.

Darien didn't say another word and Jasmine figured he had wandered away from her door. She turned her attention once again to the clothing options on her bed. A pair of black denim jeans with a cute blue top, a seersucker red dress that flowed past her knees and a body-hugging leopard-print dress.

She quickly decided against the leopard-print dress. It was too loud, too sexy. And the more that Jasmine thought about it, the denim jeans and blue top would be a little casual.

Lifting the red dress, she held it against her body and went to the mirror. She loved this dress and had been dying for an occasion to wear it. With her suede thong sandals and suede Coach purse, this outfit would be sexy but not over the top.

As she dressed, she second-guessed her decision.

With the low-cut scoop neck, maybe she looked a little *too* sexy.

But wasn't that exactly what she wanted—to show Darien just how good she could look and what he was missing out on? Seriously, she was tired of all their polite talks and easy companionship. She wanted the man to kiss her senseless already so she could see if they had the same kind of chemistry when they kissed that she imagined they would have.

That thought in mind, Jasmine left the dress on, applied a little bit of makeup—then headed out of the room to meet Darien.

Darien, who was holding a mug of something when he saw her, lowered it from his lips and simply stared at her. In fact, the look in his eyes sort of resembled that of a deer caught in the headlights.

"Wow," he said quietly. "You look…amazing."

"Thank you."

She was tempted to do a little twirl, but refrained. It was just that seeing Darien, decked out in a thin white cotton shirt and a pair of black slacks—well, the sight got her blood pumping a bit faster.

"You look pretty good yourself," Jasmine added.

"I made coffee," Darien said. "In case you wanted some before we went out."

"I'm okay," she told him.

Silently they headed outside to the car, a small, gold Nissan. It was probably a good thing that she couldn't drive it, since Jasmine wasn't sure she would remember to drive on the left side of the road.

"So, uh," she began when they reached the main road. "Where are you taking me?"

"A place called Sunshine. It's a bar-restaurant. Upbeat. Upscale but not uptight. They serve a variety of food, play good music."

For the next five minutes Jasmine pretended to be absorbed in the lush view as they drove. When they turned left onto Jeremie Street, the road that took them toward the center of town, she finally glanced Darien's way and spoke.

"I'm sorry, too," she said.

Darien glanced her way. "Excuse me?"

"About this morning. I'm sorry I left you to clean up the whole mess."

"I started the argument. It was only fitting."

Jasmine was saved from responding when Darien made an abrupt left turn. She noticed they were turning onto a street named Victoria.

A few seconds later Darien pulled up to the curb. The street was well populated, with tourists in sundresses and straw hats and shirts with loud tropical prints.

"This is it," Darien announced, his gaze going past her to the right.

The building looked like a Southern house, complete with a large wraparound porch. The exterior was all wood, painted white with yellow trim. A row of clear Christmas lights hung from the awning. Jasmine figured it was part of the decor, rather than Christmas lights that hadn't been taken down since last year.

"This is nice,'" Jasmine said, looking around at the couples sitting on the porch. She opened her door and stepped out onto the sidewalk. The beat of a reggae tune wafted out onto the street.

Darien met her at her side of the car. "You'll like this."

"I think I will," she agreed.

She started up the walkway and Darien fell into step beside her. On the porch, a dark-haired couple laughed. Beside them, another couple was holding hands across a table. And on the far side of the porch, a black woman and white man were all-out necking.

Jasmine swallowed. She couldn't help wondering why Darien had taken her here, of all places.

Darien rested his hand on the small of her back, then opened the door. "This way," he said.

Inside, the atmosphere was thankfully different. Gone were the lovebirds who only had eyes for each other. Here, men and women were dancing on a large dance floor to an upbeat reggae tune, groups of friends were eating and people populated the stools at the bar. It was definitely an upscale joint with a decided Caribbean flavor.

For a Tuesday night, the place was very busy. Then again, probably everyone in here was on vacation, so didn't have to worry about working in the morning.

A hostess greeted them with a wide smile and was soon leading them to a table on a tiered level overlooking the dance floor.

Jasmine lifted the plastic-encased drink menu and glanced at the colorful cocktails. There were the standard margaritas and coladas, as well as some drinks she'd never heard of.

"I think I'll go for the good old-fashioned rum punch," Jasmine said.

"If you're a beer drinker, you might want to give the Piton a try—it's a local beer."

"I'm not much of a beer drinker," Jasmine admitted.

"You don't know what you're missing."

"Oh, yes, I do. Bitter taste. The bloated after-effect." Jasmine shook her head. "No, thank you. I prefer wine and fruity drinks."

The waiter arrived, took their drink orders and left Jasmine and Darien to contemplate the menu.

"Just so there are no surprises," Jasmine began, "are we going Dutch on this, or what?"

Darien cut his eyes at her. "Obviously, I'm treating you."

"Okay…so what am I allowed to order?"

"Anything you want," Darien told her.

Jasmine's eyes narrowed on the lobster entrée—and she was seriously tempted to order it. But it was eighty dollars, and even if she wanted it, she wouldn't order such a high-priced item.

"I think I'll start with the shrimp cocktail and have the grilled tuna in herb sauce. What about you?"

"I had the curried chicken the last time I was here, and it was fabulous. I'm gonna stick with that."

The waiter arrived with their drinks, then took their dinner order. Jasmine sipped the rum punch—then made a face she knew was far from attractive as she winced.

"Damn. This is strong."

"Too strong?"

She took another sip. "It's flavorful, that's for sure."

"You want to order something else?"

"No. This'll do." *And maybe it's exactly what I need to get through this evening.*

Because all she could think about as she glanced around the restaurant was what the future held for her and Darien. He was so different from the guys she had dated in the past. He had such a quiet yet magnetic presence, and no matter what she told herself about keeping her guard up around him, she was drawn to him like a moth to a flame.

Five minutes passed with Jasmine sipping her drink, looking around and pretty much doing everything in her power to avoid direct eye contact with Darien. By the way he sipped his beer, thrummed his fingers on the table and glanced around, it was obvious he was doing the same thing.

"Why are we doing this?" Jasmine suddenly asked. "It's obvious you don't want to be around me."

There was shock in Darien's eyes at her words, and he held her gaze for several beats before speaking. "You really believe that?"

"It seems clear to me."

"You think I wanted us to get dressed up, head out for dinner, because I didn't want to be around you?"

"I don't know what to think."

"Then maybe you should stop thinking."

Jasmine shot Darien a confused look, but he pushed his chair back and stood. He offered her his hand.

"How about we dance?"

Bob Marley's "One Love" started as they made their way down the few steps to the main level. Moments later they were on the dance floor.

Immediately, Jasmine got into the music, swaying her hips and snapping her fingers. Darien's eyes roamed over her—something she did not miss.

Even ten minutes ago, Jasmine would have glanced away, uncomfortable. But because the rum punch had already made her heady, she kicked up her hips a notch.

Darien started to move his body back and forth to the smooth beat of the music. And damn, the man looked fine. His white shirt hung loosely over his torso, but that didn't conceal his muscular build. The man's body was scrumptious with a capital *S,* and Jasmine would as soon have him for her main course rather than the meal she'd ordered.

And not just for the sex—though she couldn't deny the strong physical pull of attraction she felt every time she looked at the man. But because she liked him, though God only knew why.

Dancing with the man, being close but not getting close, was pure torture. Jasmine glanced around. The other men and women on the floor were so close they would need to be wedged apart, yet you could fit a truck between her and Darien.

As the next song started, a funky R & B tune, Jasmine edged her body a little closer to his. Then she turned, positioning her butt in front of him, and did a little shimmy.

When she spun back around, Darien was wiping sweat from his brow. Because the view of her had gotten him hot and bothered—or because the dance floor was humid?

He offered her a smile, but she wanted more than that. Boldly, she placed a palm on Darien's chest.

Darien looked in the direction of their table. "I think the waiter just brought out our appetizers."

"They can wait a little longer, can't they?" She gyrated her hips a little faster and reached for his hand, a subtle invitation to get a little closer to her.

He did, but it was still as though there were a wall between them.

"Is that the best you have to offer?" Jasmine asked, a challenge in her voice.

"What do you mean?"

"I mean—" She did some fancy footwork combined with fast-swaying hips, and ended the move with a twirl. "I mean, can you top that?"

"Oh, you want me to step up my game."

"*If* you can," Jasmine taunted him.

"All right, then." Darien linked his fingers and stretched his knuckles, then volleyed his head from side to side. "Okay, now this I can get down to," he added when an upbeat hip-hop tune filled the room.

"Show me what you got!"

In as sexy a maneuver as Jasmine had ever seen, Darien shook his shoulders while rocking his hips back and forth. Jasmine watched him, a smile playing on her lips.

"Go on with your bad self, Big D!"

"You like that, huh?"

Jasmine clapped to the beat, encouraging him.

"Then watch this." Even though the music wasn't appropriate, Darien pulled a Michael Jackson hip-pumping move, complete with the leg maneuver, then started to moonwalk. In a few seconds, a small crowd formed around them, clapping and hooting as Darien did his thing.

He kept up his Michael Jackson impression for another minute or so, then abruptly took Jasmine's hand and pulled her close. He wrapped his arms around her, laughing as he did. Jasmine was laughing, too.

"Nice moves," a heavyset guy with a jiggling belly told Darien, and shook his hand. Then he started his own imitation of Michael Jackson's dance moves. He failed to impress, but didn't seem to notice.

"Slow down, brother," Darien joked.

He was still holding Jasmine, and whether it was for show or because he wanted to, Jasmine enjoyed the moment.

"I think someone's been drinking too many Piton beers," she mumbled, and she and Darien chuckled at that.

His hands still loosely around her waist, Darien's gaze met hers. His warm breath fanned her forehead, tickling her skin.

"You ready to get to our food?" he asked.

"I like you," Jasmine blurted out, not sure why the words came out in response to his query.

Darien's eyes narrowed in question. "Sorry—what?"

"Hey!" The big man was back, this time taking hold of Jasmine's arm. He caught her off guard, and she shot him a what-on-earth-are-you-doing look.

The man beamed. "I know who you are! Cleo, baby." He motioned anxiously for someone to come to his side. "Look who it is!"

Darien stepped back, eyeing Jasmine suspiciously. She avoided his gaze as she tucked a strand of hair behind her.

The man took one of her hands in two of his. "Oh, man. I can't believe it." He pumped her hand, over and over.

A woman joined his side, also beaming, and Jasmine figured this had to be Cleo. Cleo was a short, plump brunette.

No sooner had Cleo's boyfriend or husband released Jasmine's hand than the woman scooped it up. "My husband and I saw *The Game* just before we came here, and I absolutely *loved* it!" the woman raved in what sounded like a Texas accent.

"Thank you," Jasmine said. "Thank you so much."

"Do you mind posing for a picture with us? This is our honeymoon, and it will be the highlight of our trip."

"Of course," Jasmine said. She glanced to the left at Darien, who was still watching her curiously.

"Would your boyfriend mind?" Cleo asked.

"No, not at all. Darien, can you snap a picture of the three of us."

Cleo's husband handed Darien the digital camera. "Just point and shoot."

Cleo and her husband took a place on either side of Jasmine, and Darien snapped off a couple shots. The picture-taking attracted stares from other patrons, and Jasmine noticed a group of women on the dance floor huddle together and whisper.

Then one of them sneered at her.

"This is gorgeous," Cleo gushed as she looked at the digital camera's display. "Thank you so much!"

"You're welcome," Jasmine said quietly.

The newlyweds wandered off hand in hand, and Darien stepped toward Jasmine. "So," he began. "Seems I've underestimated your acting career."

"How do you mean?"

"I assumed you were an aspiring actress, but with the way that couple went crazy for you, you must be some big star."

"'Big star,'" Jasmine said, making air quotes, "is a serious exaggeration."

"Not to that couple."

Jasmine shrugged. "I've done a few things people might have seen." She didn't know why, but she felt she should downplay her star status—at least for now.

She wanted Darien to like her for her, not because of who she was.

Glancing around, Jasmine's gaze landed on the trio of girls who had clearly been talking about her. Now they were all staring in her direction, the looks on their faces saying that none was too pleased to see her.

"You ready to get our food?" Jasmine asked.

Darien regarded her for a beat before answering, and Jasmine knew he was wondering if she was being forthright with him.

Finally he placed a hand on her shoulder. "Yeah. Let's eat."

Chapter 14

Over the next couple hours Darien and Jasmine ate their meals, drank some more and burned off the calories on the dance floor. Darien had been perfectly aware of what Jasmine had been doing when she found an out-of-the-way spot in a corner.

Avoiding the public.

While no one else approached her, Darien hadn't missed the looks people had shot her way. Most were awestruck looks, some questioning, as if they weren't sure who they were seeing, but a few were downright peculiar.

A little scornful, really.

If Darien could dismiss the looks, he couldn't dismiss the few camera flashes by people who had tried to get close enough to snap a shot.

Obviously, Jasmine was someone that people recognized, which meant she was a bigger actress than he'd figured. Yet when he'd said that to her, she had shrugged off his comment. For the past couple hours, he had been patiently waiting for her to fill him in a bit more on who she was and what she'd been in, but other than singing off-tune and making casual conversation, she'd hadn't offered up even a smidgen of a hint.

Darien hadn't pushed the issue, mostly because he'd been absorbed with watching her move that incredibly sexy body of hers. Her looks alone were enough to attract any man, but there was something else about her. Jasmine had incredible presence—and if she was a full-fledged movie star, he could easily see why.

But what got to him most was her smile. It was natural, pure, and so bright it could light up a football stadium.

Being near her, he found himself thinking of the dreams he'd had of her before she had shown up in his life. Being near her, dancing with her, flirting with her, he found himself not thinking about what tomorrow could bring, but how he very much wanted to live in the moment.

Of exploring the reason why fate had brought them together.

Outside, Darien opened the passenger side door for her, made sure she was settled in the car, then got behind the wheel. Jasmine was grinning at him as he sat.

"What?" Darien asked. "Something on my face?"

"I'm just happy. And I wanted to say thank you for a lovely, lovely evening."

"It was fun, wasn't it?"

"Maybe we can do it again sometime."

"Sure," Darien replied.

As he put the car into gear, Jasmine ran her fingers along the top of his hand. His eyes shot to hers. She bit down on her bottom lip—and damn, did something that looked a lot like eyelash batting.

She'd only had the one rum punch and a glass of wine. Was she *that* drunk?

Pondering just that, Darien jerked his gaze ahead of him and started to drive. Jasmine's laughter had him turning to look at her again.

"What's so funny?"

"You should have seen the look on your face!" she told him, barely able to contain herself. "I was messing with you. You know—about that whole 'batting my eyelashes' thing."

For a moment Darien was confused. Then he remembered what he'd said to her earlier when they'd had their fight in the kitchen. "Ah."

"I had to get you back."

"Well." Darien swallowed his embarrassment. But when Jasmine kept chuckling, his embarrassment ebbed away and he started laughing, too.

It was nice to watch Jasmine laugh. There was something infectious about her sexy chortle, something that made him want to throw all caution to the wind and kiss her senseless. He hadn't known her long, but when he compared the spark of attraction he felt for her to what he had felt when he'd first met Sheila...well, there *was* no comparison.

So why didn't he do it—just stop the car and kiss Jasmine?

While his fear over getting involved with another woman was slowly but surely ebbing away, he realized his problem now was that he was nervous. Since he'd started dating Sheila ten years ago, he had kissed only one woman. His whole life had been wrapped up in her. His hopes for the future. His happy memories. Everything.

Not that the memories were all that wonderful. That was something Darien had only been able to admit to himself in the past few weeks. After their first couple years of marriage—and a miscarriage— Sheila had changed. And not for the better. She had become materialistic. If her best friend had a pair of designer shoes that cost a grand, she needed a pair that cost more. If someone at work went to the Bahamas for a vacation, she had to go somewhere, too. Darien had tried to please her, keep her happy, buying her nice things in hopes that she would get over the pain of losing their baby. But even though he had spent a small fortune on her, Sheila had secretly run up his credit-card debt to the point where they lost their house.

And while *she* had been the one to behave badly, it had been—according to Sheila—*his* fault. Darien should have strived for more. A higher position in the military, a part-time job, or even worked on a novel about the military in his spare time.

Darien had forgiven her behavior and her irrational blame, having seen her sudden spending as a cry for help. But he had also insisted on couple's therapy, which Sheila had agreed to. Darien had thought that all their problems would be in the past—but that wasn't the case.

"What are you thinking about?" Jasmine asked.

The question pulled Darien out of his trip down memory lane. "Nothing," he replied.

"Oh, with that serious look on your face, you were definitely thinking about something."

Darien faced her as he turned right onto John Compton Highway. "Something I'd rather forget."

"You are a man of mystery," Jasmine told him.

"I can certainly say the same about you," Darien countered. "It's obvious you've got some secrets of your own."

At that, Jasmine turned her gaze to the right, even though it was too dark to see anything out the window.

Which only proved his point. She was no more interested in talking about her past than he was in talking about his.

But it wasn't as though talking about their pasts was a prerequisite to exploring what they were feeling for each other.

"It certainly is pitch-black out here," Jasmine commented.

"Unlike big-city U.S.A., there aren't lights everywhere." Darien glanced at her, noticed she was gripping the hand rest on the door. "You scared?"

"Darien!" she cried, scaring the life out of him.

His eyes darted to the road and he saw the headlights of a truck heading toward him. It was in its own lane, though—meaning there was no risk of collision.

"What?" he asked.

"I…I just thought…it looked like that truck was coming right toward us. Lord, these roads are so narrow."

Darien reached for her hand and took it in his. "It's okay. We're almost home."

"Thank God you're comfortable behind the wheel. I can't believe how dark it is."

Darien wondered if she had a phobia of the dark, too. He wondered how much he didn't know about Jasmine…and how much he would learn.

He gave her hand a gentle squeeze. "That's the turn for our house right up there." He indicated the spot with a jerk of his head. "So, no worries."

Even though Jasmine nodded, she didn't stop clutching the hand rest until Darien had turned left onto the gravel road that led to the house. Moments later, he was putting the car in Park.

He reached for his door handle, hoping to make it out of the car to open Jasmine's door for her. But she tugged on his other hand, as though she didn't want to let him get out of the car.

"Huh?" Darien asked stupidly.

"I said something to you at the restaurant," she said quietly. "I'm not sure you heard me."

Darien's heart started to race. "Oh?"

"Yeah."

"I said that I liked you."

A beat passed. "I like you, too."

"But you don't want to kiss me."

"K-kiss you?" Darien stammered, wanting to kick himself. "What makes you say that?"

"Because you would have done it already."

Sweat popped out on Darien's palms and his mouth grew instantly dry. "That's not true," he said, then wondered why he didn't just kiss the woman. With the way she was edging her face closer to his, it was clear she wanted him to kiss her already.

So Darien edged his face toward hers, tilted his head to the side and went in for the kill. Only instead of his mouth pressing against her lips, their teeth knocked.

"Ow!" Jasmine exclaimed, jerking backward as though she had been scalded. Darien, too, pulled his head back, but if he felt any pain, it was overshadowed by extreme embarrassment.

He closed his eyes and moaned. Damn, what was wrong with him? Jasmine was going to think him a world-class loser. Finally he had decided to go for it, see what would happen when their lips connected, and he had made a complete fool of himself.

"Well, that was fun." Jasmine smiled sweetly at him, and he didn't know if she was taking the incident in stride or if she felt nothing but pity for him.

"Let me try that again."

"Ooh, I've got to go to the bathroom!" Jasmine quickly threw her door open.

Darien did the same, wondering if Jasmine had

simply come up with an excuse to let him down gently. He watched her scurry to the house and disappear inside.

"Dumb, stupid, ridiculous!" Darien groaned his frustration before heading inside. If it was the last thing he did, he was going to show Jasmine that he wasn't a bumbling moron. That he knew how to kiss a woman—and kiss her good.

But the phone was ringing when he stepped inside, so he hurried into the living room to answer it. "Hello?"

"Hi!" a woman enthused on the other end of the line. "I'm looking for Jasmine St. Clair."

"Sure," Darien said. "Just a minute."

He wandered toward the bathroom and met Jasmine as she was exiting. He extended the phone to her.

"It's for me?"

"Yeah."

"Oh. Thanks."

Jasmine took the phone from him. "Hello?" A grin erupted on her face. "Oh my God!"

Turning, she went into her nearby bedroom and closed the door. Darien went to the living room, plopped himself down onto the sofa and buried his face in his hands.

Other than her agent, Victoria, there was one person in the film business that Jasmine considered a true friend. That person was Kate Latham, who was also represented by Victoria and had, in the last couple years, made a huge name for herself as a sexy starlet. She had been in Italy shooting her latest thriller, and every time Jasmine had tried to reach her since the scandal broke, she hadn't been able to. So she was shocked when Darien handed her the phone and she heard Kate's voice.

"Kate, is that really you?" she asked as she closed her bedroom door behind her.

"Of course it's me. You knew I'd track you down one way or another."

"It's so good to hear your voice," Jasmine said.

"Back at ya," Kate replied.

"Where are you? Still in Positano?"

"I'm home now. Got back a couple hours ago. I called Victoria to find out where you were. It's not, like, two in the morning there, is it?"

"No. It's a little after nine in the evening."

"So, girl, what is going on?"

Remembering all that had happened in the last few weeks, Jasmine groaned. "You know. The typical starlet-gone-wild drama."

"I heard about it when I was in Italy! I tried calling you, but could never get through."

"I had to take my phone off the hook and turn my cell off. The media wouldn't give me a break. You'd think I proclaimed myself to be some sort of holy virgin. I finally had to take off in order to get some peace."

"So you're in St. Lucia."

"Yeah."

"What's it like?"

"A piece of heaven. Beautiful, quiet… Just what I need right now."

"Good. I'm glad to hear it."

"How was Italy?" Jasmine asked. "Did the film shoot go well?"

"Positano was *amazing*. The film shoot went well. *And*…I even fell in love."

"Kate!"

"Yeah, well, it's already over," Kate added bitterly. "I swear, you just can't trust anyone in the film business."

"Who?"

"My co-star. Amir Elfar."

"Wow. That's a surprise."

"I know. I normally go for the blond hottie types, but Amir and I made a real connection."

The way Brad and Angelina had when filming Mr. & Mrs. Smith, Jasmine thought, rolling her eyes.

"He talked about taking me to Egypt, showing me where he'd grown up, then giving me a tour of the pyramids and everything." Kate sighed her displeasure. "Then I found him in his Winnebago with some young Italian groupie. The two best weeks of my life, over like that." Kate snapped her fingers loudly enough for Jasmine to hear.

Kate was the type who fell in love hard and fast—and often. Her marriage last year had ended after two months, and Jasmine would bet there were many more in her future.

Still, she said, "I'm sorry."

"I think I should just become a nun and get this whole dating thing over and done with."

Jasmine laughed out loud at that.

"I mean, seriously. Is there something wrong with me?"

"Of course not."

"Am I no longer hot or something?"

"You know you're hot. Everyone in the world knows you're hot."

"Then why can't I find a decent guy to settle down with?"

"Clearly, you and Amir weren't meant to be. Count your blessings that you found that out now as opposed to later."

Kate was definitely a drama queen, but at her core, she was honest and decent. She was one of those rare people who, once she called herself your friend, wouldn't betray you.

Kate sighed. "Listen to me, going on an on about my own drama. Victoria said Allan was behind the release of that awful, dirty tape?"

"Uh-huh. Can you believe it?"

"And I thought screwing another woman was bad."

"Exactly."

"Allan called me," Kate said.

Jasmine's back straightened. "You talked to him?"

"No. He left me a message. Said if I got in touch with you, to tell you that he still loves you."

Unbelievable. "Please tell me that's not why you're calling."

"Of course not. I'm calling to chat to you, see how you're doing. But…I know how much you cared about him."

"He destroyed what we had when he released that tape to the media. I can never be with him again."

"Everyone makes mistakes," Kate commented.

"This was not a mistake. It was a calculated plan to benefit *his* career."

"I'm just saying, if what you had was real, it's not weak to consider forgiving him."

"Are you sure you didn't speak to him?" Jasmine asked.

"No, I didn't. And when I do, you'd better believe I'm going to give him a piece of my mind. What was he *thinking?*"

"That this was his ticket to household recognition. He didn't care how it would hurt me."

"That's so hard to believe."

"He told me that to my face, so I'm not guessing here."

"Ouch." Kate paused before saying, "I hate this. You two were so cute together. The perfect couple."

"I guess looks can be deceiving," Jasmine said, sighing softly.

"What's that supposed to mean?"

"Ever since this whole thing happened, I've been thinking. For Allan to do this to me, and how I feel about him now…maybe we didn't really have a relationship of substance to begin with. Everything fell apart so easily. Almost like…"

"Almost like you wanted a reason to get out?"

Hearing Kate put into words her own thoughts, Jasmine felt a bit shallow. "Yeah," she admitted, because she could tell Kate anything. "It's not like

I would have just left him, but maybe I needed something like this to happen for me to reevaluate the relationship."

"I could not be more shocked right now. You never said you had any doubts."

"I know…but now that it's over, I realize I want a man who makes my heart beat faster just by looking at him. Allan never made me feel that way."

"Oh my God," Kate suddenly said. "Now I get it!"

"Get what?"

"You met someone else, didn't you?"

"Why would you say something like that?" Jasmine asked, her voice suddenly sounding a little high-strung to her own ears.

"So that guy who answered the phone wasn't the butler? Or *was* he? Talk about a hot fantasy…"

"Stop!"

"Spill it," Kate demanded. "You're in St. Lucia with another man!"

"It's not what you think."

"Oh. My. God."

"Listen to me. Really, it's not what you think." Jasmine spent the next few minutes telling Kate the crazy circumstances surrounding how she and Darien had first met, and how they'd both decided they were adult enough to share the villa.

"I'll bet you are adult enough," Kate said.

"Kate…"

"Tell me, is he cute?"

Jasmine hesitated a moment. "Yes."

"Oooh! And I'll bet *he's* the kind of guy who makes your heart race with just one look."

Again, Jasmine didn't answer right away. "If you want the truth…"

Kate squealed. "Is there anything better than that first rush of attraction? New love is the best love."

And Kate should know. But Jasmine said, "I don't know. He's got an ex-wife and a lot of baggage. He took me to dinner tonight and just tried to kiss me in the car—"

"Oo-oh!" Kate crooned. Then, "Oh, no. I interrupted the start of a romantic evening, didn't I?"

"No. Not at all. You didn't let me finish. I was going to say that the attempted kiss had to be *the* most awkward moment in the history of civilization."

"Ouch."

"I think he's still hung up on his ex or something."

"Ex, schmex. That can be worked out."

"I'm not sure."

"Turn up the charm," Kate told Jasmine. "You're a hot Hollywood star. Work it, girlfriend."

"Maybe it's not just him. Maybe I'm not ready for a relationship, either. So soon after all this drama with Allan. The timing sucks."

"Oh, you can get past that."

"Hey—one minute, it sounded like you were in Allan's corner."

"Well, you sound so enamored with this guy."

"What have I said that makes you think I'm enamored?"

"I can tell," Kate responded, laughing. "How can this guy *not* want you—you're gorgeous, famous…"

If only Jasmine could be so confident. She said, "I'll see how it goes."

"Why are you still talking to me? You should be trying to seduce this guy! What's his name?"

"Darien."

"Oo-oh, I like."

"He's nice." Jasmine felt a hot flush when she remembered how he had taken her hand in the car. Just the touch of his hand had made her feel one hundred percent better. "I don't know why I like him, but I do."

"Go get your man, girl. And you had better tell me every last dirty detail!"

"I don't know…."

"Talk to you later."

Jasmine gaped. "You're going to hang up on me?"

"I'm doing this in the name of love."

"You're moving far too quickly with that love talk. I've only known this guy about ten days."

"And how long did you know Allan before you started dating him?"

"Six months," Jasmine answered.

"Exactly. And you never once sounded as nervous and excited about him as you do right now."

Did she sound excited? Or was Kate exaggerating?

"I'll call you tomorrow. Afternoon. That should give you enough time to get out of bed with this hot, new stud."

"Okay, fine. I'll talk to you later." She may as well let Kate go or the rest of the conversation would be about her love life.

"Bye. And good luck!"

Jasmine giggled, then said a decisive, "Later, Kate."

As she ended the call, her stomach danced with nerves. Maybe Kate was right and she should just go for it.

Inhaling a deep breath, Jasmine walked to her bedroom door, then opened it. She made her way down the hallway to the living room, where she planned to pick up where she and Darien had left off in the car.

"Darien?" she called.

No answer.

When she got to the living room, she understood why Darien hadn't answered her.

He was asleep on the sofa, snoring lightly.

Well, there went that.

Another missed opportunity.

Chapter 15

Even though Jasmine awoke late the next morning, she was hardly rested. Her feelings for Darien had kept her awake much of the night, and when she hadn't consciously been thinking about him, she had dreamed about him.

Gone was the confidence she'd felt last night when she had searched for him in the living room and found him sleeping. Now, she was insecure about everything—about what he possibly felt for her and where any sort of involvement between them could even lead. She lived in Los Angeles and was involved in the film world. He was a soldier. Their lives were as different as night and day.

Much of the night, she had replayed in her mind

the kiss that wasn't. Kate seemed to believe that Darien would definitely be attracted to her, and Jasmine wanted to believe that, too. But now that she had thought about last night's events ad nauseum, she had come to a different conclusion.

She was the one who'd told him she liked him. *She* had been the one who had brought up the subject of kissing. Darien had, simply to be polite, tried to oblige her. But he had been so disinterested in kissing her that he'd awkwardly knocked his teeth against hers instead.

It was time Jasmine put things in perspective. Just because she was attracted to Darien didn't mean she had the right to expect him to want her. She could find him drop-dead gorgeous, completely sexy and still share this place with him without any expectations.

Couldn't she?

Well, if she couldn't, she would have to learn how to. She was thirty-one years old. If she couldn't be mature at this age, when would she ever be?

The sudden knocking at the door pulled Jasmine from her thoughts, and in stark contrast to what she'd just told herself, her heart danced with excitement. As she got off the bed, she finger-combed her hair, then glanced in the mirror to make sure she looked presentable.

She frowned. She looked nowhere near as attractive as she had last night.

What does it matter? she asked herself. *Darien's not interested, anyway.*

With that thought, she moved forward and opened the door—and was floored to see Darien standing there with a bouquet of flowers in his hand. Red hibiscus. It had to be from the bush out front, but still, seeing the bouquet made her smile.

Then she was wary. "What are these for?" she asked.

"You will be pleased to know that I took my happy pills," Darien told her, a smile growing on his face. "And they are in full effect."

Jasmine wanted to laugh, but somehow she held it in check. "Good to know," was her response.

"About last night—"

"Don't say another word."

"No, I want to. First, I'm sorry. If that wasn't the lamest attempt at kissing a woman, I don't know what was. I can't imagine what you think of me."

"That you're a really nice guy, but one who isn't into me," Jasmine answered frankly.

"Isn't into you?"

Jasmine's eyes went to the bunch of red hibiscus. Sure, Darien's actions were saying something entirely different—that he *was* into her. At least a little bit.

Then again, it could all be part of his polite nature.

"And these flowers are a nice, respectful gesture," she went on, not wanting to believe her own words, "but I won't read anything into it."

"You have it all wrong," Darien said. "Sometimes, I'm not good at letting out my thoughts. But I hope this is as clear as it gets." He paused. "I like you. A lot. The way a man likes a woman. These flowers aren't about friendship, about being polite. I thought a guy giving a woman flowers was pretty clear."

"Well." Jasmine's gaze wandered. "I couldn't be sure."

"Be sure." He extended the flowers, and she took them.

A slow breath oozed out of her. She didn't know what to say.

"If I tell you something," Darien went on, "do you promise not to think I'm crazy?"

"It might be too late for that," she told him, but grinned a little to soften the blow.

"I knew I was going to meet you."

"Huh?" she asked, confused. And then his words made sense. Maybe all this time, he *had* known who she was—but had been acting as though he hadn't.

"I dreamed of you. Have been dreaming of you ever since I got to this island."

"You knew who I was, all this time?"

Now it was Darien's turn to look confused. "Oh, you mean because you're an actress. Honestly, I didn't know. Believe it or not, I'm one of those guys who hasn't kept up with pop culture. Now football— that's the only entertainment I need."

"You never watch movies?"

"Hardly. Don't get me wrong. I know who Tom Cruise is, Will Smith… The real big names."

"Then I don't understand what you mean when you say you dreamed about me."

"I warned you that you might think I was crazy. But when I say I dreamed of you, I mean I dreamed of you before I ever saw your face." Darien paused, let his words sink in. "Ever since I got to this island, I kept having dreams about this woman. I didn't know who she was—until you showed up at the pool. At first, with the bandage on your head, I didn't realize you were the woman from my dreams. And then it hit me, and…and I couldn't believe it. I couldn't stop staring at you, unable to believe my eyes."

Jasmine remembered the odd expression on Darien's face after his anger had passed. Now she understood why.

"You're saying you dreamed of me before you met me?"

Darien nodded. "And not sleazy dreams. That's not what I mean. I would see you here, on the island. You'd be standing outside, taking in the view. Smiling. You never said anything to me, you'd just look at me. The dreams were never sexual."

"Well, there's a surprise," Jasmine muttered.

"Excuse me?" Darien asked.

Jasmine ignored the question and sniffed the floral bouquet. "Thank you for the flowers."

She started to turn, but Darien suddenly took hold of her arm, stopping her. He said, "No, seriously. Say what's on your mind."

There had to be something wrong with her, because even though she had told herself to forget about Darien, a sexual frisson ran through her arm at his touch. She could feel the heat of his gaze on her, but she suddenly couldn't meet his eyes.

"Look at me," Darien said softly.

So she did. And swallowed when her mouth went dry from the intensity in his gaze.

"Tell me what you meant," he urged.

"I don't know." She paused. "I mean…you couldn't kiss me last night. Maybe the only reason you think you like me is because I told you that I like you."

"Is that what you believe?" Darien asked, touching her face.

As he ran his finger first along her scar, then down along her cheek, Jasmine quivered. "Please, if you don't mean this, don't do this."

"I already told you, I don't always say the right thing. Sometimes, I even put my foot in my mouth."

Jasmine held her breath.

"Hell, there's no way on earth that I couldn't be attracted to you." His gaze wandered over every inch of her face. "Look at you. Could you be more beautiful?"

White-hot heat jolted Jasmine's center.

"Don't…" Jasmine said.

Darien's finger stopped. "Don't do what?"

"Don't…don't touch me like that. Don't tease me…."

"But isn't teasing the best part?"

Something had changed. Darien was acting like a completely different person. Confident. A man who knew what he wanted and was going to get it. Jasmine should have had the sense to push him away and close her door. He was the one who'd told her

Love, Lies & Videotape

only the day before that he wasn't ready to get involved with anyone else. But she just stood there, as though she didn't have a muscle in her body, much less a brain cell.

Darien took the flowers from her hand and tossed them onto a nearby chair. Then he snaked his arms around Jasmine's waist and edged his face closer to hers.

"Oh, man. You feel incredible in my arms."

"Just how many happy pills did you take?"

Darien roared with laughter. As his laughter died, he pulled her a little closer. "I know I'm not smooth. After being married for seven years, I'm out of practice. I'm also a little afraid."

"Afraid of what?"

"Of what I'm feeling for you," Darien said. "You have no clue how much I have ached to touch you since last week. How much I've wanted to feel your skin on my lips."

Darien planted his soft, warm mouth on her cheek and Jasmine melted. She closed her eyes and moaned at the pleasure his lips brought her—and he wasn't even kissing her on the mouth!

"Please tell me that's part of the teasing," she said.

"You liked that?"

"I'll like it better if I know there's more coming."

Again, Darien laughed. "I've got nothing but time. How about you?"

"Time for?" she prompted.

"For this," he answered.

And then his mouth came down on hers—with all

the skill and confidence of a man who knew how to kiss a woman—and every delicious sensation imaginable overtook Jasmine. He suckled softly on her lips, nipped them with his teeth, tangled his tongue with hers.

Jasmine mewled and completely surrendered to the kiss. The passion between them was a living, breathing thing. It was overpowering, making Jasmine delirious.

His lips locked with hers, Darien took a few steps backward until her back was against the wall. Then, he linked fingers with her and raised her hands high above her head.

His mouth moved to her neck, and as he rained hot kisses over her skin, Jasmine moaned in pure pleasure. How could she like Darien this much? So much that she didn't want him to stop until they were naked on her bed? Never in her life had she experienced such mind-numbing sexual fervor for a man.

Darien's mouth moved from her neck to her breastbone. "I don't want to stop," he rasped.

"I don't want you to," she managed breathlessly. "Ever since I met you, I have been waiting for this moment."

Darien splayed his hand over one of her breasts, and even though she still had her shirt on, the pleasure was so intense, moisture pooled between her legs.

And then the doorbell sounded.

His lips stilling, Darien met her eyes. "Was that the doorbell?"

"I…I think so."

"Damn," Darien muttered.

Disappointment washed over Jasmine in droves. "I guess…I guess one of us should get it."

Darien pulled away from her, leaving her cold. "Right."

Jasmine stroked his arm. "I don't want you to, but—"

"I know." Darien kissed her hand. "I know."

The doorbell rang again, and now, Darien started toward Jasmine's bedroom door. "I'll get it."

Jasmine's body was still pressed against the wall. She was too weak to move. "You do that."

"I'll get rid of whoever it is," he went on. "Then we can pick up where we left off."

With those words, Darien left the room.

Jasmine closed her eyes and sighed.

Chapter 16

Jasmine had barely pulled herself together by the time Darien came back to her room. "Looks like you have a visitor," he announced.

Jasmine eyed Darien curiously. "A visitor?"

"I'm pretty sure he's not here for me," he went on, and Jasmine's heart leaped to her throat.

"What does he look like?" she asked.

"Don't look so panicked. He's your new friend. Or should I say, my competition?"

Jasmine's heart didn't stop beating overtime until she went to the foyer and peered out the window into the front yard. There, she spotted Luc. He was tossing rocks into the brush.

"Oh, Luc."

"You sound relieved." Darien looked at her pointedly. "You thought it was someone else."

"No," Jasmine lied, though she'd been afraid that Allan had somehow tracked her down. Especially after the call from Kate. "No one knows I'm here."

She started past Darien for the door, but he took her by the arm. "I'm not sure this is a good idea."

"Seeing Luc?"

"I don't think it's smart for you two to get too close."

Jasmine guffawed. "And why not?"

"Because. You know nothing about him. Sure, he's charming. But what if he's got an agenda?"

"He came to my aid, Darien."

"Which is great, but…"

"But what?"

"Just be careful," he said.

Jasmine rolled her eyes as she pulled her arm free of Darien's grip. "He's a boy, Darien. Don't be so suspicious."

She threw one quick glance over her shoulder before opening the front door. "Hey, Luc!"

Hearing her, Luc turned, and instantly his lips formed a brilliant smile.

"Look at that face," Jasmine said to Darien. "How can you think he's up to no good?"

Darien threw his hands up in a sign of surrender, and it was just as well. However, as she went outside to meet Luc, she couldn't help wondering what in Darien's past had made him so distrustful.

"Hello, Miss Jasmine."

Jasmine sauntered out to the front yard to meet Luc, who also started toward her. "What are you doing here?" she asked.

"Just came to visit," he replied. "I almost lef', since no one come to da door."

"We were just, uh, busy with something."

"Going to da beach?" Luc asked. "Cuz I could be your bodyguard again."

"Um." Jasmine looked over her shoulder at the house. She saw Darien peering out the window at her.

"Come on," Luc urged. "It's gon' be fun."

"Well, I…" Talk about awful timing. But as Jasmine looked at the boy's happy face, she couldn't find it in her heart to say no. "All right. Give me a few minutes to get my stuff."

Jasmine turned and went back into the house, where she immediately had to face Darien and his disapproving stare.

"Where are you going?" he asked her.

"To the beach," she replied. "Just the beach, no big deal."

"Maybe I should go with you. Especially after yesterday."

The idea was tempting, but Jasmine could tell Darien wasn't Luc's biggest fan. There was no point in him going along.

"I won't stay long," Jasmine told him. "And don't worry—no one will bother me with Luc around."

"I'll be here when you get back, then."

Jasmine went into her bedroom, where she

changed into her swimsuit and a cover-up. Then she filled her beach bag with sunscreen and a towel. Yesterday, she'd noticed some vendors at the beach, so she also took some cash should she decide to buy a soda or a straw hat.

Darien wasn't in the living room when she exited her bedroom, and it was just as well. She didn't want him telling her again that he thought her getting close to Luc was a bad idea.

Because as far as she was concerned, Darien couldn't be more wrong.

Hearing the door close, Darien left the kitchen and went to look out the front window. His heart slammed into his chest at the sight of Jasmine in a red bikini with a sheer red kimono cover.

Lord have mercy, the woman was sexy. And wearing the color red, she wasn't just sexy, she was as hot as fire.

And so was his libido.

Unable to take his eyes off her, Darien watched her saunter down the driveway with Luc. She smiled affectionately at the kid as they walked, and he at her. A stranger regarding them would think they had a bond that went beyond their meeting the day before.

Jasmine seemed happy, and so did the kid. But Darien—he was suspicious.

He watched them disappear behind the brush, then frowned. He didn't know why, but he didn't entirely trust Luc. Yeah, he was just a boy, as Jasmine had said—but even kids knew how to con unsuspecting victims. Especially a kid who didn't have much money and hoped to steal some from a tourist.

It wasn't that Darien wanted to think the worst of Luc. But it didn't hurt to be cautious. For Jasmine's sake, he hoped Luc had nothing but honorable intentions.

Darien stepped back from the window. Of course, it was possible that his problems with the kid stemmed from the boy's poor timing. If not for Luc showing up when he did, he and Jasmine would likely be making love right now—something Darien found he wanted more than he had imagined possible.

Just days earlier, he had feared the very idea of getting close to Jasmine. But now…

Now, he knew he couldn't leave this island without getting to know her a whole lot better.

After an hour passed—then two—Darien knew he couldn't stay in the house twiddling his thumbs. He had to get out. Part of him wanted to head to the beach and walk up and down until he located Jasmine and knew she was okay. Another part told him he was being extremely paranoid, letting what had happened to Sheila cloud his thoughts about what could happen to Jasmine.

And with good reason. What had happened to Sheila while Darien had been on a tour of duty in Iraq was, according to her, what had led her to turn to another man for comfort.

Then again, Sheila had blamed Darien for all the problems in their marriage, while accepting no blame herself.

"Don't think about it, man," Darien told himself. "Don't think about it." No good came of thinking about what had happened.

And for the first time since his wife's betrayal, Darien truly felt as though he was ready to move on.

With Jasmine?

Time would tell how things would work out for them, but right now, his heart was telling him that he wanted to pursue something with her.

Darien went to his bedroom and got his wallet and car keys, then headed outside. Though he had planned to go straight to his car, he walked to the edge of the cliff that overlooked the beach. He scanned the stretch of sand below. It didn't take him long to spot Jasmine in that sexy red bathing suit. She was on the sand, as was Luc.

At least she was all right.

Moments later Darien was behind the wheel of the Nissan. Soon, he turned left onto John Compton Highway, heading north toward Choco Bay and his favorite spot on the island.

The Pit Stop was a local bar, and unlike the bars at resorts and on other parts of the island, this place was authentic St. Lucia. It was the kind of place that most tourists entered and quickly left when they saw the high number of men with dark skin and dreadlocks.

Darien had felt at home here from the moment he'd walked through the door. The islanders had welcomed him with open arms, making him feel comfortable. The place was never overcrowded, the music never overbearing, and for the most part, there weren't tourists here hoping to score a dime bag of weed.

Darien liked this place because it was a man's bar, the kind where soccer and football played on the television. A guy could forget about his problems in this place. Drink a few beers and enjoy male camaraderie.

It was the first place Darien had found after coming to the island that had helped him take his mind off of his ex, Sheila. Everywhere else he'd been, he had been bombarded with happy couples unable to keep their hands off of each other. Mostly newlyweds. Darien would watch them and wonder how long it would be before their relationships would sour. Who would betray whom? Were they really truly in love, or were they in lust? Who among them had stabbed a best friend or family member in the back to get to this happy moment?

No, seeing all those happy couples had been too much for Darien to bear. Maybe if Sheila hadn't betrayed him with his own brother…

Darien pushed that thought out of his mind as he parked his car. Less than a minute later, he was entering the establishment, a room about two thousand square feet in size. It was simple in decor: two long metal bars on either side of the room, shelves above the bar made of bamboo and well stocked with liquor and a dance floor in the middle of the room. Reggae music filled the place, and even though it was only noon and a Wednesday, the place had about a twenty locals milling about.

Darien took a seat at the end of the bar closest to

the door. "Hey, Buddy," he said, greeting the owner of the place who doubled as a bartender, whose name was indeed Buddy.

"Haven't seen you in a long while, mon," Buddy said, his voice thick with his Patois accent. He knocked his knuckles against Darien's.

"I'll have a Piton," Darien said, referring to the island's famous beer.

In one smooth move, Buddy reached below the bar and produced a bottle of Piton, then popped the lid off. Darien tipped his head back and sipped some of the cold brew.

"Ah-hh. That hit the spot, man. Thanks."

Buddy made his way down the bar, dealing with other customers. Darien glanced up at the television, figuring he'd see some sports game on the screen. Instead he saw the words "Entertainment Talk" in the bottom right-hand corner, and some striking blond woman who looked like a host.

"Hey, Buddy," Darien said when the owner wandered back his way. "What's with the TV? No sports on?"

"You naw hear yet, mon?"

"Hear what?"

"There's a real celebrity in town. Some big-time movie star."

Darien brought the mouth of the bottle to his lips. Then nearly choked on his swig of beer when he saw a familiar face.

Jasmine's.

"Buddy," Darien said. "Turn that up."

Without saying a word, Buddy reached for the remote control on a shelf behind him and turned up the volume.

"…but in spite of that fact, the film is doing extremely well at the box office, still holding the number-one spot for the third week in a row. Which lends credence to the old adage, 'there's no such thing as bad publicity.'"

The camera panned to a wide-screen television on the set of *Entertainment Talk,* on which there was a blond man standing on a beach. He and the woman could easily be mistaken for Barbie and Ken.

"Let's face it, Colleen," the man said. "A good Hollywood scandal can certainly help an actor's career. Look what happened to Paris Hilton. Once her sexy tape became public, her television career and celebrity status skyrocketed."

Scandal? Darien wondered. *What scandal?*

The camera went back to the woman. "Exactly. And since this latest scandal has rocked Tinsel Town, we can tell you that Jasmine St. Clair has been the most Googled celebrity on the Internet." The woman paused and a different camera picked up the shot of her from another angle. "But with this new fame there is controversy. Some groups have lashed out. Church groups all across the South are calling for a boycott of Jasmine's latest film. Many people say they looked up to Jasmine as a role model, and many parents are spitting mad. Here's a scene outside a movie theater in Jackson, Mississippi, just yesterday."

The television now showed video footage of a crowd outside a movie theater, walking in formation, bouncing signs in the air. Signs reading Shame on you, Jasmine! and Sellout and Our Girls Need a New Role Model.

"Where is Jasmine now?" the woman asked, her voice saying she knew a secret. "We can give you one hint—somewhere in the Caribbean. Isn't that right, Mark?"

"Right you are. And I can tell you, this island is arguably the most beautiful in the Caribbean."

"We've got the scoop," Colleen said, her smile from ear to ear, "right after the break."

The television went to commercial. Darien swigged his beer. What the heck was going on? Jasmine was definitely some movie star, big enough that the media was interested in her whereabouts. But what was this scandal the hosts were referring to?

If only he'd entered the establishment a little earlier.

He knew she was running from something, just as she knew the same about him. He hadn't exactly spilled his guts to her. Could he really blame her for not doing the same?

Still, Darien was curious. He cared for Jasmine now. Whatever she was going through, he wanted to know.

He wanted to be there for her.

A hair commercial ended and *Entertainment Talk* started again. Darien had to suffer through minutes of talk about this movie and that, which celebrity couple was having a baby and who was getting divorced, before the hosts started talking about Jasmine again.

"So," Mark said, stretching his arms wide. "Where in the Caribbean am I? That, Colleen, would be the beautiful island of St. Lucia."

The camera panned to give a spectacular view of the two signature volcanic mountains St. Lucia was famous for—the Pitons.

"This piece of paradise," Mark went on, "is where Jasmine St. Clair is reported to be staying."

"Is that rumor or fact?" Colleen asked.

"That is the million-dollar question, Colleen, and I can tell you today that it *is* fact." The man started to walk along the sand, and the camera followed his movements. "Just last night, Jasmine was seen by many American tourists at a restaurant called Sunshine. And we've got the pictures to prove it."

Darien's stomach jumped. Pictures? How on earth did the media have pictures of Jasmine at Sunshine? Instantly the answer came to him. The people who'd snapped photos of Jasmine at the restaurant. They had seemed so happy to see a real, live star. They had seemed harmless. Yet at least one of them had contacted the tabloids to sell a photo of her.

"According to witnesses, Jasmine was dancing up a storm with an unidentified hunk. We're not sure if he's from the island or somewhere else. But here's a picture of Jasmine taken last night, and it's clear that she's having a great time."

A candid photo of Jasmine with her arms in the air appeared on the screen. Her lips were open as she sang, her eyes almost shut. At the far right of the photo Darien could see only a part of his white shirt and both his hands.

All too quickly, *Entertainment Talk* went on to another story, something about plastic surgeries gone bad.

So not only was Jasmine a major actress, she was the kind whose whereabouts were of interest to the entertainment community.

And scandal? What kind of scandal? She did mention she'd had a bad breakup, so maybe she'd been with some high-profile actor or producer who had cheated on her. Darien would bet his last dollar that she hadn't cheated on him.

At least, he wanted to believe she wasn't the type.

He sipped more beer, then shook his head. He more than wanted to believe that Jasmine wasn't the type to screw a man over—he needed to believe it. He was interested in her. They had almost made love earlier. He didn't want to give that all up so soon.

Staring straight ahead, Darien thrummed his fingers on the bar. The plot had certainly thickened. Just who was Jasmine St. Clair and what exactly was she running from?

There was only one way to find out.

Darien finished off his beer, then put some cash on the bar to pay for it.

Buddy settled in front of Darien, resting his elbows on the bar. "Leavin' so soon, mon?"

"Yeah." Darien got off his stool, then scratched the back of his neck. "Got some things to do in town."

"Don' be a stranga, eh?"

"No problem, man. I'll be back."

Once again, he and Buddy knocked knuckles. Then Darien left and sped all the way back to the house.

Chapter 17

Darien had every intention of telling Jasmine that the media knew where she was, and of asking her what the "scandal" was when he got back home—provided she had returned from the beach. However, he had to put his plans on the back burner when he stepped into the house and saw that yes, Jasmine was there, but that she wasn't alone.

Luc was with her.

Luc's eyes met Darien's, and he looked a little surprised. No, more than surprised. He looked—

Giving Jasmine a hasty hug around the waist, the kid said, "See you again, Miss Jasmine."

Then he headed out the door.

"Hello to you, too," Darien muttered, watching the kid disappear.

"Hey, you," Jasmine said. "See—I'm back, and all is good."

Darien narrowed his eyes, thinking. "What was that about? Why did Luc take off so quickly?"

"I guess he's not keen on seeing you. He knows you haven't exactly warmed to him."

Darien's radar was picking up a signal he didn't like. "Did you bring cash with you to the beach?"

"Yeah."

"Then check your wallet."

"Are you trying to say—"

"Just humor me."

"Fine." Jasmine pulled the zipper on the side pocket to her bag. Darien saw the truth in her eyes when they widened in shock. "My God."

"Your money's gone, right?"

She thrust her fingers completely into the pouch, feeling every space. "I don't believe it. I had five hundred dollars in there!"

"I told you. I had that kid pegged from the moment I saw him. Wait a minute. Five *hundred*? You took five hundred dollars for a trip to the beach?"

Jasmine didn't respond. Instead she opened the door and darted outside. "Hey!" she called. "Luc!"

Darien stepped outside in time to see Luc turn to look at Jasmine, then the realization that streaked across the kid's face. Instead of stopping—which he'd do if he hadn't taken her money—he bolted.

Jasmine gave chase. Darien trotted behind her, observing everything.

"Luc, you stop right now!"

The kid didn't stop. As he rounded the bend toward the road, he picked up speed. Jasmine gained on him, continuing to call his name. But Luc went full steam ahead.

Darien saw what was about to happen, but he couldn't do a thing to stop it. By the way Jasmine stopped short and called Luc's name in desperation, she saw it, too.

But Luc's momentum was too forceful as he escaped down the sloped driveway at the speed he was going.

Even though the road was there, Luc didn't stop. And as he vaulted into the roadway, car tires screamed in a desperate effort to avoid a collision.

But it was in vain, because the car slammed into Luc's body and sent him flying at least thirty feet.

Jasmine screamed.

Jasmine drew up short when she saw the collision—but only for a moment. As the car screeched to a stop, as well as other traffic, she darted to the side of the road where Luc's body had landed.

"Luc!" she screamed as she came to his side. His limbs looked as limp as a rag doll's, there was a nasty gash on his forehead and his eyes were closed. Jasmine quickly lowered the side of her face to his nose to see if she could feel his breath.

It was faint, but Luc was definitely breathing.

Darien dropped to the ground beside her. "Oh, man," he moaned. "I can't believe he ran into the road like that."

Jasmine was aware of people having gotten out of their cars. A woman was crying and explaining that the kid had just run into the road, that she didn't have a chance to stop.

Jasmine stroked Luc's forehead. "Luc? Luc, can you hear me?"

A few moments passed—then a miracle happened. Luc opened his eyes.

Relief flooded Jasmine. "Oh, thank God." She quickly turned to see Darien. "He's okay!"

Darien placed a comforting hand on her shoulder and squeezed.

As traffic backed up, horns started to blare. The middle-aged woman who'd hit Luc cried a steady stream of tears. She was inconsolable.

Groaning, Luc tried to lift his head.

"No, don't move," Jasmine told him.

"I all right," Luc insisted, but winced as he got to a sitting position.

"I don't know if you should do that," Darien said.

"One ting about me, I's tough."

Jasmine grinned, relieved. She admired this young boy's spirit. He had to be in serious pain, yet he still wanted to get up.

"The traffic here needs to get moving," Darien said. "Let me talk to the lady who hit him, then I'll help you get Luc back across the street."

Feisty little Luc tried standing on his own. Jasmine quickly threw an arm around his body to support him. The side of his face was scraped badly, and he was bleeding, but that didn't stop him from trying to get up and go.

Darien returned and supported Luc from his other side. Then, he and Jasmine helped him across the street and back to the long driveway that led to the house where Jasmine and Darien were staying. Less than a minute later, the woman who'd hit Luc pulled into the driveway. She got out, still crying and shaking.

"Is all right," Luc told her. "I's fine."

"Should we call the police?" Jasmine asked. "File an official report?"

"The police ain't gon' care about me," Luc said.

"At the very least, we need to get you to a hospital," Jasmine insisted.

"Let's set him down," Darien said, already easing Luc's body downward to the ground. "He's very, very lucky that he landed in the brush, but still, he ought to be checked out by a doctor."

"I don' need no docta," Luc protested.

Darien went toward the crying woman, and Jasmine saw how he placed his hands steadily on her shoulders to comfort her. He assured her the accident wasn't her fault, and asked her if she knew where a hospital was.

The woman went on to say that she didn't have the money to cover any hospital bills.

"Tell her it's okay," Jasmine said. "I'll pay for it." She looked at Luc and added, "And I know just where I'll get the money."

After a moment the woman approached Luc. She gently stroked his face. "I sorry, I so sorry."

"I's fine," Luc said bravely.

Jasmine squeezed the woman's hands. "It's okay. It wasn't your fault. I'll take good care of him."

"Thank you," the woman said. "Thank you. You is an angel."

The woman hugged Darien before getting into her car and slowly driving off.

"Let's get him to my car," Darien said. "That lady told me where to find the hospital."

"Nah, mon. I's fine."

"Maybe he is," Jasmine said. She looked him over from head to toe, felt for broken bones.

"He could have a concussion, internal bleeding."

"Maybe we should take him in the house, lie him down, then try to reach his family," Jasmine suggested. "Then head to the hospital."

Darien hesitated, but agreed after a moment. "All right. That's not a bad idea."

Darien carried the boy into the house. Jasmine ran to the linen closet and withdrew a large towel, then placed it on the sofa before Darien set Luc down.

"Please, no docta," Luc said. "Please."

"Why don't you want to go to the doctor?" Jasmine asked him.

"I just want rest. Then I'll be fine."

Jasmine looked from Luc's face to Darien's. Darien shrugged. "I'm no doctor, but I learned a thing or two in the military. I can do a pseudo-exam, see if anything seems seriously wrong."

"Pseudo what?" Luc asked, his eyes bulging.

Whatever you said about Luc, you couldn't say he

didn't have spunk. Apparently not even getting hit by a car could knock that out of him.

"Lie back," Darien began, and Luc obeyed.

Darien spent the next few minutes extending and bending Luc's arms and legs, pressing fingers into his stomach area and back, and asking if anything hurt. Whether or not he was being truthful, Luc answered no each time.

"Well?" Jasmine asked. "What's your diagnosis?"

Darien looked up at her. "I say this is one lucky kid."

Jasmine blew out a relieved breath. "You think he's okay?"

"It was a very lucky break that he landed in the brush. That cushioned his fall."

Smiling bravely, Luc got to his feet. Then wobbled. Jasmine threw her arms out to catch him.

"Darien?" she said, her eyes flying to his.

"Take it easy there, sport." Darien ran his hand over Luc's head.

Jasmine cradled his head to her chest. "We should call your parents."

"No!"

At his outright refusal, Jasmine couldn't help staring down at him in question. "You should tell them what happened."

Luc shook his head.

Stubborn as a mule. She settled Luc on the sofa and told him not to move. "I'm going to get a warm rag to wipe your face."

Less than a minute later, Jasmine was back.

Darien had gotten the boy a glass of orange juice, which he held to his lips.

"You think afta this, I can rest?"

"I think Darien and I should take you to your house."

Luc reached for her hand and squeezed. And for the first time, she realized he was afraid.

Afraid of going home?

"All right," she said softly. "You can rest here."

Maybe she was a sucker, but she didn't have the heart to turn him away.

Hours later, Darien peered through the crack in Jasmine's door. She was curled up on the armchair beside the bed where Luc slept.

He stared at the two for a moment before he entered the room, thinking this was as odd a picture as any. It was clear that even though Luc had stolen from her, Jasmine still had a soft spot in her heart for the kid.

Darien pushed the door open and Jasmine's gaze flew to his.

"How's he doing?" he asked. It was a widely held view that a person shouldn't go to sleep immediately after a possible head injury, and while Luc had seemed to be okay, Darien and Jasmine had kept him up for a couple hours by feeding him. To their surprise, Luc had consumed enough to feed a large family. For an eleven-year-old kid, he had a voracious appetite—and a bottomless stomach.

"He's still breathing," Jasmine said quietly. "I've been watching, to make sure."

"You really like him." It was a statement, not a question.

"I do," Jasmine said.

"Even though he stole your money."

"I think he more than paid the price for that, don't you? Besides, I think he needed the money. He's wearing the same shirt and shorts that he had on yesterday. It's obvious he doesn't have much. And I'm a bit worried about what's going on in his home life. When he squeezed my hand, he seemed afraid."

Something pulled at Darien's gut. Something about the way Jasmine had so easily fallen into the role of caregiver for Luc.

Not only was she a beautiful person on the outside, she was also beautiful on the inside.

He stroked her hair. *What happened to make you leave the U.S.?* he thought. *Did someone hurt you, did you hurt someone, and why does Hollywood care?*

He wanted to ask her about it, but this wasn't the time.

Instead he pushed the thought aside and asked, "Can I make you a cup of tea? Fresh peppermint?"

"Yes, please."

"I'll be back in a few minutes."

"Thank you."

Darien stroked her hair again. Jasmine smiled up at him, one that made him feel good all over.

Was he a fool to think she was an honest woman, the type who didn't manipulate? She certainly seemed honest. In fact, she was a pleasant breath of fresh air after Sheila, who had been a drama queen for much of their marriage. Sure, he'd known Jasmine for less than two weeks, but they had spent practically every hour of every day together since she got here. She was beautiful, but not sleazy, so he didn't see her as the type who slept her way into film roles.

She was a good woman.

Darien knew that in his heart.

Chapter 18

The moment he heard her name, everything else ceased to matter. Not where he was and why he was there, and certainly not the menu that fell from his hands. The craving he'd had for thick Belgian waffles smothered with whipped cream and maple syrup seemed to dissipate into thin air. He was no longer hungry. Not even the cup of black coffee the waitress had placed before him got his attention, and for Allan Jackson, the first cup of coffee in the morning was as precious as gold.

His attention, instead, was riveted on the small color television ten feet away. As though the broadcast were airing specifically for him, he watched and listened with more interest than he'd ever watched or listened to anything in his life.

"Yes, it's true. Ms. St. Clair has been spotted on the island of St. Lucia. And she's not alone. This photo of her at a restaurant on the island surfaced yesterday. You can see her on the dance floor, but what you can't see is the man who's with her. And sources say she was *very* comfortable with him."

"Allan." A finger snapped loudly before his face. "Earth to Allan."

Momentarily surprised to find his friend Donnie sitting across the table from him, Allan stared at the man as though he didn't know how he got there.

"Allan, you look like you've seen a ghost."

"Sorry," he said, remembering the importance of this breakfast meeting. Donnie was the friend of a friend who had a connection to Will Smith. He was a producer with some B movies to his credit, but was looking for that great script that would send him to the A-List. Allan was meeting with him to talk about the script he was writing on spec. Only he *wasn't* writing it because he was stressed over not being able to find Jasmine.

And now he was learning that she was in St. Lucia—*with some other man?*

"…nearly four weeks since that shocking sex tape of her surfaced," the woman newscaster continued, "and three weeks since she went into hiding. Her most recent film, *The Game,* is still number one at the box office."

"Allan?"

"Huh?"

Donnie threw his gaze over his shoulder, following his line of sight to the television. Turning back to him, he raised an eyebrow. "Ah, I get it. Jasmine. I heard on the news last night that she's in St. Lucia. Did you know?"

"Uh, I…no…" Allan cleared his throat. "I mean, I knew she was going away, but…"

"I thought you two were gonna get married," Donnie said. "But she just dropped you cold."

"She did *not* drop me!" Allan snapped. Then he had to take a moment to breathe and calm himself down. It would do no good getting mad at Donnie.

"She just needed time, is all," Allan went on. "For God's sake, you'd think the media would be tired of this story already."

"Yeah. Yeah, of course she needed time," Donnie said, but didn't sound convinced. His eyes scanned the menu. "What are you going to have?"

Allan threw a quick glance at the television, but seeing the waitress arriving at their table, he picked up his mug and half finished its contents in one gulp.

"You two ready to order?"

"I'm gonna have the St. Clair waffles," Allan said. "And plenty of coffee."

"The *what* waffles?" the waitress asked.

Allan's heart stopped as he realized what he'd said, but Donnie seemed oblivious of his faux pas as he studied the menu.

"Uh, the Belgian waffles." He chuckled nervously. "Bottom-right corner."

"Sounds good to me," Donnie said. "I'll have the same."

When the waitress disappeared, Donnie faced Allan and said, "Now, this script you're writing for Will. How's it coming along?"

"It's going well," Allan lied. He had no choice.

"When can I see a draft?"

"You know me, man. I'm a strict perfectionist. If you're gonna pass this script along to Will Smith, then it's got to be in top shape. And that means I don't want anyone reading it until it's good and polished."

Donnie nodded his understanding. "All right. How long do you think it'll be?"

Allan shrugged. "Maybe six weeks, two months? And you know what, my man Will is gonna love this."

"It's that good?"

"It's that good."

"You've got me excited, man."

"You should be," Allan said. And then his eyes wandered to the television.

The news broadcast was already on to something else, and he frowned. He was hoping to find out exactly where in St. Lucia his girlfriend was.

Because he had to go there. No matter the cost, he had to go there and work things out. The newscast had mentioned something about her being there with a guy, but he knew how the media was. They wanted salacious stories, even if they had to manufacture them. It's not as if they'd shown Jasmine in the arms of some other man.

"Allan?"

Allan's eyes flew to Donnie's. "Sorry, man. What'd you say?"

"I asked where you're setting the story. You did say there'd be a couple foreign locations."

"Right. And, uh, I was thinking St. Lucia."

Donnie's blue eyes widened with shock. "I thought you said something about Africa."

Before Allan could answer, the waitress appeared with more coffee, which he gratefully accepted. It gave him time to think of how to respond.

"I was thinking about Africa—you know, after the success of *Sahara* and other movies. But what if St. Lucia is cheaper? And how many films are shot there? We might get the location for a great price."

Donnie nodded. "Good point. If Will Smith says yes to the project, a studio will green-light it, but still, the budget can't be over the top."

"You know, it just came to me since I'm gonna be heading there to see Jasmine." Allan gulped at his coffee.

"You're going to St. Lucia to see Jasmine?"

"Yeah. She called. Left me a message. Said she misses me. I'm gonna surprise her with a ring, man."

Donnie nodded, but his eyes said he was wondering why Allan was talking about Jasmine. "Hey, good for you. I know you love her."

"Sorry, Donnie," Allan said. "I need about three cups of coffee in the morning before my brain starts working. I don't mean to be going on about Jasmine."

"Don't even sweat it."

Allan nodded. "I can picture this really fun action sequence, where Will's character follows the bad guys to St. Lucia. There'll be gunfire on the sand, lots of hot bods...." Allan had no clue what he was talking about, but hoped it sounded good to Donnie.

"Like I said, I can't wait." Donnie clapped his hands together. "This could be the big break for both of us."

"Excuse me a minute, Donnie?"

"Sure."

"Just gotta run to the bathroom," Allan went on, slipping out of his side of the booth.

Moments later he was in the bathroom. He banged a fist against the tile wall and stifled a scream.

What the hell was Jasmine doing in St. Lucia?

The more Allan thought about the newscast, the angrier he felt. He'd gone ring shopping. Ring shopping, for God's sake. And Jasmine had the nerve to be living it up in St. Lucia with some other man?

Allan went to the sink, where he splashed cool water over his face. "Pull yourself together, man," he told his reflection. "Look at the bright side."

The bright side was that he *hadn't* called the media when he'd gone ring shopping, because now he would look like a fool. But, he would call them soon and do some damage control. Start the rumor that she was on the island with a brother. No one had to know that Jasmine's only brother had died when he was a kid.

Hell, Allan would send a freakin' telegram announcing that he and Jasmine were in St. Lucia and secretly planning to marry away from the glare of the paparazzi's cameras.

Allan clenched his fists. Seriously, what was

Jasmine thinking? She'd been so damn worried that she'd been perceived as a whore when their sex tape had been released, and now she was off gallivanting with some man? Did she think *that* showed her virtue?

"Calm down," Allan said to himself. "You know the media exaggerates everything."

Clinging to that thought, Allan's anger began to dissipate. Of course Jasmine wasn't in St. Lucia screwing some other guy. She was there trying to escape the vultures who'd made her life a living hell.

And soon, Allan would be there with her.

Chapter 19

"Hey there," Jasmine said, her lips pulling into a smile when she saw Luc's eyes open. "You're finally awake."

Luc's eyes darted around the room, as though he was confused. Then he abruptly sat up.

"Take it easy," Jasmine said.

Luc winced, letting Jasmine know that he was in pain.

"How long I been here?" Luc asked.

"About eight hours."

"What time it is?"

"It's after seven. I was worried about you, but I kept checking to make sure you were breathing, and you were."

"Seven in the night?"

"Yes."

Luc threw the covers off. "I been here too long."

Jasmine hurried to his side. "What do you think you're doing?"

"Mi motha, she gon' wonder where I is."

"I know. And we should call her."

"No. I jus have ta leave."

Jasmine frowned. "So, that's it. You just plan to take off?"

"Sorry." Luc blew out a frazzled breath. "I 'preciate you lettin' me stay here. I 'preciate you helping me."

"Of course I would help you. You got hit by a car."

"But I tek your money."

"I know." Jasmine stroked the boy's face. "And I forgive you."

Luc's eyes filled with tears, which broke Jasmine's heart. It was easy to tell that this kid was in financial need, and she had plenty. How could she be mad at him under the circumstances? Sure, she would have preferred he ask for money rather than steal it, but she understood. And ultimately she believed that he was a good person.

"Thank you, Miss Jasmine. You too nice."

"Listen, Luc. You've been here all day. We need to contact your parents, let them know you're okay."

"Is all right. I gonna go."

"No, it's not all right. They need to know you were hurt. Thank God it wasn't worse, but if you were my child and you didn't come home... You know your parents will be worried."

Luc didn't say a word.

"You must live nearby."

"Dere's no phone at da house."

"Then we can drive you there. I'm sure your family wants to see you."

Ever so slightly, Luc shook his head.

Which made Jasmine frown. She could only remember that horrible night when her brother had been hit by a car, how if by some miracle he'd survived, she and her parents would have hugged him for days, not wanting to let go.

"You don't think they'll be mad, do you?" Jasmine asked.

"If you tell mi fatha, he'll beat me."

"What? Oh, Luc—don't worry about that. I won't tell them you took my money. I wouldn't do that."

"He'll still beat me."

"For getting hit by a car?" The idea was so preposterous, she frowned skeptically. But when Luc's eyes once again filled with tears, she knew he was telling the truth.

"You're serious."

"Miss Jasmine, he get mad…"

"My God." She paused, blew out a breath. "I can talk to your mother, then, if you like."

"Mi motha—she sick real bad."

Good Lord, this poor child. He was dealing with far more than he should ever have to.

"Is she in the hospital?" Jasmine asked.

Luc shook his head.

And then something Luc had said when she'd

first met him clicked. At the time, Jasmine had thought he'd been particularly astute. Now, she realized he had to be talking from experience.

He had asked her if a man had hit her and caused her scar. Did his father regularly beat on his wife and children?

"Where's the bathroom, Miss Jasmine?"

Jasmine led Luc out into the hallway and pointed him toward the bathroom. Then she sauntered into the living room. Seeing her, Darien asked immediately, "Is he up?"

"Yeah."

"And he's okay?"

"Yes." She frowned. "And no."

Darien stood from the armchair. "What does that mean?"

"I think that Luc has an awful home life. It sounds like his father beats him. I saw some scars on his back when he went into the sea, but at the time, I thought nothing of it. And his mother's ill. He didn't say what, exactly, but it sounds serious."

Darien flashed a skeptical look. "That's what he said?"

Jasmine planted her hands on her hips. "You think he's lying?"

"He stole from you and wants to gain your sympathy. Yeah, I think he's lying."

"You didn't see him," Jasmine said. "You didn't see his eyes fill with tears as he talked to me."

"You're too kindhearted."

"How can you say that?"

"I bet you any money the kid wouldn't have told me that story."

"Probably because he can tell you don't have a sympathetic bone in your body!"

"I'm just saying you have to keep your guard up."

"Don't be so cold, Darien." Jasmine paused, closed her eyes. "Don't be so…"

"Hey." Darien placed his hands on her shoulders. "What is it?"

"You didn't see his face when he was talking to me. This kid has been through a lot."

Darien's eyes narrowed as he stared at Jasmine. "I know it wasn't easy seeing that kid get hit, but against all odds, he seems perfectly okay. Something else is going on. My God, you're trembling."

Darien didn't think. He simply gathered Jasmine in his arms. And when she started crying, he knew her tears weren't for Luc.

"What is it?" he whispered as he stroked her hair.

She pulled out of his arms. "I'm going to check on Luc."

Brushing at her tears, Jasmine padded off down the hallway. Tons of questions floating around in his mind, Darien watched her disappear around the corner.

Then saw, seconds later, when she came running back toward him.

Darien's eyes widened. "What is it?"

"Luc…"

"Is he—"

"He's gone! Darien, he's gone!"

Darien charged toward her. "What do you mean, he's gone?"

"He's not in the bathroom. He's not in the bedroom!"

"Oh, man."

Darien moved past Jasmine. He opened her bedroom door. No Luc. He opened the bathroom door. No Luc.

He opened his bedroom door. And instantly saw that the doors leading to the patio were wide open.

Jasmine ran into the room. "Luc!" She ran to the patio doors. *"Luc!"*

"I guess this is your money." At his words, Jasmine turned to face him. Darien held up the five crumpled one-hundred-dollar bills. "This was on the bed."

"Oh, Luc."

"I bet he's long gone," Darien said.

Jasmine sprinted past him out of his bedroom. He followed her down the hallway to the front door.

Moments later Jasmine was outside. Her head went this way and that in search of Luc.

"He's gone," Darien insisted.

Jasmine spun around to face him. "We have to find him. What if he doesn't make it home? What if he collapses somewhere?"

Darien nodded. "You're right. Let me get the car keys."

They spent the next half an hour driving north and south, and along remote off roads, but their search was in vain.

Luc was nowhere.

As Darien parked the car in their driveway, Jasmine was sulking. He reached for her hand. "Think of the bright side. We didn't see him anywhere. That means he probably got home okay."

Jasmine nodded, but her body language said she wasn't convinced. And then, out of the blue, she started crying.

Something was seriously wrong, and Darien would bet his last dollar that it had nothing to do with Luc. He got out of the car, made his way around to Jasmine's door, then helped her out. She was crying so hard now that he had to hold her up as he walked to the villa's door.

Safely inside, he sat her down on the sofa. "Jasmine," he said softly, "what's really going on here?"

She didn't answer right away. Slowly she raised her eyes to his. "My brother...he died that way."

It took a couple moments for Darien to understand Jasmine's meaning. "He was hit by a car?"

Jasmine nodded. "He was with me, and he darted into the road.... I couldn't stop him...."

"Oh my God." Darien pulled her close. "Sweetie, I'm so sorry."

"I was walking with my brother. We'd left the playground because it was raining. I was eleven, he was five. I was holding our soccer ball, but I stumbled on the sidewalk and the ball fell from my hand. It bounced into the road...and my brother—

he just ran. Ran right into the road after the ball."
Jasmine now sobbed, and she had to stop talking.

Darien stroked her head. "My God. How horrible for you."

"For me?" She pulled her head back to look at him.
"My brother got run over by a car." She balled her
hands into fists against his chest. "And it was my fault."

"Shh. Don't say that. It wasn't your fault."

"If I hadn't dropped the ball—"

"It was a terrible, terrible accident."

"My parents blamed me," she went on.

"I don't believe that."

"It's true."

"They said that? They came right out and told you
that you were at fault?"

"Not in so many words, no. But I could tell. They
looked at me differently. I was supposed to protect
my brother, and I failed."

Darien didn't know what to do, so he just held her.
Held her and let her cry. He couldn't imagine parents
so insensitive that they'd blame their eleven-year-old
child for a younger child's death. It was an unspeakable burden that Jasmine had had to witness the
tragic accident in the first place, but to not assure her
that she was in no way responsible—in Darien's
eyes, that was unfathomable.

"Even if they don't blame me, they changed after
my brother's death. A very real part of them died.
Never since that day have I ever seen them smile the
way they used to when he was alive. They exist, they
go to work, but they don't have a spark anymore."

"I can't imagine what it's like to lose a child," Darien said.

"I understand their pain, of course. But after a long time passed, I thought I'd see my parents smile, get excited when I got a great grade. I did everything in my power to make them happy again, but they just…they just existed. I worked so hard to make them proud…."

"I'm sure they are."

"I don't think so."

"You're an actress—a successful one. What parent wouldn't be proud of that fact?"

Jasmine got off the sofa and walked toward the front window. She peered outside, as if hopeful she'd see Luc in the darkness. "They don't disapprove of what I do. But I doubt they're proud."

Darien moved behind her, and again placed his hands on her shoulders. "I'm sorry you lost your brother. And in that way."

And now Darien understood why Jasmine had taken Luc under her wing the way she had.

"Not a day goes by that I don't wish I could redo the day. That I hadn't stubbed my foot on the sidewalk. That I'd held the ball tighter."

"I can't even imagine what that was like," Darien said softly, pressing his mouth to her hair. "But I want you to know I'm here for you."

She just nodded.

"Luc was okay. He was here all day. He'll make it home just fine."

"If something happens to him—"

Darien whirled Jasmine around in his arms. "It won't be your fault."

She didn't meet his eyes. "I…"

"Hey." He framed her face. "You and I did everything for him."

"I should have insisted that he give me his address. Heck, his full name."

"Shh." Darien cradled Jasmine's head. "Don't bear this burden. You are a beautiful, caring woman. A good woman."

Jasmine looked up at him, and with the pads of his thumbs Darien wiped away her tears.

"You're special, Jasmine. You really are."

And in that instant, with Darien staring into Jasmine's glistening eyes, something changed between them. The sadness disappeared, replaced with something else. Something that made Darien's groin tighten and his stomach clench nervously.

Gently, Jasmine placed one of her hands on his face. Her eyes never leaving his, her fingers skimmed his cheek, then his jawline and finally his lips.

Before Darien knew what was happening, they were kissing.

It was a kiss full of emotion, of heat and of need. It was deep and passionate. Tender, not lustful. The kind of kiss that said there was meaning to what they were about to do.

"Oh, Jasmine." Darien moaned into her mouth. "Baby…"

She wrapped her arms around his neck and held him tight, letting him know that she was completely surrendering to him. "Make love to me, Darien. Please…"

Darien deepened the kiss. His tongue twisted with hers while his hands wandered to her back. He moved his hands up and down her shirt.

The fabric was in the way. He slipped his hands under the shirt and pressed his hands to her skin.

Jasmine moaned her pleasure. "Mmm…"

Her pleasure urged him on. Darien tore his mouth from hers and trailed it along her jaw, then lower to her neck. Jasmine arched her head to give him more access to her. Her skin was so incredibly soft, the light scent of her perfume heady. Darien was consumed with his need for her.

Jasmine eased her body away from his to pull her shirt over her head, leaving her in a black, lacy bra. Then she lay back on the sofa.

"You are so incredibly beautiful," Darien said.

Jasmine reached for him, inviting him closer.

Darien lowered his body over hers, reaching for one of her breasts as he did. His palm played over her bra, feeling the nipple beneath.

Desire shot through him like liquid fire.

"I did mean it when I said I like you," he said slowly, clearly. "A lot."

He heard the faint sigh that escaped Jasmine's mouth, and that tiny sound had his groin tightening.

"And it's not just this," he went on, running a finger along her jawbone. "It's everything about you. I look at you and…" Darien's voice trailed off. He wasn't sure he could put into words what he felt for Jasmine.

So he kissed her.

A smoldering kiss that released all the pent-up passion he'd held in check for days.

When Darien stopped kissing her, Jasmine gazed up into his eyes. "What is it?" she asked him.

He didn't answer right away. Instead he ran the tip of his finger along her cheek, then gave her a soft kiss. "I don't want you to think I'm doing this because…because I'm a man, and you're a woman, and we're sharing this house."

"Huh?"

"That came out wrong." Darien planted a kiss on her chin. "I'm trying to say, this isn't about a man and a woman who are spending time together ultimately deciding they should try out sex. At least not for me."

"I understand," Jasmine said.

But did she? *Could* she? Hell, Darien knew that his words had sounded jumbled. He was trying to let her know, before they crossed the line, that what he was about to do with her meant more than just a physical release.

It was a huge step for him, being able to move past the pain Sheila had caused him.

"Darien?" Jasmine said, pulling him from this thoughts.

"Yeah?"

She snaked her hand around the back of his head and lowered his face to hers. "Please don't think I'm having any doubts. I want this. Need this."

"Are you sure?" he asked Jasmine.

She smiled. "I couldn't be more sure. All I want to feel right now is you…inside me."

Needing no further encouragement, he brought his mouth to her skin and kissed the soft mound of one breast. It wasn't enough. Not nearly enough. Thankfully the snap on her bra was at the front, and Darien opened it. Jasmine's full breasts spilled free.

"Oh…" Darien rasped. He ran his finger lightly over her nipple. "Man."

The sensations swirling inside Darien were overwhelming. Had he ever felt so aroused?

Slowly, he moved his lips over the flesh of her breast. A kiss here, a kiss there. And then he swirled his tongue around Jasmine's nipple, and a shuddery sigh oozed out of her.

"Darien, *ohhh*…" Jasmine ran her hands over his head, pulling him closer.

He drew her nipple completely into his mouth and suckled it. Softly at first, then with more fervor. Soon, he was breathing heavily, moving his mouth from one breast to another, and Jasmine was moaning and writhing beneath him.

She wrapped a leg around Darien's waist. "Please," she begged. "I have never felt this wonderful in all my life. Make love to me."

Slipping her hand between them, she reached for his arousal. Darien groaned as she stroked him through his jeans.

Then Jasmine was kissing him again, kissing him while she grabbed at his shirt, pulled at the snap on his jeans.

Darien whipped his shirt off and tossed it onto the floor. Jasmine started raining hot kisses along his chest.

Gripping her by the shoulders, he pulled her up. "Let's move this to the bedroom."

"Do you have condoms?" Jasmine asked.

He nodded. "Yeah. I, uh, picked some up a couple days ago."

One of Jasmine's eyebrows shot up. "You did?"

Darien's face flushed. "I wanted be ready. In case."

Jasmine placed her palm on his cheek. "It's okay. More than okay."

Then she kissed him again, and damn if her soft mewling sound wasn't his undoing. He pulled her upward, hastily urging her legs around his waist, then walked with her that way to the bedroom while their tongues danced in one another's mouths.

Darien placed her on his bed, and she moaned in disappointment when he released her. He opened the bedside drawer and found the box of condoms.

By the time he turned around, Jasmine was completely naked and lying on her back with one leg bent at the knee.

He blew out a low whistle. "Believe me when I say this, you take my breath away."

Jasmine didn't take her eyes off his body as he stripped out of his jeans, then his briefs.

"Wow," Jasmine said, her eyes eating up the sight of his manhood.

He joined her on the bed, ravaged her mouth with his, then tore open the condom package.

"Let me put it on for you."

Darien lay back on the bed, exposing himself completely. And even though this was going to be his first time with Jasmine, he felt totally comfortable with her.

Like it was right.

Jasmine rolled the condom onto him, then stretched her body over his and lowered her mouth to his. Their lips met in a deep and tender kiss.

And when Darien entered her, made sweet love to her for the next two hours, he was at long last complete.

Chapter 20

Jasmine awoke with a smile on her face. She stretched her arms, rolled over—and bumped smack into Darien's body.

Seeing the cause for her early morning bliss, her smile widened.

What a night! Jasmine settled her head on her pillow and sighed. Her thought that Darien might only be interested in her because of her attraction to him had been blown into orbit with her first orgasm. Reinforced with her second.

And after that… Well, Jasmine could safely say that her night of lovemaking with Darien had been the best night of her life.

Ever.

Angling her head toward him on the pillow, she watched the steady rise and fall of his chest. He was still sleeping. Which was no surprise. The guy had stamina, she had to give him that.

Her body still thrummed from the onslaught of carnal pleasure she had enjoyed during their marathon lovemaking session. And yet she wanted more. She wanted to wake Darien up with a slow kiss and have sex with him another time.

She giggled. The man had unleashed the inner sexual monster she hadn't known was alive inside her!

How was it that she had been with Allan for two years and never once felt this invigorated after making love?

And maybe Jasmine was a fool, but the way she and Darien had connected…it was spectacular not only on a physical level, but on an emotional one. It was as if they'd poured everything from their hearts and souls into the act.

Just remembering their tender and passionate kisses had Jasmine closing her eyes and shivering. What had started as a way to assuage her grief had turned into something more. Much more. What they'd shared last night had meant something. Jasmine was sure of it.

Darien stirred. Jasmine planted her lips on his cheek. As his eyes popped open, she kissed him on the mouth.

"Hey, you." He snaked an arm around her waist.

"Hey."

"I know that tone. You're not ready for another round, are you?"

Jasmine played with the hairs on his chest. "Well…"

"You're insatiable."

"Only with you."

"Woman, you know how to tempt a guy."

"Oh?" Beneath the sheet, Jasmine settled her body on top of Darien's. *"Ohhh."*

"Exactly," Darien said.

It was amazing how comfortable Jasmine felt lying with Darien like this. "You know, this is a pretty amazing way to wake up in the morning."

Jasmine lowered her mouth to Darien's, but as she started to kiss him, the doorbell rang. Her mouth stilled and they both looked at each other.

"Luc," they said in unison.

Jasmine scrambled off the bed, her eyes scanning the room for something to wear. The only thing nearby was one of Darien's black T-shirts casually thrown over the back of a chair.

Jasmine grabbed it and pulled it over her head. It reached her at midthigh. Not nearly long enough, but at least it covered her nakedness.

She hurried out of the bedroom and to the front door. As she'd suspected, Luc was standing outside.

Alarm shot through her at the sight of tears streaming down the boy's face. "Luc!" she exclaimed, planting a hand on his shoulder and pulling him inside. "What is it, sweetie?"

"Please…you have ta help."

"What's going on? You feel hurt somewhere?"

"It's mi motha."

Darien appeared just then, wearing only his pair of black jeans. Jasmine felt a little thrill at the delicious sight of him. But Luc's sniffling soon brought her back to the emergency at hand.

"Your mother."

He started to cry harder and Jasmine folded him into her arms. "You have to tell me what's wrong."

"Maybe this is all a play for sympathy," Darien muttered from behind her.

Jasmine's head whipped around at lightning speed. "Darien!"

"The more he cries, the more you're going to overlook the fact that he stole money from you."

"He gave it back!"

"Could be all part of his act."

Jasmine's mouth fell open in horror. Where was the loving man who had made her feel so special last night? The man she knew had a good heart?

Luc huddled closer to Jasmine, as though she needed to keep him safe from Darien.

"Don't let what happened with your brother cloud your judgment," Darien advised.

"How dare you." Jasmine shook her head in disbelief as she scowled at Darien. "How dare you use what I told you about my brother against me!"

"That's not what I'm doing."

"You have the gall to give this kid the third degree when he's obviously upset?" Once again, Darien had gone from hot to cold—and Jasmine didn't like it one bit.

"Stop!" Luc suddenly cried. He wiped his tears with the back of his hand, then continued. "Mr. Darien is right. I shouldn't 'a tek da money."

"You don't have to talk about this now," Jasmine told him, and saw Darien roll his eyes in her peripheral vision.

"Yes. I have ta mek Mr. Darien understand. Mi naw have no money. And mi mother—she's sick. Dat's why I never wanted to go to da hospital. I need money to tek mi motha to the docta."

"And what's wrong with your mother?" Darien asked, his voice full of doubt.

Now Luc's eyes filled with tears again. "She sick. Real bad. In da night, she was just cryin' and cryin'."

"We have to help her," Jasmine said. "Darien, will you drive us to his house?"

Darien didn't say anything right away, and Jasmine held her breath. *Please don't tell me the man I just made love to can have such a cold heart....*

"Of course," Darien said. "If his mother is as sick as he says, it sounds like she needs immediate medical attention. We can get her to a doctor."

"Thank you, Darien. Luc, you wait here. I'm going to get my clothes on." Just mentioning clothes, Jasmine remembered last night. She glanced over her shoulder and saw her bra on the sofa, plus her blouse and Darien's shirt on the floor.

Luc would no doubt notice it, too.

As Jasmine started off toward the bedroom, she felt Darien's fingers wrap around her upper arm. She turned to look at him.

"I'm not an unfeeling jerk, Jasmine. Just cautious."

"Sure," she said, but knew she sounded less than convincing. But she was worried about Luc, his mother…and suddenly worrying that she might have made a mistake last night.

No, she told herself as she entered her bedroom. Not a mistake. What had she expected after making love with Darien? That they would sail off in the St. Lucia sunset and live happily ever after? She was a grown woman who had wanted a physical connection with another man, and she'd gotten it.

It was as simple as that.

End of story.

Right now she had more important things to worry about—like getting to Luc's mother and making sure the woman was okay.

A few minutes later they all piled into Darien's car and set off. Luc gave the directions, and ten minutes after they'd started driving, they were pulling up in front of a small, dilapidated house with a metal roof. Jasmine had never seen anything so frail-looking pass for a family dwelling, and it broke her heart.

"This is your house?" she asked around the lump in her throat.

"Mmm-hmm."

Luc led the way inside, and Jasmine and Darien followed him. The house had one large living-dining-kitchen area—though it looked like it also doubled as a bedroom, if the blankets and pillows on the floor were any indication.

"How many people live here?" Jasmine asked.

"Five," Luc replied. "Six, when mi father come around."

"Four children live here?" Jasmine didn't know why she was so shocked. Maybe because she'd seen the beautiful resorts and gorgeous beaches—all the superficial things that brought people to the island. But there were residents who lived here—residents you didn't see on the glossy brochures.

It was the same scenario in Jamaica, so she shouldn't have expected anything different on this island.

"Where's your mother?" Darien asked.

"In here."

Luc opened one of the two doors in the house and started inside. Darien was the first to follow him, then Jasmine stepped cautiously into the small bedroom.

There was a woman on the single bed in the middle of the room. She looked beyond frail. The bed, which was small, appeared too big for her.

"Mama?" Luc said, walking toward the bed.

After a moment the woman stirred, a movement that seemed very difficult for her. Her eyes opened and when she saw her son, they lit up.

That instant of happiness quickly passed and the woman gripped her stomach and groaned in pain. The groan was so intense, Jasmine could hardly stand to witness the woman's suffering.

"What's wrong with her?" she asked.

Luc stroked his mother's brow. "We don' know. Four days now she been sick. Bad, bad chills. Pain in the shoulders. An' her stomach sick bad, too."

Jasmine said, "Clearly, she needs to see a doctor right away."

"That's why I took de money," Luc explained. "So I could tek mi motha to de docta." His eyes filled with fear and tears, both of which Jasmine knew were genuine.

"I say we get her to a hospital right away." Darien placed his hand on Jasmine's shoulder. "Is your father around?"

Luc shook his head. "He ain't been around since before she got sick."

"What about brothers and sisters?" Darien asked. "Any young children outside somewhere who shouldn't be left alone?"

Again Luc shook his head. "I's the youngest. Everybody gone to the market, tryin' to sell some fruit to mek some money."

"All right, then." Darien faced Jasmine. "I'll carry her to the car. You get the doors for me, okay?"

"Of course."

At the woman's bedside, Darien explained, "Ma'am, we're going to help you. We're going to get you to a doctor."

"Thank you," she said, her voice a grave whisper, and it broke Jasmine's heart.

Luc kissed his mother's cheek before Darien lifted the woman into his arms. And then the tears started. Jasmine gave Luc a long, hard hug.

She followed Darien out of the room, hoping the woman wasn't dying. She certainly was in enough pain, but Jasmine hoped that whatever ailed her, it wasn't fatal.

Outside, she opened the car door for Darien and

he gently placed Luc's mother on the backseat. Luc got in beside her and cradled his mother's head on his lap.

Jasmine made her way to the front of the car, all the while wondering how people lived with so little. A small house to provide shelter for six people, no money for medical care… She hadn't grown up with plenty, but by these standards, she had been spoiled.

Darien turned and started toward the main roadway. As he drove, Jasmine couldn't help feeling a modicum of shame. She'd acted as though the release of that sex tape had been the worst thing in the world, when the truth was, people suffered far worse every day. People were dying of incurable diseases, they were displaced from their homes because of drastic weather and they were dying on battlefields overseas. Yes, Allan's betrayal had been devastating, but given the big picture of life, it hardly mattered. Her family was alive. She had lots of money in the bank. If people chose to hate her because of that stupid sex tape, then so be it.

There were far more important things in the world.

Jasmine glanced over her shoulder, noting the concern in Luc's eyes and the pain etched on his mother's face. She drew in a deep breath and said a silent prayer that she would be all right.

As she finished her prayer, Darien squeezed her hand. Jasmine's eyes flew to his.

"At least that woman yesterday told me where Victoria Hospital is, so I'm going to take her there,"

Darien said. "I don't see any point in finding a family doctor. I don't know what's wrong, but if it's been going on for days, she needs emergency care."

Jasmine nodded.

"We'll get this sorted out," Darien went on. "She'll be okay."

Life offered no guarantees. But Jasmine certainly hoped that Darien was right.

Chapter 21

Jasmine and Darien passed the time in the crowded hospital waiting area as the doctor examined Luc's mother, but Luc refused to leave her side. Jasmine couldn't blame him. If either of her parents were ill, she would be glued to their side, as well.

Life could change in the blink of an eye, a lesson Jasmine had learned in the most painful way when she'd lost her brother. Again, she felt regret—regret that she didn't see her parents often, or even talk to them regularly. That was something she was going to have to rectify when she got back to the U.S.

Maybe the scandal, although painful, had a silver lining she hadn't considered before. She was gaining some much needed perspective, always a plus.

And she'd met Darien.

She glanced his way and he offered her a small smile.

About an hour into their emergency room wait, the doctor appeared at the door and called their names. Darien stood and Jasmine followed his lead. He reached for her hand and held it, as though offering her support in case the news was bad.

"Gall stones," the doctor announced.

A gigantic wave of relief rolled through Jasmine, escaping her mouth in a loud sigh. "Gall stones?" she repeated, to be sure.

The doctor nodded and said yes.

Jasmine looked from Darien's face to the doctor's. "So she'll be all right."

"Yes. Your timing was impeccable. The problem had to have started quite some time earlier, but became critical in the past few days. It was very smart bringing her here now, or it could have been much worse. She will need immediate surgery."

Jasmine nodded. "Right."

"Now, the bad news," the doctor said. "She told me she does not have any insurance."

"I'll pay for it," Jasmine said.

"It will be a few thousand dollars," the doctor said, enunciating his words. "*American* dollars."

"We'll pay," Darien said.

Jasmine looked up at him, and he down at her. Then he squeezed her hand.

"Then there'll be the cost of medicine…." the doctor went on.

"Whatever it costs, don't worry about it. We just want to make sure she's okay."

The doctor nodded. "Very well. We'll need you to sign some paperwork."

It dawned on Jasmine as the doctor walked away that she didn't even know Luc's mother's name. But that didn't matter. As far as she was concerned, it was more than tragic that the poor woman had suffered in incredible pain at home, all because she didn't have money for medical care.

She was in a position to help and she would.

"Gall stones," Darien said as they went back to their seats. "Can you believe it?"

"I'm glad it's not something more serious. I was so worried."

"I know."

A few beats of silence passed then Darien said, "I'm glad we were here. Something so simple, yet the poor woman wasn't even able to see a doctor."

"It's heartbreaking."

"I'd better ask if they take credit cards," Darien went on.

"No need. I've got cash back at the house."

Darien gave her a questioning look and before Jasmine could say a word, the door to the waiting room opened. Luc emerged and bounded toward them. He ran right to Jasmine, threw his arms around her and hugged her with all his might.

"Thank you, thank you!"

"You're welcome, Luc." Jasmine squeezed him back. "I just wish you'd told me about your mother when you first met me. I would have helped, even then."

Luc lifted his gaze to hers. "Miss Jasmine, God sent you to me. As mi angel."

The boy softly sobbed and Darien couldn't watch the interaction without feeling touched. In such a short time, they had all been through so much. It had bonded them.

A woman emerged and called Jasmine's name. She had the paperwork prepared for Renee Vance ready, and Jasmine signed on the dotted line saying she would be responsible for the cost of the surgery.

As soon as Jasmine got back to her seat, Luc climbed onto her lap and wrapped his arms around her neck. Anyone observing them would think that they were mother and child.

"I suppose we can leave now," Jasmine said. "Come back later."

"Did they say when?" Darien asked.

"I forgot to ask," Jasmine replied.

Darien got to his feet. "Let me go ask, then."

He headed to the reception desk and asked to see the doctor. The older man came to see him within a few minutes.

"Doctor, how long will the surgery take?" Darien asked the man.

"There's a newer surgical procedure for this, which takes about one and a half hours, but depending on the damage she may need the old-fashioned surgery, which will take longer."

"What does that mean?" Darien asked.

"In either case, Mrs. Vance will need to rest tonight. But what it means is that in terms of recovery, with the new surgical procedure she will have to stay in hospital only twenty-four hours after surgery, and in two weeks she will be as good as new. With the other surgery, she will need to be in hospital for at least a week, and recovery time will be around six weeks."

"That's a big difference."

"I'm hopeful I can do this the easiest way," the doctor went on, "but won't know for sure until I begin surgery how complicated things are internally."

"So there's no point in sticking around?"

"I was on my way out to tell you that you may as well head home. Leave a contact number, in case of any problem, but otherwise, you can come back in the morning."

Darien offered the man his hand. "Thank you, Doctor. Take care of her."

"I will."

They didn't go straight home. Instead they went into town and did some shopping. Jasmine bought Luc several new outfits, including two pairs of sneakers and one pair of dress shoes.

Luc's excitement and gratitude brought visible tears to Jasmine's eyes, and Darien found himself feeling a bit emotional, as well. Even yesterday, he was a bit wary of the kid, but that was completely gone now. Luc was a down-on-his-luck kid with a bad home life—helping him and his family just felt right.

When they returned to the house, Luc couldn't

wait to sport his new swimming trunks so he and Jasmine went to the pool. Darien let them have their alone time and went to his room to rest for a bit.

He was still tired from the previous night's lovemaking. But he also felt good. Real good.

It was almost hard to believe, but somehow, in such a short time, Jasmine had gotten under his skin.

In the hospital, as she'd leaned her head on his shoulder, he found himself daydreaming of the moment he could get her in his bed again. The place had been completely inappropriate, but he hadn't been able to prevent himself from his racy thoughts, especially when, as she'd leaned against him, one of her soft breasts pressed against his arm.

He would seduce her now, even though he was tired, if not for Luc.

Not even his attraction to Sheila had been this intense.

Was this the beginning of something real with Jasmine? Had his dreams been right, predicting the woman he would spend the rest of his life with?

Darien sure hoped so, because he couldn't imagine going forward without her in his life.

Hours later, when Luc finally fell asleep, Darien got his chance to seduce Jasmine. And it was well worth the wait.

The next week was spent with Luc and his mother. Luckily, Renee had been able to undergo the newer surgical procedure, which meant she could return home earlier and would ultimately heal faster.

Jasmine and Darien brought Renee home from the hospital the day after her surgery and, along with the Vance children, helped care for her. By the sixth day, she was feeling much better and walking around on her own.

Cautiously, of course, but she was well on the road to recovery.

The father still hadn't made an appearance, which Jasmine supposed was just as well. It sounded as though the family was better off without him. She'd bet money that he had another woman somewhere, maybe even another child or two. Anyone who could neglect his wife and children, no matter the reason, was the lowest kind of human being on the planet in Jasmine's mind.

Today, as they'd been doing every day, Darien and Jasmine worked together to make a meal for the family. They brought over a pot of chicken and a pot of rice as well as a bowl of salad. For Renee, Jasmine also made some chicken broth, since she didn't have much of an appetite since the surgery.

"Hello, Brian." Jasmine smiled when Luc's oldest of three brothers, the sixteen-year-old, opened the door. "We've got dinner."

"Thank you again, Miss Jasmine," the teenager said, beaming. "And Mr. Darien. Come in."

Jasmine stepped into the house. "How's your mother?"

"Well. Today she's very well."

"That's great." Jasmine set her pot down on the table and Darien did the same. "Is she in the bedroom? Darien and I aren't going to stay this evening, so I'd like to say a quick hi—"

"Nonsense," came the soft voice from behind her.

Jasmine turned to see Renee standing about ten feet behind her, leaning her weight on a cane. "Hello, Renee."

"You will stay," Renee said. "Break bread with us."

Neither Jasmine nor Darien argued, as the first evening they'd tried that, Renee would have none of it. So they ate dinner with the family.

Once Renee finished her soup, she announced she was tired and excused herself to go to the bedroom. Luc left his partially finished meal and went with her.

A short while later, after Jasmine, Darien and the other boys finished eating, Jasmine headed to the bedroom to tell Luc and his mother goodbye. She rapped softly on the door before entering.

"Luc," she said, entering the bedroom where his mother now slept. He was curled up next to her on the bed. "Darien and I are going to head off now, but we'll be back tomorrow."

"Okay."

Jasmine reached for his hand, and he not only squeezed it, he kissed it. He had thanked her a million times in the last few days for her help and still her eyes misted when he showed her any gratitude.

Jasmine remembered watching an Oprah show where audience members were encouraged to "pay it forward"—do something charitable for others, simply for the sake of giving. Jasmine could attest to the fact that there was a definite joy in giving. She'd felt it while helping Luc. And knowing she could make a difference in his mother's life—she wasn't sure there was a better feeling.

The night that *The Game* had premiered, Jasmine had thought she'd been on top of the world. But right now, knowing she had helped save a person's life—now she really knew what it was to feel high.

She had done something that, in the grand scheme of things, really mattered.

In the car she said to Darien, "It really feels good, doesn't it? To help someone in need?"

"Absolutely. When I was in Iraq, helping the displaced civilians there was always a highlight. Sometimes it was providing food for the needy or getting an injured child much needed medical care…and it always felt incredible. There's nothing better."

"I've always given to charity," Jasmine went on. "But you don't see firsthand how your money helps people. Seeing that smile on Luc's face—and his mother's—I'm telling you, the feeling was nothing like I've ever experienced."

"I know."

"And it got me thinking," Jasmine continued as Darien started to drive. "I'm in a position to help a lot of people. I'm not the richest woman in the world, but I've made a lot of cash in Hollywood. Maybe it's time I set up some sort of foundation and give back."

"Doing what?"

"Helping battered women, for one. Help them

learn job skills so they can support themselves.
That's something I think about every time I look at
Renee." Whether Renee was actually battered or just
neglected, the result was the same—she was the type
of woman who needed to learn a trade so she could
be self-sufficient. "Or donating to orphanages,"
Jasmine continued. "Anything, really."

Before they reached the main road, Darien
abruptly jerked the car to the side of the road.

"What are you doing?" Jasmine asked.

"Kiss me," Darien said.

Jasmine's eyes widened as she stared at him.
"What?"

"You heard me."

"We'll be home in a few minutes."

"I know. But I feel like kissing you now."

He took her hand in his and gently pulled her
toward him.

"Darien!"

"I can't get enough of you," he said. "It's like I've
got a fever for you I just can't shake."

"There must be a bug going around," Jasmine
whispered. "'Cause I've got that fever, too."

He kissed her and Jasmine's body felt like it was
thrown into an inferno of passion. She would never
bore of his touch, his kiss, his skin against hers while
they made love.

Darien's hands trailed down her neck, to the area
between her breasts. Giggling, Jasmine pulled away
from him. "We do have a bed," she pointed out. "Just
about ten minutes from here."

Darien stroked her face. "I know. But this is fun, isn't it? Spontaneous?"

"Spontaneous it is. And, as much as I enjoy the excitement of necking in the car like a couple of teenagers, I say we go for the comfort of your bed. It'll be better for the positions I have in mind."

Darien threw the car into Drive. "A guy needs no further encouragement than that."

"You know," Jasmine said after a moment, "I haven't even asked you how old you are."

"I'm forty."

"And already retired from the military?"

"You can retire after twenty years. You can work longer, if you like, but I was ready to get out."

Jasmine placed her hand on his arm. "I can't imagine the horrors you saw."

"It's not something I like to talk about. But I came home in one piece. I was one of the lucky ones."

Lucky, yes—but did he still have nightmares about what he'd seen?

"Then, my marriage was in serious trouble. I thought when I got back, we'd be able to work on fixing it."

The mention of his marriage made Jasmine feel a spate of jealousy. "Something else we haven't talked about."

Even in the darkness of the car, Jasmine saw the bitterness that streaked across Darien's face. "My wife cheated on me."

"I'm so sorry—"

"With my brother."

Silence. Then Jasmine asked, "Are you serious?"

"As a heart attack."

"I don't know what to say."

"There's nothing to say. She blames me."

"What?"

"She was pregnant when I left. A few months along. About a month after I left for Iraq, someone attacked her at an ATM. It was the middle of the day and she was banged up pretty good. As a result, she lost the baby."

"No, Darien."

"It was her third miscarriage. My feeling is that she might have lost the baby regardless of the attack. Maybe not, I don't know. It didn't make the loss any easier to deal with."

"Three babies? That's got to be utterly devastating."

"It was. When I found out, I wanted to see if I could go home, but she said not to bother. As the months passed, every time I talked to her, I could tell she was slipping away. There was nothing I could have done, even if I'd been home, but she was angry with me. When I got home, she said I hadn't been there for her, that I hadn't even tried to get a leave…."

"But you said that she was the one who told you not to bother."

"Exactly." Darien sighed. "It's complicated. Or maybe it isn't. She turned to my brother, who'd been there for her. My own brother."

"I'm sorry."

"It was hard." Darien faced her. "But I'm moving on."

A couple minutes later they were at the house. And by the time they got out of the car, they were necking like two people who couldn't keep their hands off each other.

By the time they made it to the door, Jasmine's blouse was unbuttoned and her bra opened.

"Hey," Darien suddenly said. "You didn't tell me how old you are."

"I'm thirty-one."

"Phew. As long as you're not eighteen!" he joked.

"Eighteen? Right, that was likely."

"Well, you do have a body as fit as a teenager's." Darien ran his hands over her butt.

"And you have the body of a god."

Their lips locked again and they walked that way into the house. Before long, they were in Darien's bedroom.

Jasmine was the first to break the kiss. "I've got an idea."

Darien's eyebrows shot up. "Something better than making love? 'Cause I'm seriously hot and bothered here."

"Then let's cool off in the pool. Naked."

"What?"

"How's that for spontaneous?"

"Very. But—"

"Last one in is a dirty rotten egg!"

Jasmine made quick work of taking her clothes off. Darien followed her lead. She ran to the patio door and threw it open, and seconds later was diving into the pool.

Darien made a huge splash as he canonballed after her. Jasmine screamed with delight.

Darien swam to her and pulled her into his arms. "I could get used to this," he said after a moment. "Hell, I already am."

Jasmine stared into his eyes. The lights surrounding the patio glistened on the surface of the pool. Above, the sky was filled with stars and the moon was full. The atmosphere couldn't be more romantic.

Was that why Jasmine almost wanted to say something that seemed inconceivable? Her heart told her she was falling in love with Darien, but was it real love? Or just a special bond because they'd been through so much together?

"To spending time here—or with me?" Jasmine asked. She wanted to know what he was feeling for her, other than the obvious physical connection.

"Both," Darien replied.

"Is this real?" Jasmine asked softly. "What's happening between us? Or are you going to go your separate way and I go mine…?"

Darien hesitated before answering, but held her closer. "I want to tell you something."

"Oh, no. You're going to let me down easy."

He kissed her on the forehead. "Hear me out."

"Okay."

"After Sheila," Darien began, "I never thought I'd love again. I didn't think I knew how. My marriage had taken everything from me—even my happiness, my hope for the future. When I came here, I was at a really low point in my life and needed to escape everything. Then I started dreaming about this woman, night after night, and I had no clue why. Then I actually met her. Met you…" Darien kissed the edge of her mouth. "I didn't let myself believe anything could happen between us. Let's face it— we're from vastly different worlds. But somewhere along the way, Jasmine, something inside me changed. My heart opened up again. Because of you."

"Oh, baby." That was the sweetest thing anyone had ever said to her. Jasmine placed her hand on Darien's cheek and he turned his lips into her palm so he could kiss it.

"I don't say things like that lightly," Darien told her.

"I believe it. I do—because I know what you mean. I think of the past and it's like a distant memory. Before Allan, I never dated anyone for more than a few months at a time. I was all about my career. About trying to do something to make my parents proud—make them smile again after my brother's death. I didn't even realize how unhappy I was and that I couldn't give my heart because a part of me was broken inside. But now I know I'm different. I've found a sense of peace, a sense of purpose, of happiness—all after a few weeks on this island. Heck, I look forward to going snorkeling with you, when before I would never set foot in the ocean." Darien chuckled at that, and so did she. "I feel content here, with you," Jasmine continued. "All that matters to me is here and now…and us. Sometimes, I think I could seriously stay here and be happy. Forget Hollywood and all the craziness of the film business."

Jasmine pressed her mouth to Darien's and kissed this man she was falling for, kissed him with tenderness and love.

Darien was the first to pull away from her. "What is it?" Jasmine asked. She wrapped her legs around his waist, the water easily holding her up. "You don't want to make love out here?"

"It's not that. It's just that you reminded me of something I've been meaning to ask you."

"Oh?"

"Yeah. The day Luc got hit by that car, I was at a local bar while you two were at the beach. And there was something about you on the news. There was mention of some scandal."

Jasmine's gut twisted. "There…there was?"

"I missed what it was about, but the media knew you were here on this island."

"What?" Jasmine lowered her legs.

"I guess that night we went out, someone sold a picture of you to the media."

Jasmine shook her head in dismay. "You are kidding."

"I meant to tell you already, but once Luc got hurt, then the ordeal with his mother…"

Jasmine nodded absently.

"So." Darien planted his lips on her cheek. "What was this 'scandal'?"

Jasmine gazed up into Darien's eyes, saw his care for her, his trust. And she wanted to tell him all about the scandal. She really did. But they'd gotten so close, how could she ruin what was the first good thing to happen to her in ages? Darien had just said that they were from vastly different worlds. Would he, a no-nonsense military man who hardly even watched movies, react well to the truth about the sex tape? Or would it remind him of just how different their worlds were?

Even if he believed her—that she didn't know she was being taped—how well would he deal with the fact that she was in a sex tape that millions of people the world over had no doubt watched on the Internet by now?

It wasn't the kind of news your average man would be comfortable with. Not to mention he would have to start wondering what life with her back in the real world would be like. Paparazzi stalking them, giving them no peace whatsoever. The real world was a far cry from right here, right now.

So as much as Jasmine wanted to share the truth with Darien, she couldn't. At least not yet.

"It was a high-profile Hollywood breakup," she finally said. "My ex started dishing dirt about me, and it got ugly." She paused. "You're absolutely sure the media knows where I am?"

"I saw it with my own eyes on television."

"Well, they obviously don't know about this villa or they would have been here already. Thank God for that."

"It's okay," Darien told her. He gave her a soft kiss on the lips. "I'll keep you safe."

Was she safe? Or were the paparazzi lurking in the bushes? Had they found this hideaway?

Suddenly she didn't feel comfortable being naked in the pool.

Jasmine slipped out of Darien's arms and started to swim toward the edge of the pool. "Ready to head back inside?"

Darien swam toward her. "I thought you'd never ask."

Chapter 22

The next morning Jasmine's illusion that the villa was her safe hideaway was shattered.

The doorbell rang as she and Darien were having their morning coffee. Jasmine's eyes met his across the table in question.

"You think that's Luc?" she asked, not expecting him so early if at all.

Darien shrugged. "Who else would it be?"

Jasmine pushed her chair back and stood. "I hope everything's okay."

There was a small chance his mother might have some complications due to the surgery, and as she walked to the door, she worried her bottom lip.

When she opened the door, the camera flash

caught her off guard. She was immediately startled, but it took her no more than an instant to figure out what was going on.

Her safe house had been discovered.

She tried to slam the door shut, but the photographer stuck his foot between the door and frame, preventing her.

"Is it true that you have a secret love child on this island?" the man asked.

"What?" Jasmine shrieked.

"The boy you were at the hospital with. You two seem *very* close."

The man's words were too shocking for Jasmine to comprehend, so she didn't bother to respond. Once again she tried to force the door closed, but the man was too strong. She turned to call Darien, but saw that he was already there.

"What the hell is going on here?" he barked.

"So this is the new man," the wiry, balding man said. "Is he the reason you called off your engagement to Allan Jackson?"

Jasmine's eyes widened in horror, then she threw her gaze to Darien's. She saw the flash of confusion on his face.

Not that she owed this intruder any answers, but she faced him and said, "I have no idea what you're talking about. Allan and I were never engaged."

"I'll bet you're getting ready to make a new sex video," the man went on. "Considering the last one was such a hit. Perhaps one using that beautiful pool out back."

The man's words made Jasmine remember the previous night. The worry that someone might be observing her very intimate moments with Darien.

"You son of a bitch!" Jasmine screamed, and lunged at the man.

He jumped backward, still snapping photos, then started to run. Darien gave chase, quickly catching up to the thin man. He ripped the expensive camera from his hands, forced the back open and tore out the film roll.

The man cried out in frustration. "You can't take my film, man! That's worth thousands!"

Jasmine slapped a hand to her forehead in relief. "Thank God it's not a digital camera."

Darien stood over the man in a menacing gesture. As quickly as a person could snap their fingers, he had gone into combat mode. No doubt from years of training in the military.

"Any more where this came from?" The man moaned in pain in response to Darien's question. Darien raised his voice. "Any more?"

"N-no! That's it, man."

"It's a Saturday morning," Jasmine said. "Don't you vultures ever take a break?" Her heart was racing from fear—fear that her hiding place had been discovered and the fact that God only knew how many other reporters would show up. And fear of what Darien would think of her now, given the things the so-called reporter had said.

She wanted to ask how he had found her, but the truth was, it didn't matter. Since he'd mentioned the hospital, she would bet that once she'd signed her name on that document authorizing payment for Renee's surgery, someone had let the news slip.

Darien forced the lens off the camera, then threw it past the hibiscus bushes. It easily sailed over the cliff.

"Noooo!" the man wailed.

"And you're not getting the rest of it back, either," Darien told the man. "Now get the hell out of here, because if you're still around when the cops arrive, you're going to jail."

Darien's voice said he meant business. The man scrambled to his feet and bolted.

Jasmine was surprised to feel the sting of hot tears on her cheeks. Slowly she walked over to Darien and placed her hand on his upper arm. "Thank you. I don't know what I would have done if you weren't here."

Instead of curling her into his arms, Darien looked down at her and shook his head with disappointment. Then he marched toward the house.

"Darien," Jasmine called. He didn't stop. "Darien!"

She dragged a hand over her face. Obviously he was mad. More than mad. Jasmine had hoped that he would dismiss what he'd heard the vulture say, or at least ask her about it, but clearly, that was wishful thinking.

She followed him into the house. He whirled to face her and spoke before she could. "We need to talk."

"I know. And let me start by telling you I'm sorry."

"Just last night, I asked you about the 'scandal.'" He made air quotes when he said the word.

"It's not what you think."

"Then why did you lie to my face?"

Jasmine grimaced. "I didn't exactly lie. I told you that I didn't want to talk about it at the time."

"And it's no wonder. A sex tape? My God."

Darien rushed toward his bedroom.

Jasmine raced after him. "No, you're wrong. I didn't even know! I mean, I didn't know my ex had made that tape. He betrayed me. Made it and leaked it to the media for his own personal gain."

Darien opened his closet door, then faced her. "If it was so innocent, why didn't you just tell me?"

"Because—"

"I knew things were going downhill with Sheila when she stopped being truthful. Started hiding things."

"I was going to tell you. I was. But last night…it wasn't the right time."

Darien hauled out his suitcase. "You think that guy was here last night, watching us?"

"What are you doing?" Jasmine walked farther into the room. "You—you're *leaving?*"

The phone rang, saving Darien from having to answer. Jasmine might not understand his decision, but it was easier this way. He was already falling in love with her and if their relationship couldn't work—whatever the reason—it was better to end it now, before he got too involved.

Hurrying to the room phone, Darien snatched up the receiver. "Hello?" There was no answer. "Hello?"

The dial tone sounded in his ear.

"There was no answer?" Jasmine asked.

"Probably the media, right?"

"I don't know."

Darien went back to the closet and started grabbing clothes off the hangers.

The phone rang again. This time, Darien ignored it. Jasmine marched to the bedside table and snatched up the receiver. "Hello?" she snapped. Then, "How did you get this number?"

Darien hesitated a moment, looked at her. She really was a vision of loveliness. He had meant the words he'd said to her in the pool—that his heart had opened up again because of her.

In the pool where a reporter might have been spying on them...

That thought urging him on, Darien continued dropping his clothes into his suitcase.

"Oh my God," Jasmine said.

Darien didn't want to face her, didn't want to worry about her. But just because he thought they couldn't have a relationship didn't mean he'd suddenly stopped caring.

He looked at her, noting the wary expression on her face. "What is it?"

She hugged her torso and took a few steps toward him. "That was, um, my ex."

"Your ex?" Just saying the word made Darien's stomach tighten painfully.

"Yeah. The one who made that tape."

"Right." Darien clenched his fists at his sides. "What'd he want?"

"I don't know how he found me, but he said he wants me back."

"Look at that. Perfect timing."

"Don't say that, Darien."

"The guy sounds like he's really into you. You should call him back."

Jasmine stalked toward him, her hands akimbo. "How dare you? You don't want to be with me anymore, fine, but don't say something like that after what I told you about Allan."

"I'm sorry," Darien said. And he was. In fact, he ached to reach out and curl Jasmine into an embrace, hold her and never let her go.

"Please," Jasmine said. "Don't leave."

Darien looked down, then met her eyes but still said nothing.

"I'm sorry about the tape. I know I could have told you a long time ago. I should have. But—"

"It's not just the tape," Darien said, cutting her off.

Jasmine's eyes narrowed in question.

"I guess it took that reporter showing up at the door for me to realize the truth. I said it before, that we're from vastly different worlds. I thought it didn't matter, but…"

Jasmine closed the distance between them now, but he wouldn't meet her eyes. "It doesn't matter, Darien."

"Probably everywhere you go, you've got the media following you. I'm not used to that. And you've got your career in L.A. I'm newly retired and have to figure out what I'm going to do with the rest of my life."

"Figure it out with me."

He would like to. Oh, how he would like to. But would Darien ever fit in with the Hollywood scene?

Here, on this island, their time together had been easy. Not challenged by their real lives.

Darien grabbed the last of his clothes in one armful, then dumped them into his suitcase. He hastily zipped the luggage.

"I can't believe this," Jasmine said, and he could hear the emotion in her voice.

"Tell me, Jasmine. Where will I fit in your life? When you're off around the world shooting films or going to all those fancy award shows, where will I fit in your life?"

"You can be with me."

"And what am I supposed to do to make a living?"

"I can support both of us."

Darien chuckled, but the sound held no mirth. "Right. I'm supposed to sit back and let you support me. Do you see that this can't work?"

"I love you," Jasmine said, her eyes glistening with tears. "Do you love me?"

A lump lodged in Darien's throat, one full of emotion—and pain. He knew what she wanted to hear, knew what his heart told him he should say. And yet…

What good would come of prolonging this relationship? What did love matter when their worlds could never merge?

"Maybe I don't know how to love," Darien answered quietly.

Jasmine burst into tears.

Doing his best to ignore her, he went to the drawer and took out his passport and other important papers. Jasmine must have realized there was no point saying anything else to him, because she left the room without a word.

Darien closed the door behind her, then dropped to his knees and closed his eyes. Already, this hurt. Hurt like hell.

All the more reason for him to get away now. His heart couldn't handle the kind of intense heartbreak he'd suffered with Sheila again. Jasmine might be in pain now, but she'd find some actor sooner rather than later. Hollywood types always did. Even if he stayed with Jasmine, how long before she tired of him and moved on to some powerful man with billions in the bank?

Darien couldn't compete with that.

Half an hour later he called the airport and learned a flight was leaving for Miami in four hours. He could make that flight.

If he left now.

His luggage in tow, Darien exited the bedroom. When he got to the foyer, he saw Jasmine sitting on the armchair in the living room. Her face was stained with tears, a sight that ripped his heart in two.

"I'm not saying it's over," Darien said softly. "But I need some time. Need to figure out my life. Need to put things in perspective. And I don't think it will hurt for you to do the same."

Jasmine didn't say a word.

Darien placed a slip of paper on the decorative table in the foyer. "This is my information. When you're ready—when you're back in the States—you can call me."

"Nice," Jasmine muttered.

"And I was kinda hoping you'd leave a way for me to reach you."

Jasmine shot to her feet. "I'm right here. *Right here.* You want to reach me, you do it now."

"I need time—"

"Then go. Take all the time you want."

Darien groaned. "You don't know what I went through with my wife. You're a star, Jasmine. How long before you get bored with an average Joe like me?"

"I'm not like that."

"Maybe you're not, but I can't be sure—"

"So you need a guarantee? I'm sorry to tell you, life doesn't offer guarantees to anyone!"

"Do you see what I mean? Already, things are falling apart."

"Because this is what you wanted from the beginning. An excuse. An excuse to cut and run at the first sign of trouble. Nice way to live."

Jasmine dashed out of the living room and to her bedroom, leaving Darien standing there. He glanced at his contact information on the slip of paper.

He had a feeling she would never call.

Allan pulled his copy of *Hollywood Life* out of his jacket pocket, unfolded it and stared at the front page for the umpteenth time. No matter how many times he'd seen it, he was still unable to tear his eyes away from the photo on the first page.

The caption read: Starlet Disses Old Love, Finds New Flame in the Tropics.

As much as Allan wanted to dismiss this picture as some sort of trick in the editing room, he knew it wasn't. The woman on the front page—the one resting her head on the shoulder of some guy he'd never seen—was Jasmine.

And she wasn't just leaning on this guy—they were holding hands, their fingers linked as though they couldn't get enough of each other.

He'd read the article when he first saw the rag at LAX, and it talked about how Jasmine had clearly ended her alleged engagement to him and had found someone else. Some new guy she'd met in St. Lucia whom she was totally "hot" for.

"You little bitch," Allan muttered. She had made a laughingstock of him. Just last week he'd announced his engagement to Jasmine, and the media had greedily snapped photos of the three-carat ring he'd splurged on. Now, they were telling the whole world he had been dissed—and Allan couldn't be more humiliated.

He'd wanted to rip the newspaper to shreds on sight, but he'd somehow managed to keep his composure. Instead of destroying the paper, he'd carried it with him on the plane, had read and reread the article. Had studied the photo closely to make sure it wasn't trick photography.

He'd concluded, angrily, that it was legit.

So had his contact in St. Lucia, when he'd called the guy before boarding the plane.

After everything he had done for Jasmine, after how hard he had worked to help her achieve her success! She actually thought she could diss him and move on without so much as a backward glance?

It was bad enough when he thought she was sleeping with Terrence Green, but now he *knew* that she was screwing this guy.

Her behavior was evil, selfish. Whorish.

Unforgivable.

The plane had barely landed before he'd used his cell phone to call her. And the ungrateful whore didn't even have the decency to chat with him for a minute. Instead she'd hung up on him.

He hadn't even gotten to tell her that he would be seeing her soon.

Allan grinned. He could imagine the look on her face when he surprised her.

In the end, he might forgive her, but first she would have to pay.

In due time, he told himself.

His luggage in hand, Allan went to a quiet corner of the airport and pulled his cell phone out of his carry-on bag. Then he placed the call to the person who would tell him everything he needed to know.

Chapter 23

Hurtful words are like bullets; once fired, they can't be taken back. And when they pierce the skin with razor-sharp aim, they go straight for the heart.

For years Darien's wife had been shooting him with words, wounding him, making him bleed slowly and painfully. Everything was his fault, he didn't love her enough, he wasn't man enough to make her happy. If anyone knew the pain words could bring, it was Darien. And yet he'd lashed out at Jasmine in a way that he knew would definitely hurt her.

Point-blank, she had asked him if he loved her. And he hadn't been able to say yes. Not because he didn't feel love for her in his heart, but because he had figured it would be easier for her to move on if he didn't give her hope.

Now, Darien couldn't get over the pain he'd seen in her eyes. In fact, it was killing him. Because despite everything, he knew he loved Jasmine, and what he wanted most in the world was to have a normal, loving relationship with her.

But who was he kidding? Jasmine would be better off with someone else. With some high-profile actor, perhaps, or a director. Someone from the world she was used to, who could wine and dine her, buy her a big fancy house and hire nannies to take care of their children. This time he'd spent with her in St. Lucia…well, it was borrowed time. Something Darien had known from the beginning.

Ugly reality reared its head this morning, and just like that, his time in paradise was over.

No point worrying about it. It was time to pick up the pieces and move on.

He told himself that as he drove his car back to the local man he'd rented it from, and repeated the mantra as a taxi had taken him the rest of the way to the airport. He'd stared at the beautiful landscape of this island that had been his home for two months and tried to be grateful for his time here.

Tried to be grateful for reconnecting with a woman, even if it wasn't meant to last.

He had wanted to stop to see Luc one last time, but knew that would be hard, as well. The kid wouldn't understand his sudden departure. And Darien didn't have the heart to explain it.

At the airport, Darien's heart was heavy as he headed to the American Airlines ticket counter. His heart told him he should turn around, go back to Jasmine.

But his brain told him that some things just weren't meant to be.

"Hello, sir," the woman behind the ticket counter said to him, her smile bright. "How may I help you today?"

"I have a seat reserved on the four o'clock flight to Miami."

"I can help you with that. Passport, please."

Darien dug into his laptop case and removed his passport. He handed it to the smiling woman who had no clue his heart was breaking.

Jasmine hugged her body as she stood near the hill's edge. The sun was starting to dip in the sky. Another couple hours and there would be another magnificent sunset.

One Darien wouldn't be here to see with her.

Jasmine stifled a cry. She shouldn't have let Darien leave. She should have swallowed her pride, thrown her body in front of the door—or better, in front of the car. Anything to stop him from walking out of her life.

Instead she'd let the words spoken in anger be the last words they would say to each other.

A tear ran down her face and she hastily brushed it away. What was the point in crying now? Darien was gone. Out of her life forever.

The sooner she accepted that fact, the better.

She might have grown to love the man, but by his own account, he didn't know how to love. Yet every time he'd made love to her, had touched her, had offered her comfort…there had been love in all his actions, even if he hadn't said the words.

Jasmine drew in a deep breath, one meant to soothe her, and it failed miserably. She went back to the patio and sat at the round table. Sat and watched the sun, drank wine, cried. She wasn't sure how much time passed before the sun was noticeably lower, its hue changed from yellow to orangey-red.

Where was Darien now? On a flight back to the U.S.? Was he missing her as much as she was missing him?

She reached for the bottle of wine, then lowered her hand. She'd already had two liberal glasses. Her head was getting light. She didn't need another drink—she needed food in her stomach.

Slowly, Jasmine forced herself to rise from her seat. She headed to the back door off the kitchen and entered the house.

And thought she heard a noise. Her heart filling with hope, she raced through the kitchen and into the living room. "Darien?" she called.

Her eyes volleyed left and right, into the formal dining room and then past the foyer. But once again she heard something and now knew he must have returned.

The bedroom. He was putting his things in the bedroom!

She raced out of the living room and down the

hallway, a smile dancing on her lips. "Darien, baby—"

Jasmine stopped dead in her tracks when she reached Darien's bedroom door, her body turning to a block of ice.

"Hello, Jasmine. It's been a long time."

Chapter 24

Jasmine swallowed. Hard.

"Don't you have anything to say to me?" Allan Jackson asked. "Not even hello?"

Jasmine didn't say a word, but her heart raced out of control. "Allan. H-how—"

"How'd I find you?" he finished for her, a grin forming on his lips. A cold, smug grin, not one full of warmth. "Well, babe," he began. "Where there's a will, there's a way."

Jasmine quickly assessed her options and came to the sad realization that she didn't have any. If she tried to run, Allan would chase her down. She didn't have a car to escape. She could only hope he wasn't here to do her harm.

Allan strolled toward the foyer, and Jasmine didn't know what to do. Follow him? Stay where she was?

"Nice pad," Allan announced, glancing around before his gaze settled on her once more. "I see why you haven't been in a hurry to return to L.A."

"Yeah, um. It's nice here."

"I always thought sunsets in Los Angeles were to die for. But, man, this place. Love it."

Jasmine drew in a shaky breath.

"Hey, you don't have to be nervous." Allan crossed the foyer to stand in front of her. "You haven't been doing anything *scandalous* here, right? Nothing that would make me mad?"

Allan ended his question on a note that made Jasmine shiver. Almost as though he was baiting her, and anything she said would be the wrong thing.

"Of course not," he went on. But his gaze kept moving around, as if he was looking for someone. "You could have been a little nicer to me when I called earlier, however. You just hung up on me, like you and I don't go way back. It was one thing when I thought you probably hadn't gotten around to checking your voice mail. But now I know you were avoiding me."

Jasmine crossed her arms over her chest, hoping that would make her appear strong and ready to deal with Allan. But the truth was, she was terrified. "Why are you here?" she asked him.

"For one thing, I wanted to make sure you were okay. Since you didn't get back to me. And I also wanted to make sure you weren't holed up here with some guy. I'm not sure how I could handle it if I found out you were cheating on me with some guy named Martin or Lee. Or maybe *Darien*."

Jasmine's fear intensified. "Allan—"

"What? It's not what I think?" His smile immediately disappeared, replaced by an evil scowl.

"I was going to say," Jasmine began slowly, "that I didn't cheat on you."

"Then who was this guy *Darien* you were calling out to?" He reached into his pocket and pulled out a newspaper. "Is this him?"

Jasmine swallowed at the sight of her and Darien in the hospital waiting room. They were holding hands and she was leaning her head against his shoulder.

Where had anyone gotten such a photo? Had someone in the waiting room been armed with a camera?

It didn't matter. "You and I are not together anymore, Allan. After what you did—"

"And I told you I was sorry!" Allan yelled, spittle flying from his mouth. "Sorry! I went to the media, told them I leaked the tape. I was trying to make amends, damn it. I did everything to make it up to you, even bought you a huge diamond ring."

"You…you what?"

"I know you knew. Don't pretend you didn't know."

"I haven't seen a television since I got here."

"The point is, I had a plan. A plan to do right by you. Once I told the media we were engaged, they didn't care about that damn video. But days later, you're seen all over this island with some other guy? Making a fool of me?"

"I don't know what you want me to say." She shrugged. "I don't know what you expect from me."

"Expect?" Allan all but shouted as he advanced. "I guess what I expect is a little gratitude. Something that tells me you know I did right by you. You're so concerned with your damn image, but you're forgetting that I helped you get to where you were." His expression softened. "And I can help you get there again."

Jasmine stared at Allan, wondering if she had ever known him.

"What if I said I don't want it anymore?"

Allan chuckled mirthlessly. "I don't believe that."

"I found myself," Jasmine told him. "Part of me I didn't even know had been missing for years. Right here on this island. I was so consumed with succeeding as an actress that nothing else mattered. And I finally discovered why. I believed that if I could play other people, live out happy endings on film, then I could live vicariously through my roles."

"What are you talking about?"

What *was* she rambling about? She was saying words she'd never even *thought* before, much less said. And yet, it made sense.

Jasmine had always believed that her career was the most important thing in the world to her, and Darien believed that, too. But that wasn't entirely true. She wanted this career, yes, but she also wanted more. Such as a happy relationship with a man who made her smile simply by being in the room with her. Such as to see her parents truly get over the pain of losing their only son, which would require her being there for them, even doing family therapy if necessary.

"You really aren't going to forgive me," Allan said. "I came all the way here—"

"I have forgiven you," she said, meaning her words.

A grin erupted on Allan's face. He stepped toward her and wrapped his arms around her waist. "That's what I wanted to hear, babe. I don't care about this guy. He's nobody."

Jasmine stood still as Allan rained kisses all over her face. But when he planted his lips on hers, she stepped backward, away from him.

He stared down at her in confusion. "What is it? What's the matter?"

Jasmine considered her words. "Allan, I've forgiven you. I really have. But that doesn't mean…it doesn't mean I want to be with you anymore."

"What?"

"But we can still be friends," she quickly added. And knew right away that she'd said the wrong thing.

"*Friends?* Two years together, one mistake, and all you want is to be my friend?"

Now that Jasmine had spoken her thoughts, she couldn't take them back. And she wouldn't. Finally she'd fallen in love. Real love. She wasn't about to settle for less than that, even if she never saw Darien again.

"I took this time to find myself," Jasmine ex-

plained. "And while I cared for you—I really did—
I realized that we didn't have the kind of love you
can base a marriage on. The kind of love that gets
you through the darkest of days."

Slap. Jasmine's head flew to the side as Allan violently slapped her.

She was so stunned that she didn't even cry out.
She just palmed her injured cheek and stared at Allan
in disbelief.

"After everything I did for you," he said through
clenched teeth.

"Allan—what's gotten into—"

He didn't let her get the rest of her question out.
He gripped her by her shoulders—hard—and shook
her. "You're not going to leave me. I won't let you."

"You're hurting me!"

"You'll be a lot more than hurt when I'm finished with you."

Even though Jasmine had dated Allan for two
years, even though she never would have thought
him capable of violence, she was certain that he
meant to kill her. Kill her because she didn't love
him.

She wiggled and struggled until she freed herself
from his arms. "You...you stay away from me." Her
gaze flew to the phone. She wondered how long it
would take for the police to arrive if she was able to
reach the phone to call them.

Allan followed her line of sight. "You think you
have a chance?" he asked her. "Go for it, bitch. Give
me yet another reason to hurt you. Because I could

strangle you and dump your body over that cliff behind this house before the police even arrive."

Despite her resolve to stay strong, Jasmine whimpered. "Why are you acting like this?"

"Just tell me that you still love me. That you're willing to give me a second chance. That's all I ask."

Jasmine stared at Allan, knowing that she was looking into the eyes of a madman. Had he always been crazy or had losing her sent him over the edge?

How easy would it be to tell him what he wanted to hear? *Yes, Allan—I still love you.* It was certainly the smart thing to say. And if she didn't, God only knew what Allan would do to her.

And yet she couldn't bring herself to say what wasn't in her heart.

Besides, if she told Allan she loved him, it wasn't as though she could turn around and leave. They were alone here, and he would no doubt want to take her to bed.

And that was something Jasmine couldn't fake.

"I…" she began, buying time. She took a tentative step in the direction of the phone, then another.

"What are you doing?"

Jasmine ran across the living room and grabbed the receiver the moment it was in reach. But she didn't get to put it to her ear, because Allan grabbed her by the hair and yanked her backward. Jasmine went down screaming, but she wasn't about to give up. She kicked her feet as hard as she could, hoping to hit Allan where it hurt.

But Allan was stronger than she was. He snagged

one of her feet and twisted her ankle until a sharp pain shot through her leg.

"Allan, please!"

He dropped her leg and tears filled Jasmine's eyes from the pain. She knew she couldn't stand on it, so she tried dragging her body by using her arms and the one uninjured leg. The phone wasn't that far. If she could get to it—

Allan bent down and grabbed her by her shirt, pulling her to a sitting position. "All you have to do is say it." He spoke through clenched teeth. "Say the words I want to hear and I'll forgive you."

Jasmine's chest rose and fell with her labored breathing. She stared Allan dead in the eye—then raised her hand and dug her nails into his face. If he was going to kill her, she was going to have his DNA under her nails so the police could nab him.

"Damn it!" he screamed.

Once again he slapped her, and this time Jasmine tasted blood in her mouth. But she didn't give up. With her uninjured leg, she kneed Allan in his groin.

He let out a loud, agony-filled moan and went down. As he writhed on the floor, Jasmine tried to stand. But her ankle was in such pain, it couldn't support her weight.

The best she could do was try to crawl to the door. Outside, she had a hope of trying to hide. In here, even if she got to the phone—

A foot landed in her solar plexus, winding Jasmine and sending her face-first to the floor. Allan grabbed her, spun her onto her back and straddled her.

"I wanted to give you a chance," he said. "God, I wanted to give you a chance. But I was too stupid to see the truth." He wrapped his hands around her neck. "You're not worth my love. You never were."

Allan started to squeeze. Jasmine grabbed at his hands, scratched them with her nails, but he didn't loosen his grip.

"Die," he growled. "Just die and put me out of my misery."

Jasmine tried frantically to gasp in air, but she couldn't. Her eyes were losing focus, her head growing light. Any second and she would pass out.

She would die at Allan's hands, and there was nothing she could do about it.

Her eyes fluttered shut. She said a silent prayer that it would end quickly and that her parents wouldn't be utterly devastated.

And then, miraculously, Allan let go.

She was gasping in a huge gulp of air when she realized that Allan was sprawled backward on the floor—and that there was another set of legs in the room. Her eyes followed the length of those legs and her heart filled with a feeling she would never be able to put into words.

Darien, she tried to say, but no sound escaped her throat.

But Darien wasn't looking at her. His focus was solely on Allan. Allan jumped to his feet and starting throwing punches. Darien easily landed a punch to Allan's face that landed him flat on his back.

Allan groaned, but didn't move.

Finally, Darien's gaze landed on Jasmine. He rushed to her and gathered her in his arms, then hugged her long and hard.

"Oh, baby," he said, brushing her hair back. "Oh my God."

"You came back," she managed, but her voice was a croak.

"I was a coward, and I'm sorry. But I couldn't do it. I couldn't really leave. I was supposed to get on the plane, and I just couldn't." He planted his mouth on hers.

Was this for real, or was Jasmine hallucinating?

"I don't need time," he went on. "I know I want to be with you."

"Darien!" Jasmine screamed.

He threw his gaze over his shoulder in time to see Allan raising his foot to kick him in the head. With lightning speed, Darien deflected the kick, then gripped Allan's leg and twisted.

Jasmine heard a sickening crack, followed by a high-pitched squeal she didn't imagine Allan capable of. Then Allan was bawling like a baby, and Jasmine knew the nightmare was over.

She started to cry.

Once again, Darien gathered her in his arms. He shushed her and wiped away her tears. "It's okay now. He's not gonna hurt anyone."

"I know." Jasmine blew out a shuddery breath. "That's Allan, in case you were wondering."

"Allan." Darien's eyes narrowed. "He found you?"

"Apparently. We need to call the police."

"We will." Darien sighed softly. "But first I want to get something off my chest." His eyes roamed over her face. He smoothed her hair, wiped her face until it was dry. "When I said that I didn't want to get hurt, I meant that. No one wants to get hurt."

"I understand," Jasmine said.

"No, no you don't. You were right when you said that life gives no one any guarantees. I thought I could protect my heart by walking away, but I realized how wrong I was. At the airport, I was already in pain. I couldn't stop thinking about you. I wasn't protecting my heart. I was giving myself a reason to grieve. Suddenly, leaving you made no sense. And my God, how could I have lived with myself if anything had happened to you."

Darien glanced over his shoulder in Allan's direction, then his eyes misted. Jasmine stroked his face. "You saved me," she said, wanting him to concentrate on the good, not the bad. "Because you came back."

"I know." Darien swallowed. "What I'm trying to say is that whether I have only one more hour with you, or fifty years—I don't want to spend that time being afraid I'll lose you. I want to spend that time loving you like there's no tomorrow."

And despite the fact that Allan was crying like a baby behind them, Darien cradled Jasmine's face in his hands, lowered his head to hers and kissed her.

Kissed her as though this moment in time was all they had.

Epilogue

Six months later...

It was a simple wedding. There was a chill in the air as the bride met her groom on the sand, but the scene couldn't have been more beautiful. Palm trees swayed and waves gently lapped at the shore as a gospel singer serenaded the happy couple. Fifty seats had been laid out on the sand for the guests, and every seat was occupied.

At the altar, the bride smiled at the man she loved. She was simply radiant, and not just because of the megawatt smile on her face, but because she also had a maternal glow. Her pregnant belly was not only obvious but highlighted by the shape of her knee-length dress. Even though she'd clearly gotten pregnant before her wedding, she was proud of the baby and wanted the world to know.

Jasmine glanced at Darien, and he at her. He squeezed her hand.

It was a true testament to the power of love and forgiveness that Jasmine and Darien were even here in Key West, attending his brother's wedding to Sheila. Jasmine had worried that it might be too much for him, but he assured her that he'd put the pain of his marriage in the past. His love for Jasmine was all that mattered now, so much so that he and his brother had started talking again. Their relationship would never be the same as it had been before, but at least they weren't at odds.

As Jasmine listened to the bride and groom exchange their vows, she couldn't help thinking that if she and Darien got married, they would have to do it in St. Lucia. After all, it was the place where they'd fallen in love.

The past six months had been insane. The story of the attack on Jasmine's life had been huge news. This time, instead of portraying her as a sex-starved starlet, the media had showcased her as a woman brave enough to fight for her life against the man who had so cruelly tried to destroy her career.

Allan Jackson, who was currently in jail awaiting his trial, had been painted as a monster so insecure because of his girlfriend's success that he first tried to bring her down, then had ultimately tried to murder her.

Sadly, the media's slant hadn't been a slant at all. Everything they'd printed in papers and stated on the news had been true.

The trial was still ahead of her, but with Darien by her side, Jasmine had no doubt she'd get through it all right.

She had a lot to be grateful for. Her parents, after learning of her near murder, had had an awakening of sorts. When she got to Florida and saw them, they'd never hugged her so hard or so long. And for the first time in forever, Jasmine had seen them genuinely smile when they'd greeted Darien—the man who'd saved her and the man she had announced she was in love with.

Knowing that they'd almost lost her had jolted them into appreciating every moment they had left with her. They were embracing life again, embracing happiness, and Jasmine once again had a real relationship with her parents, rather than a superficial one. A relationship that wasn't mired in the pain and guilt of Rickey's death, but in the joy of love and hope for tomorrow.

And things couldn't be better for her and Darien. They'd spent much of the last six months together, even though they still had their respective homes in Ohio and California. Their passion was alive and well. Even as the ceremony ended and they headed back to the hotel, they didn't stop holding hands.

Couldn't.

A casual observer might think they were the ones getting married.

In the hotel lobby, Jasmine's purse vibrated. It was a Saturday, and she frowned, but opened her clutch to retrieve her BlackBerry. She saw her agent's phone number on the display.

"It's my agent," she told Darien. "Should I answer it?"

"Why not?"

For six months, Victoria had been calling Jasmine about film roles. The offers had been steady and lucrative, but she had declined each and every one. Victoria didn't understand; neither did her friends. But Jasmine had been torn. She wasn't sure she was ready to forgive Hollywood so quickly. One day, she had been a shooting star. The next, Tinsel Town had sent her crashing down to earth without a care. Now, she was the good girl again?

She attached her earpiece and answered the call. "Victoria?"

"How's my favorite client?" Victoria asked sweetly. "Ready to get back to the daily grind?"

"Can we talk later? I'm at that wedding in Key West I told you about. Remember?"

"Right. Well, I'll be quick. *Will Smith's leading lady.* I know you've been taking a break, but this... this is the kind of opportunity you don't say no to, not even if you're dead."

"Are you serious?" Jasmine asked. Despite herself, she was getting excited.

"He asked for you personally."

"Oh my goodness."

Beside her, Darien mouthed "What?"

"Will Smith," she answered. Then, to Victoria, "What's the part?"

"Action-adventure romance. *Huge.* At least three other big names are attached. Jasmine…"

"I know." She bit down on her bottom lip to keep her excitement in check. "*I know.* And I'd love to talk more about it, but I'm heading into the reception. Can I call you later?"

"Please tell me you're not even remotely thinking of turning this one down."

"I'll call you later."

"Jasmine…"

"Tomorrow at the latest."

"Jasmine!"

Jasmine chuckled. "Love you, Victoria. Bye."

"You're going to send my blood pressure through the roof!"

Jasmine ended the call, then turned to Darien. Squealing, she launched herself into his arms.

"Will Smith?" he asked.

"Will Smith wants me," Jasmine bragged.

"He wants you?" Darien's eyes widened with excitement, then they narrowed. "Wait a minute. What do you mean he *wants* you?"

"He wants me to play his romantic lead!"

"Oh. Well, all right then. 'Cause if it was anything other than that, I might have to head to Beverly Hills and hurt a brother."

Giggling, Jasmine moved her arms from Darien's waist to his neck. "You know I only have eyes for you."

"Still, I think I'd better be on set for every day of the shooting," Darien joked. "Just in case…"

"I want you to be there."

A beat passed. "You gonna say yes?"

"I think I'd be crazy not to. Besides, for the first time in months, I got excited about Victoria's call. That tells me I'm ready."

"Good."

"Are you sure? You want me to do the film?"

"I want you to do what makes you happy," Darien said.

"It will," Jasmine said. "At least, I think it will. And since I promised to put Luc and his brothers through college, I can't exactly stop working."

"And then there are trips to St. Lucia to visit him and his family. Make sure they're okay."

"Didn't they look radiant in that last photo they sent?" Jasmine asked. "Healthy and happy."

"And the new house looked pretty good, too."

"Yeah," Jasmine said, wistful. "It was so nice to be able to do that for them."

Sheila and Rodney came into the lobby hand in hand, and Darien looked their way. Jasmine waited

for his body to tense—show some sign of discom-
fort—but it didn't.

The bride and groom approached. Darien released
Jasmine to give first his brother a hug, then his ex-wife.
"Congratulations," he said. "You both look happy."

"We are." Sheila beamed and patted her belly.
"All three of us."

Rodney threw his arms around Darien again and
squeezed him hard. Squeezed him as though he
didn't want to let him go.

"It's okay," Darien said, patting his brother's back.
"It's all good."

"Thank you." Rodney broke the hug and stood
back. "For everything."

"Like I said, it's all good."

Rodney turned to Jasmine. "And, Jasmine, you
take care of my brother."

"I plan on it."

The bride, groom, maid of honor and best man
wandered off in the direction of the reception. "I'm
proud of you," Jasmine told Darien.

"I told you—the past is the past. You're my future."

"I guess we should head inside."

"Wait—I have a surprise."

"A surprise?" Jasmine repeated. Then eyed
Darien skeptically. "You're not going to—"

"Propose to you at my own brother's wedding? To
my ex-wife? Uh-uh. Though, now that I think about
it, that's a story the tabloids would trip over themselves trying to report first…."

"Don't even think about it!"

Darien pressed his lips to Jasmine's forehead. "No worries, baby."

"Then what's the surprise?"

"Well. I've been talking to Realtors in Los Angeles. Trying to see if I can make my dream of becoming a chef a reality."

A slow smile spread across Jasmine's face. "Darien!"

"It's not a done deal by any means, but there's one place that seems promising. It'll be a huge leap, though, investing in my own restaurant, creating my own menu...."

"So you're moving to L.A.?"

"That's the plan, yeah."

Jasmine screamed and squeezed the life out of Darien. "This is incredible!"

"Who knows what'll happen. I'm taking tentative first steps here."

"It's going to be fabulous, sweetheart. And we are going to make such a team!"

"I love your excitement," Darien told her. "I love the way you support me. I love the way I feel around you." He paused. "I love you, period."

"Oh, baby. I love you, too."

"I can't even believe that last summer I felt so hopeless. Now I'm in love again, and I'm happy. It just goes to show you never know when life can change in a heartbeat—and give you a second chance at love."

"One that will last a lifetime," Jasmine said.

"You'd better believe it. Because I have no plans of letting you go."

"Just what I like to hear, sweetheart. Just what I like to hear."

And then Jasmine tipped on her toes and pressed her lips to Darien's. With love flowing through her veins, she kissed this man who had been her second chance. The one she knew in her heart that she would love forever.

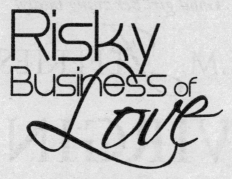

Some men will promise a woman anything…
only to break her heart.

ESSENCE BESTSELLING AUTHOR

FRANCIS RAY

Silken Betrayal

Jordan Hamilton has a vendetta against Lauren Bennett's seemingly untouchable father-in-law—and sees Lauren as the key to revenge. But he never counted on falling for the sexy single mother…or her irresistible young son. Suddenly, Jordan is torn between his powerful feelings and his need for vengeance.

"Francis Ray creates characters and stories that we all love to read about. Her stories are written from the heart."
—*New York Times* bestselling author
Eric Jerome Dickey

Available the first week of August wherever books are sold.

ARABESQUE®

www.kimanipress.com

KPFR0170807

Essence bestselling author

PATRICIA HALEY

Still Waters

A poignant and memorable story about a once-loving
husband who has lost his way…and his spiritual wife
who has grown weary from constantly praying for
the marriage. Greg and Laurie Wright are perched at
the edge of an all-out crisis—and only a miracle can
restore what's been lost.

"Patricia Haley has written a unique work of
Christian fiction that should not be missed."
—*Rawsistaz Reviewers* on *No Regrets*

*Available the first week of August
wherever books are sold.*

Adversity can strengthen your faith....

TIME FOR *Hope*

MAXINE BILLINGS

**A poignant new novel about the nature
of faith and of friendship...and the ways
in which each can save us.**

Two years ago, Hope Mason was cruelly betrayed by
her husband and best friend. Now, with no desire or
energy to socialize, Hope believes the fewer friends
one has, the better. But when she's asked to train
young Tyla Jefferson, Tyla shows Hope how to open
up again—and helps Hope discover that life is not
nearly as hopeless as she thinks.

*Available the first week of August
wherever books are sold.*